Voices of Hell's Kitchen

To David —

Best Wishes —

John V[...]

To order additional copies, please contact us.
BookSurge, LLC
www.booksurge.com
1-866-308-6235
orders@booksurge.com

Voices of Hell's Kitchen

John V. Amodeo

2006

Voices of Hell's Kitchen

Writing a book about this great neighborhood would not have been possible without the support and encouragement of family, friends and associates. Many people who make up the exciting, diverse and always changing neighborhood had much to say that ultimately became Voices of Hell's Kitchen. I would be remiss if I did not thank my mom, Florence Bochette Amodeo and my late father, Vincent A. Amodeo; my sisters, Carol Krajewski and Linda Gulli and their children for their encouragement. I especially want to thank my nephew, Ed Krajewski for timely giving me a book for first-time authors at Christmas. Also my nieces Leslie Armstrong, Lisa Polsinello, Amelia Ambrosino, my nephew Nick Gulli, Jr. and my brothers-in-law, Nick Gulli and the late Ed Krajewski, Sr.

I had the pleasure of attending a writing seminar on the Queen Mary 2 with the mystery writer, Ms. P.D. James. Her insight into writing style, use of setting, scents and dialogue was a great help.

In addition, people of Hell's Kitchen, such as the real dog walker, Rose Pollio, friends such as Linda Ivey, Joe Chen, Lars Jose, Bob Jundelin and Ed Jenkins were always positive and encouraged me to finish, as did Lee Collings, Paula Stark, Al Goodman, the late Edith Goodman, Rev. Owen Lafferty, Dr. Louis Gioia and my neighbor, Virginia Miller.

Scott Cirelli of Mid-City as well as Anthony Cavaleri gave me added insight on protein shakes, so essential for body building. Personal trainers, such as Anthony Preischell, Jeremy Simmons, Eric Mercado and workers Michelle and Baron were a great help. Special thanks for letters, emails and calls from Terry Grayson, Dwight Walters, Stan Blitz, and Adrian Patterson.

Gerard Guglielmo of Amy's Bread on 9th Avenue gave me additional information concerning the preparation of food; Lois Feigen of Hello New York allowed me to continue my tours of Manhattan. At Mercy College, Monica Foote and Javier Perez were very supportive.

The staff at the sprawling Manhattan Plaza, where I reside, were also very helpful, including Richard Hunnings, Paulette Woodside and Susan Bernstein as well as the competent and wonderful security and maintenance staff.

To you all, a heartfelt thank you!

John V. Amodeo
Amodeo/Voices.....

CHAPTER I

Dawn again, it always comes too early, especially on a cold, dark overcast January morning, Frankie thought as he glanced out the shadeless, dirty window while the odors of the city crept in—the cold breeze was a relief from the fifth floor walkup with its musty walls that had seen better days. "The place reeks as if someone barfed up a six pack," he said to himself, as he threw off the soiled blanket in no apparent fashion, allowing it to fall onto a rugless, wooden floor in need of cleaning. Reaching for the small, rectangular box blurting out static, the all-news station told him what he already realized: "It's 22, snowing with major tie-ups on the Jackie Robinson and Belt Parkway." Then, the overzealous announcer, as if to test his nerves, added, "Enjoy the beauty of a New York moment." "Hell," Frankie yelled aloud to the otherwise empty apartment, "I don't need this bullshit." Shutting off the radio, he donned his warm-up blue Nike jacket, pulled his cap over a do-rag, grabbed a pair of well-used, black gloves and soiled Adidas sneakers and headed down the stairs and onto the street.

Within two minutes, the familiar routine found Frankie on his five mile journey along the West Side Highway, past the auto showrooms on 11th Avenue, the warehouses along 12th Avenue, and he headed towards Battery Park and back along the Hudson. It was always the same routine—a quick mile, then jab-jogging shadow boxing for the next two miles, followed by a brisk 'cool down' consisting of a two mile walk, then returning to his flat on West 48th Street where the entire program ended by jumping rope for a full 15 minutes. Then, off to the C train at 8th Avenue and 50th Street, to 14th Street Boxing Gym which consisted of a three-round, quick spar, another jump-roping routine, getting weighed, a quick shower and then the moment of truth with the man himself, his trainer, Max. All of these routines, draining and challenging to anyone, were easy for Frankie. After all, he was just two weeks away from his debut at the Garden as the main challenger in the middle weight division.

As New York's newest gladiator, he was Max's number one prospect and, despite the early hour of 7:30 AM, he was in great spirits and ready for anything thrown at him from Max.

The climb up the old, iron stairs leading up to Max's office never looked so inviting. He knew that he was in top physical form. "I hope he's in a good mood today and feeling a little better than yesterday," Frankie said to himself. He knew he had accomplished all the demands outlined by Max—the daily, cardio exercise plus the sparring. "I felt sick yesterday, but I couldn't let Max know," he told one of his sparring partners, Hector Rosado. "I overdid it, that's why it was so hard to get up today, but today is different and I'm one day closer to my goal and I'm focused." In fact, the frigid New York in January made him ever more determined. "The snow makes me move a little more carefully and I'm reinvigorated and stronger." Climbing the rusty, iron, black stairs, making a noise that seemed to get louder with every step, he caught sight of Max at his perpetually cluttered desk, forever chomping on an unlit cigar, open to the <u>Daily News </u>sports' section atop a bundle of old, yellowed envelopes.

"Frankie." Max smiled as he entered. "Today I want you to spar with Tyrone. I know you showered and finished your warm-ups, but he's cool, even-tempered and thinks on his feet—he's destined to be a good challenger some day." Frankie knew that

Max's gruff but fair assessment of "T", as he was known at the gym, was correct. A 19 year old from Brownsville, Brooklyn, he needed to polish his performance before Max would commit him to a bout. "He's not Garden material like you, but with our help, he'll get there," Max added as he brushed off a few papers from his desk, nodding to Frankie to pull up the one chair adjacent to the overstuffed trash receptacle.

Max remembered telling Frankie that T had been through all the sparring to test his will and fiber and passed the "Max Test," which meant getting to the gym on time, leaving your attitude outside the door, and most of all, taking advice from Max and the other trainers in the gym, Joey Restivo and Roosevelt Graham, whom everyone called Rosey.

It's all an act with Max, he thought, but the old man was now like family and he knew that ole Max was his real chance, a meal ticket from his poor beginnings to a possible career with money to boot. Everyone wanted to impress Max and to get his blessing meant you were on your way. Frankie had seen boxers come and go. He was glad that Tyrone had shaped up and left behind his ghetto anger when in the gym. Many of the young men who had come and gone were frustrated once the tedious routines became daily. Many just couldn't give up the time or ignore their girlfriends who demanded more attention, feeling neglected and threatening to leave them. "You need the drive, the hunger, the 'gut,'" as Max often reminded new boxers. Max called it motivation. Frankie knew it was more than that—it was growing up, facing responsibility and being accountable and he knew he, like T, wanted it badly. That made him a fighter. The constant hunger and motivation. Frankie stayed with it and his big day was just around the corner.

"Frankie," Max shouted. He seemed unusually restless, as he rearranged an already untidy desk for the fifth time this morning into no apparent organization. Just shuffled old newspapers and fliers into a big pile. Frankie couldn't help but notice that the newspaper was open to the sports page. He glanced at the yellow-stained walls, much in need of a paint job and the posters of past gladiators that adorned them, a testament to old days of boxing at the Garden. Boxers who had come and gone, many of whom the world had long forgotten. But not Max. Every boxer who made it out of this smelly, rancid atmosphere was added to the Hall of Fame posted in Max's office. "Someday when I'm long gone, maybe a future Max will remember me and have my picture up there, too," he once remarked in a moment of weakness.

"Got some news that will be of interest to you."

"Great." Frankie was relieved that the mood was good today. He knew something was up from the smiling Max with the cigar, upturned much like the old FDR cigarette holder caricature familiar to old timers. He felt something big was about to happen.

"Look at page 64, not bad, eh?" Max slowly got up from his desk. Despite his doctor's warning about his fatty diet, he was now overweight and diabetic, a condition that had plagued his forebears and now him.

Max showed Frankie Ceteno the latest edition of <u>Boxer,</u> the bible of aspiring pugilists. Getting noticed in the <u>Boxer</u> was like a weightlifter, like Victor Martinez being featured in <u>Muscles and Fitness</u> or J-Lo in <u>People.</u> At once, Frankie Ceteno's name would be out there, making him the envy of the gym and getting the attention from the boxing world.

Nervously reading the article, Frankie couldn't believe his eyes. Glancing quickly at the cover which showed his hero, an aging Holyfield making a comeback, he quickly turned to page 64 and saw the picture of himself sparring with Tyrone taken two weeks earlier. He remembered Max was unusually quiet, listening intently to a loud middle-aged woman and man, looking too cosmetic and clean for the joint, talking on and on, occasionally looking at Frankie and nodding approvingly. He went on with his routine, thinking nothing of the strange company Max was keeping that Tuesday. "Maybe family, who knows?" he remarked.

"Perhaps the best boxer to look at with a future in the upcoming Garden bout is the young Frankie Ceteno. At 21, he's 5' 11", 174 solid pounds with a jab as quick and powerful not seen since Marvelous Marvin Hagler. The young, handsome, hazel-eyed southpaw, originally from Southern Boulevard in the South Bronx, is the biggest hope of Max Segal, the iconoclastic, gruff, aging manager of the 14 Street Boxing Gym, often called the best trainer since Cus D'Amato who modeled another young upstart in the heavyweight division, Mike Tyson. Ceteno, despite the charm and good looks, is a focused, tough, self-starter who listens well to Segal. His talent was at once recognized at age 16, when he got his first taste of victory in the ring by outlasting all his other opponents at the very competitive 2001 Golden Gloves. Segal, always looking for raw talent, took young Frankie under his aegis and today has the best shot at winning the middle weight title. I predict...."

"Yo, Max, this is it!" he said, not able to finish the paragraph. For the first time, Frankie's emotions started to get to him as he gave Max a bear hug.

"All right," Max shouted, unused to such a display of affection, as he gently pushed Frankie away, lest others see him in a weak moment. "Well, I'll admit, I've been a little rough on you and now you know why. You proved you're not a quitter and that's what I respect. You're like the son I never had, Ceteno. Hell, I know you weren't feeling 100% yesterday and that you had to be in the Bronx for your grandfather's funeral last week. But, I'll say this to your face—you got guts and damn it, you're the best fighter to come out of this stinking hole in seven years and if my goddamn blood pressure and diabetes don't make me history, I'll be there for you. Remember that piece in the magazine means bullshit until you prove to yourself that you got it. So now that you been noticed, big shot, you still belong to this place and you work for me and you got work to do, so get out there, train and watch the hell what you eat—*comprende?*"

"*Si, si, comprende todo.*" Frankie never remembered Max being so real. Frankie's mother always said that Max was a soft touch from the moment he introduced her to him at the Christmas party at the gym the year before. Both Max and Maria Ceteno knew life wasn't always fair—she was the middle of six children of Puerto Rican immigrants from Caguas, while Max's grandparents and his young mother fled Russia during anti-Semitic pogroms in Czarist Russia.

Mrs. Ceteno worked in the garment district on West 37th Street and 9th Avenue as a button sewer where she met her husband, Raul, a fellow Puerto Rican garment worker, born in Mayaguez. Their marriage produced three children. Frankie, the youngest, was her pride and joy.

After being abandoned by Raul, she labored six days a week to make sure she could pay the tuition for the parochial school on nearby Burnside Avenue for her Frankie. Yes, Frankie would make it. He was her best hope. At 46, the years had taken a toll on her once beautiful jet-black hair, mixed now with gray. She knew that Frankie, unlike his older brother Carlos, a drop-out and drug dealer who was finishing a six year term at Fishkill Correctional, was no quitter. She also knew Frankie wouldn't let her down. Then there was Rosa, her oldest child. Married at 16, she was now welfare dependent with four children, after two failed marriages. Like her mother, the stress of abandonment compromised a once-beautiful young woman into a corpulent and desperate woman who never seemed to make ends meet. Then, of course, there was Max, her hero. It was the balding, overweight, sixtyish Max with the owlish features who made her Frankie take his chances at fame seriously, providing him with a one-room SRO in Hell's Kitchen just off 11th Avenue on 48th Street. It was Max who instructed and modeled him by his constant pressure to lay off the high calorie diet of rice and beans and called him every day on a cell phone he provided to ensure that his morning regimen was done. "Yeah, I know the old man has a big heart," Maria often said. He saw what Maria saw in her son— a determination to make it against the odds and make his dream a reality. Max had even called Maria when he heard of her father's death two weeks ago and ended showing up with three other boxers at Ortiz Funeral on Alexander Avenue in the South Bronx.

Frankie left the gym, stopping at the newsstand at the corner of 8th Avenue and 14th Street, buying three copies of the <u>Boxer.</u> "Why so many?" asked Mahmoud, the Egyptian vendor who always greeted Ceteno as entered the subway. "I'm in it—page 64—check it out, my man. One's for me and other two are for my mom and my girl, Cynthia."

Cynthia Lopez, his girlfriend, still lived with her mother on 182 Street in the Bronx. Max made sure that he stayed away from all temptations, thus the reason why Frankie's apartment was in Hell's Kitchen, far away from Cynthia. "Stay focused, the broads will come later," Max always pointed out to every serious boxer.

Mahmoud gave Frankie a high five gesture of his hand as he descended into the subway on his way to 48th Street. He knew nothing could stop him now. The uptown C local was coming into the station. The world, it seems, was his, at least for today. He would make his mother, Cynthia and Max proud. Then it happened in an instant!

"Are you feeling better, young man?"

Frankie opened his eyes to a peculiar smell that reminded him of Lysol and disinfectant, that same smell when his mother cleaned the bathroom. In front of him was a petite, angelic figure clad in an immaculate white uniform. He saw a name tag—Aurelia Rios, RN. In one hand, she seemed to be carrying something—yes, he could now see it clearer—it was not disinfectant, but a small plastic cup with two capsules.

"What's this for?" he begged, trying to adjust to his new surroundings. The Filipino nurse knew that her patient would have a lot of questions. "What happened and where am I?"

"Here, take these two pills—you're a very lucky man, Mr. Ceteno."

"Lucky, you must be nuts. My right hand hurts like hell. What am I doing in this place? Where's my mother and Max? I got to know; I got to know!"

"Relax a minute and we'll explain everything." He saw Ms. Rios smile and felt a little less scared, as she went on to tell him that he just returned from the recovery room after a two-hour operation performed on his right hand. She went further to say that the injured hand would mend well and that the two best orthopedic surgeons at Bellevue, Dr. Carl Rubin and Dr. Henry Liu were pleased at the results. Seeing the puzzled look on Frankie's face, she added; "Dr. Rubin told your mom and your friend that if you didn't have such great strength, you might be in much worse condition."

"What's wrong? What's wrong? You don't understand—I'm a boxer and have a fight at the Garden in just three weeks. I have to be there. I got to be there!"

"Slow down. First, be thankful that you're going to be alright." Frankie was about to say something, but the nurse put her finger to her lips for him to be quiet while she added, "We know about the boxing thing. Dr. Rubin is going to come in and talk to you. It could have been much worse. You're still in the game, they tell me. Max and your mom, by the way, are outside and I know you're anxious to talk to them and your doctors. Now, just take a deep breath and I'll send for them, ok?"

"Yeah, thanks, I need to find out the deal here." Frankie was near tears as he looked at his right arm in a heavy caste.

Max Segal and Maria Ceteno were waiting for Frankie to wake, and when told he was lucid, entered his fifth floor hospital room at Bellevue's west wing. Seeing Max and his mother, still in the customary, 'old school habit' of wearing black for his grandfather, he immediately felt the emotion overpowering him. His mother smiled and kissed him on the forehead, sobbing silently. She quickly regained her composure said in a loud, firm voice, "You'll be fine, *mi hijo precioso.* They'll find the bastards who did this to you, that much I'm sure."

Max, ever deliberate in his arthritic step, said softly, "The doctors assured your mom and me that you have a good chance of getting full use of that arm."

"Max, I want to know what the hell happened! I had this weird feeling before I went into that station that someone was following me. All I really remember is being pushed by someone and falling onto the tracks and hearing a woman screaming. The next thing I saw was the train and I thought I covered myself as it passed over me. I don't know anything else except that I woke up here smelling the smells of my mother's bathroom."

The comment brought a laugh from both Max and Maria. Max said, "Whatever you did, you did instinctively and it seems to have saved your life. This incident happened five hours ago. Your mom and I have talked to the surgeons to find out what's up; I want you to just get well—you hear? Focus only on that right now. This is a raw, rotten deal, but we'll find a way out, believe me and believe in yourself. You can do it. Your family has been through tough times before, so don't let these bastards have their way—you listening?"

"Son, listen to Max, he makes a lot of sense," Maria Ceteno added, now dabbing her eyes with her handkerchief.

"Who would do this to me—why?" Frankie said to no one in particular, as he stared at the white-washed walls, barren save for a small Monet still-life adjacent to a porcelain sink.

"The police are on this—the officer, I think his name is Donnelly, came by just one hour ago to check on you and is now conducting an investigation. He was very decent, this officer. I don't watch that much 'Law and Order,' but he reminded me of Jerry Orbach. When I told him about you and the boxing and how things were coming your way, I saw the expression on his face. If looks could kill. I hope he'll get to the bottom of this crap." Max shook his head and couldn't go on.

At this point, an elderly doctor entered the room. It was Dr. Carl Rubin.

Carl Rubin had a reputation of being the best orthopedic surgeon at Bellevue, if not all New York. When told his young patient was an aspiring boxer, he immediately wanted to help. A product himself of the Lower East Side, he graduated tops in his medical class at Cornell and stayed true to his roots in New York. Cited by many medical professional organizations and writing for the <u>New England Journal of Medicine</u> and <u>JAMA</u>, he was the proud recipient of many awards in his field, including the prestigious NYC Make a Difference Award in 2002, having put in long hours after 9/11 terrorist attack on the World Trade Center attending to broken limbs. He was past president of the NYC AMA chapter and was well respected for his innovative rehab techniques with people suffering joint injuries. He had seen many cases, like Frankie's, and was steadfastly determined to mend his right hand to full usage.

"Young man, how about ten rounds?" Everyone, even Frankie, let out a hearty laugh. "Let me get right to the point, because you're going to ask me sooner or later. The fracture you sustained isn't as bad as we anticipated. You did suffer bone fractures in your right hand, and in layman's terms, with proper rehabilitation, it will take 11 months until you have complete use of your hand. I know this is not the news you want to hear, but you're going to have to put your boxing career on hold for a year."

"No, no, no, Christ, no. I'll do anything, work 24 hours to get this damn hand in working condition and I'll show you doc and everyone else, I will. I'll do it, I'll do it!" Frankie didn't want to hear anything else from Rubin. For the first time in years, he buried his head in his pillow and cried aloud.

The next morning, Frankie was greeted by several surprises—three bouquets of flowers, over 25 emails sent to Bellevue's main website and a box of Godiva chocolates. "I guess I can forget my diet, anyway," he said to the orderly who brought his goodies.

An attractive nurse, Evelyn Corello, entered and said, "So, here's our famous patient."

"I'm not famous. I'm pissed! What the hell is left? Sorry, I just don't know why I'm here-I'm supposed to be a fighter. See these hands? I'm nothing without them. I'm nothing if I can't use them. I'm sorry nurse; I don't even know your name and I'm here carrying on." Frankie rolled over, covering his face with his good arm. Evelyn had seen many patients frustrated and angry over their condition, but she could see a determination on the part of her young patient with the piercing eyes and look of determination.

"The newspapers, the press and TV have shown your story; you are famous," Evelyn said..

"That's ok—my name's Evelyn and I'll be here for you. And if it's any consolation, Dr. Rubin said it could have been a lot worse. You're alive and there's plenty of people who are much worse off than you, young man. You're young, tough and alive and, like I said, pretty famous. Your buddies at the gym called and the press wants some information on you too. So, just take it slow and we'll get you back to your old self." The smile on Frankie's face was assurance from Evelyn that she had made her point.

"He's a cutey," she said to herself as she exited his room.

"Still no suspects, Donnelly," Commander Jeff Norris, a tall, powerfully-built black man shouted at Donnelly as he passed his desk at the 10th Precinct. Mike Donnelly knew from the start that this was not an ordinary investigation—something in his 10 years on the job as a detective told him to dig deeper concerning the incident on the subway with Frankie Ceteno. As he passed Norris' desk to pick up his daily docket before inspection, he couldn't help but give Norris a nod of reassurance that this case needed quick attention and was becoming more intriguing as the facts unfolded. Michael Donnelly always considered himself a cop first—a tough cop in the proud tradition from his immigrant Irish roots which saw his father, grandfather and two uncles on the force. He was now the third generation, an Emerald Society leader and a scout master in his Long Island town of Carle Place. However, the 6' 2" short-haired detective was puzzled. Something was bugging him in the back of his mind, as he poured a cup of black coffee and loosened his tie. "Why this kid? Why? There had been older, more vulnerable people, as well as a family visiting from South Dakota, on the subway platform that would have been easier marks. Robbery was not the motive. Frankie still had $22.00 on him when he was brought into the emergency ward at Bellevue. "What was it; what was it?"

As he pored over the facts, he remembered he was with his partner, Catherine Reid at the 28th subway station checking on a possible push-in at a nearby Thai restaurant, when the call came over that there was a subway incident at 14th Street. Reid, his partner for the last three years, was the analyst—if there was a car accident report to be written, she checked and rechecked all the facts, concisely, neatly, taking copious notes from eyewitnesses. Donnelly first found her micro-management style of incident reports to be too time-consuming and unnecessary; he now valued her insight. Indeed, a quick look at her reports offered the reader the next best thing to being at the scene. He was grateful that she got the two witnesses, Mabel Green and Nicholas Pappas, to come down to the precinct and meet with the sketch artist for a wanted poster to be placed in the midtown and downtown subway stations. The composite the artist drew showed a light-skinned Hispanic male with a pencil moustache, closely-cropped hair and an earring on the right ear.

Donnelly distinctly recalled that Ms. Green, the witness, said, "He looked like he was strongly built and went right for the young man." Just as he was about to show Green and Pappas photos of wanted felons that matched the description, the phone rang.

" Answering the phone, he got up in a rush when someone on the line yelled: "Get over to Bellevue right now—that Ceteno kid. Someone tried to get to him."

Christ, thought Donnelly, *we should have placed him in protective custody.* Racing out the door, he nearly tripped on the icy pavement before telling Reid to hightail it to nearby Bellevue.

Frankie Ceteno never encountered the suspect. Elias Matos was known on the streets as "Lucky." By the time Reid and Donnelly made it up to Frankie's eighth floor room, Max had recognized Lucky, eyed him over and when Matos saw Max, he immediately raced to the elevator, shouting, "Oh shit." A Bellevue security guard, Oliver Flowers, was a pro and was able to overpower Lucky before he reached the open elevator door. Security guard Flowers held Matos until additional staff arrived. All the while, Matos was very vocal, shouting racial obscenities to the three black security guards who held him. Thanks to the action of the Bellevue security staff, Reid and Donnelly were able to arrest Lucky, after having discovered a knife in his camouflaged jeans. Max knew Matos was a bad seed; he had been ejected from his gym twice for refusing to follow orders, threatening boxers and Max. It was Frankie who had ended any chance for Matos to succeed at the gym when, during several sparring events a year before, he defeated Lucky without much effort. Lucy's chances at getting a spot in the Golden Gloves and an ensuing career in boxing were forever crushed and it was, according to Lucky, all Frankie Ceteno's fault.

Lucky was brought to the precinct on 6th Street and after a one hour interrogation, was placed in a lineup and picked out by both Green and Pappas, the eyewitnesses. Rather than run the risk of a lengthy and costly trial, the assistant district attorney, Ethel Lehrman, and Matos' appointed defense attorney, Sheldon Harris, got Matos a guilty plea. Charges were reduced from attempted murder to felonious assault and he agreed to a 12 year stint at Otisville, a medium upstate correctional facility in the New York prison system. Donnelly and the ever vigilant Reid filed their report for Norris, knowing that they helped save a life. The solving of the vicious, premeditated revenge crime in the subway made Donnelly and Reid heroes in their unit. Lucky, like many New Yorkers, had seen the front page article on Frankie in the <u>Post</u> entitled: "Boxer Pushed on Way to Fame." His desperate attempt to finish the job failed.

Eight months had passed since that fateful encounter with Elias Matos on the subway on that cold January afternoon. It was now September, autumn in New York, which meant that tourists were flocking to Manhattan with Europeans enjoying a bank rate that allowed for nearly a two-for-one exchange on the Euro. Too early for a frost, not hot or humid, the visitors seemed to prefer the city at this time of year. Like the song, "Autumn in New York," it was the best time of year to be in New York. It was also Frankie Ceteno's time.

While the tourists made somber stops at Ground Zero, they also saw a newly-invigorated city with Harlem's 125th landmark street teeming with people shopping at Old Navy, Gap and sipping cappuccinos at Starbuck's while taking pictures of Bill Clinton's office building. "This is part of the new New York," the double-decker tour bus guide shouted as he showed the site of the new Marriott Hotel to be built at the corner of Park and 125th Street, a tribute to the entrepreneurial spirit envisioned by Clinton and local politicos like Charlie Rangel. The churches on Sunday were full of German, French, British, Italian and Japanese who came to hear the angelic and full-range gospel sounds from the choirs of Shiloh Baptist, Riverside and Abyssinian Church. These same tourists were eager to spend their coins at Macys, go to Broadway's newest hit "Spamalot," eat in Chinatown, Little Italy, Restaurant Row and take countless pictures to share with family and friends back home. Yes, it was a good time in New York, a city that had been punched, but not beaten and rose back to face the challenges. In that regard, New York and Frankie Ceteno were one and the same. For Frankie, autumn was a dream come true.

One place the tourists may not have put on their tour agenda was the Garden. Madison Square Garden had been given more national attention with the 2004 renomination of George W. Bush, the first time the city hosted the GOP in the overwhelmingly liberal bastion of Manhattan.

The Garden was always the place to go—to see the Knicks or the Rangers or watch a sold-out Springsteen concert. If these same tourists traded their "Spamalot" tickets for one special September night at the Garden, they would have seen theater unlike any other Broadway venue.

Yes, it was theater of the highest form. Surprise, action and melodrama would play out tonight, for this was Frankie Ceteno's big night.

My eyes are playing tricks on me, thought Frankie as his name was announced to a thunderous ovation upon entering the Garden in his gold and black ensemble of trunks and robe. People everywhere were on their feet, cheering, stomping their feet, screaming, "Frankie! Frankie!" Among the onlookers were Donnelly and Reid in front row seats, Dr. Rubin and Dr. Liu plus many of the nurses at Bellevue who were off duty that night. Seated next to Detectives Donnelly and Reid were Ms. Green and Mr. Pappas. Then there was poor Cynthia, who had endured so much sacrifice by staying away while Frankie went through an agonizing and painful recuperation. Finally, there was his mother with Max's wife, Sophie. The <u>Times, Newsday, Post</u> and <u>Daily News</u> were all on hand. "Not just an ovation, but an uproarious, spontaneous response from the crowd for the young, scrappy Ceteno," wrote Dave Anderson of the <u>Times.</u> The entire city, yes, even the entire world had read about the young man, living in the Hell's Kitchen walkup with a big dream.

Determined to make it to the Garden, young Frankie had made his mark in just six months, getting back his strength, weight and full use of his damaged right hand intense therapy at the Rusk Rehabilitation Center. "Truly a miracle," noted Penny Crone of Fox News. People had followed his progress from the initial news reports to the interviews at Rusk, allowing even Sal Marciano to tell of his tough regimen as prescribed by his doctors. In fact, all New York made his story their story, bonding ever so close with Frankie every day. Students at Norman Thomas High School, where he graduated, sent a huge billboard; more emails came into Bellevue during his two-month stay. Japanese sumo wrestlers sent him a Buddhist greeting to ensure a speedy recovery and Gov. Pataki of New York stopped by in a surprise visit to say hello. The flowers numbered in the dozens and Frankie, ever the gentleman, sent them to children's wards, nursing homes and to HIV patients.

Here he was, ready to challenge the titleholder, Lloyd Hopkins, a man with an impressive 12-1 record. Hopkins was formidable; he had knocked-out fighters eight times and lost only once after a controversial ruling in Prague that gave the fight to an upstart from the Georgia republic. The champ, Hopkins, was given a big greeting by the Garden fans, but he knew the deal—people were coming to see if Ceteno, 'The Comeback Kid,' could withstand the challenge. It was considered a pipedream just a few short weeks ago. Ceteno had thought for a moment of giving up the effort but Max, ever the optimist, wouldn't allow Ceteno to indulge in such trash talk. "I've seen boxers for 40 years from the tough Irish and Italian neighborhoods and now Latino and blacks—you have what it takes so don't discourage yourself—you'll never live with yourself! You'll do it, goddamn it, you'll do it or what's your life all about?"

Unwittingly, Elias Matos had made Frankie Ceteno a hero. Instead of eliminating him, he elevated him to the most talked-about continuing saga that is always uniquely New York. Time completed an interview with him, giving him exposure of which he never would have dreamed. His piercing hazel eyes, complemented by a Roman nose, short-cropped hair, infectious grin and a solid body, soon made him an icon idol to many young girls. Even Stallone, Tyson and Lenox Lewis, plus a host of other boxers emerged, encouraging and telling him to hang tough and persevere. Leno had the audience cheering for him when the normally taciturn Ceteno appeared for a few nervous moments. Typically Leno, he got the audience on their feet roaring for him when he said, "You set this up to get the publicity, right—well it worked!"

Even foreign journalists, discussing subway safety in New York, cited the Ceteno case and his story made the headlines in Le Monde, Manchester Guardian, Corriere della Sera and Der Spiegel. Subsequently, he was invited to fight in Britain, France and Italy. And Frankie was humbled by seeing the less-fortunate who had lost limbs in accidents and falls.

Caroline Kennedy Schlossberg, California Governor Schwarzenegger and the Shriver family invited him to the Special Olympics memorial run for Rosemary Kennedy. Even the archbishop of New York, Edward Cardinal Egan, cited Frankie as an inspirational figure who would not give up, inviting him to the 10:15AM High Mass at St. Patrick's Cathedral and the entire congregation was on their feet when he introduced young Ceteno saying, "He represents all that is good and never once asked for pity or sought vengeance against his attacker."

Like it or not, one can make history under the most trying conditions. Frankie, now a celebrity, drew big crowds to the 14th Street Gym. Max even thought of charging admission to see Frankie spar in preparation for his debut bout. "These damn newspaper people are always calling but they wouldn't be here at all if this was just a normal fight," he said.

Max was right again. He usually was. Yet, Max and everyone else knew that this was no ordinary night, no ordinary fight. Max knew it, the press knew it and Hopkins knew it too. Was it worth it? Did he really stand a chance against the powerhouse that was Hopkins? A decent and affable man, he was known as the Jamaican Torpedo, and had the fastest jabs since Sugar Ray Leonard. Ceteno respected him and knew that he would be formidable in the ring.

But it wasn't just Frankie's night. He hadn't done it alone. Parts of everyone who helped Frankie were in the ring too. Day after day, physical therapists, with their strenuous exercises, challenged him to the max. "It hurt like hell, but I had to stay focused on the prize," he often said. He became what Max always suspected—determined, strong and a visionary. "This kid's got guts; I saw it in his eyes the first day he stepped into the gym," he said. Even Dr. Rubin, always the realist, told him not to expect 100% usage of his right arm. But, as a southpaw, he knew he could overcome the obstacle and get his hand working like it did before the accident. The therapy, advice, prayers and motivation all seemed to come together. Indeed, Rubin expected 10 months before any fight activity; Frankie had outdone it by a full two months and the media picked up on it with a series of interviews, labeling him "The Comeback Kid." Even Donald Trump set up a mini-gym during his therapy at Bellevue, which Frankie donated to Bellevue's therapy department when he was released and entered Rusk Rehabilitation Center. He never forgot the doctors, nurses, security and cafeteria staff who had come by to see him as his story unfolded. The headline in the tabloid <u>Post</u> said it all with bold headlines: **New York's Hometown Hero Goes Home.**

The routine—the beautiful, painful routine—had returned as if it never left. The gym, with its faded yellow walls and torn posters never looked so beautiful. Even the odor of the place was a familiar welcome for him. The stale, musty locker room smell Soon the routine came back with the determination that helped him so quickly recover. Jogging, sprinting, jump roping and the added arm curls from the trainer at Bally's was put into the mix to make Ceteno the full package. His right hand and overall body responded as if that fateful afternoon on the subway never happened. Once again, diet and exercise became his religion and he was the devoted communicant.

Within four months, Max, chomping nervously on his always unlit cigar and running his fingers through his matted hair, blurted out: "He's ready—he's ready."

So it all came down to this night. This beautiful autumn night. As tourists flocked to the Empire State Building, the new musicals, restaurants, museums and the free concert by Sting at the Sheep Meadow of Central Park, they surely missed out on the biggest ticket of the year—the debut of Frankie Ceteno. Political conventions, concerts and sporting events with the Knicks and Rangers paled in comparison to this emotional roller coaster that made it such a uniquely New York story. The Hell's Kitchen resident brought out the best in all of New York. Tonight, the Garden was electrified like a political convention.

Jimmy Breslin, ever the peripatetic journalist, wrote in Newsday, "Ceteno has brought out the best not only in a boxer, but also every person with a dream. This young man united the whole city. Winning is immaterial at this point. Ceteno, even if he's knocked out in the first round, is the winner. He's won over New York from the medical profession who never gave up on him to some 14-year-old kid in Bushwick who sees his story and wonders—maybe me. He represents the best that is New York, a city that has seen its share of troubles and heartaches. Yes, he's won over New Yorkers of every race, creed and economic status. But the most important person this young man has won over is himself. All he has to do is step into the ring—he's already a winner who gave this city something to believe in and gave us hope and made dreams come true again. He's the biggest winner of all."

Round I began and Ceteno and Hopkins faced each other. The Garden was still. Whatever the outcome, Breslin, as usual, was right on target—the real winner was the Ceteno in all of us.

CHAPTER 2

"Professor, can I leave early? I have to get my daughter at the center on East 110 Street," said Katherine Lopez.

Joan Conway, adjunct professor of history at the Manhattan campus of Mercy College, located directly across from Macy's on West 35th Street, knew her students well. Many of her students were single mothers and needed an extra few minutes to pick up their children or needed to get to a jobsite and leave class early. "Sure," she replied. Katherine Lopez was one of her best students. Katherine, like many in her class of undergraduates in American history from 1877 to the present, were recent arrivals to the US and tried desperately to learn English and better themselves and their children. She was an Ecuadorian and loved American history and the manner in which Conway taught.

Joan knew that Katherine would make up any extra work and appreciated her concern. A single mother herself, Joan had empathy for all struggling students, having gone through tough times herself. Katherine quietly left, giving a thumbs up to Professor Conway. Katherine reminded her of her young days when she was a struggling student at a time when women were expected to marry and raise families. "She'll be fine," she said to herself as she continued her lecture: "Effects of the Great Depression on New York City."

Joan Conway, unlike most of her students, was a native New Yorker, born to Irish-Polish parents at St. Clare's Hospital in 1946. She excelled at Sacred Heart School and later at Cathedral High School, winning a scholarship to Fordham University where she received both her BA and MA in 20th Century American history on a Pell grant. That was the only way she could complete her education—through financial aid. Ever a diligent student, she was pursuing her PhD at NYU on a scholarship, when she met Jason Scarborough, a lanky, blue-eyed, blond graduate student from Memphis. Scarborough, like Conway, was a PhD candidate. Scarborough's expertise, however, was in European history, specializing in the Renaissance and Reformation . In fact, his doctoral thesis examined the role of the printing press in the spread of Lutheranism in Northern Europe. Entitled, "Gutenberg's Contribution to the Spirit of Free Thought," it was destined to be published. He was also given a grant and traveled to both Upsala University in Sweden and Wittenberg, Germany, where he was given access to primary documents showing the impact of the written words of Martin Luther in the vernacular throughout the German and Scandinavian countryside. Just back and about to defend his thesis, he met Joan while walking in nearby Washington Square on an unusually warm April morn. She sat at a nearby bench just under the Washington Arch, relaxing while completing the <u>Times</u> crossword puzzle to pass the time before going to her afternoon lecture on the New Deal by Professor Johnson.

Joan remembered looking up and seeing Jason. H e was 6'1" with thick blond hair and Robert Redford looks, pale blue bedroom eyes, wearing a short sleeved, white Polo shirt that revealed a Mark Spitz-like body. "He was beautiful," she fondly recalled. She couldn't help but look at such a sight.

Their eyes met.

"Hi," he said. "I see you in the library often."

Joan remembered this first encounter when Jason, in an effort to make small talk, remarked how unusual it was to have a 90 degree day in April and proceeded at once to tell her that he thought her blond hair and dark eyes were a distraction when he was studying at the library. Joan, shy and a bit unassuming, got the nerve to ask Jason to sit. Although a tough New Yorker, she had a soft touch and Jason was a visiting Adonis. She prayed that the butterflies swirling in her stomach wouldn't last.

"Yes, I've seen you at the library. In fact, you were there last night sitting by the window on the fifth level." Jason added, "You're always so intense in your studies. I like that."

"Well, I'm trying to focus on my graduate work in history," Joan replied in a whisper, hoping she didn't make a fool of herself.

"Well, we have something in common--I like European history and am pursuing my doctorate on the effects of the printing press on free thought."

"Sounds pretty heavy, but I know what you mean. The research can be challenging," Joan responded.

"Yes, we have something in common—history, although my area is American 20th century."

"By the way, my name's Jason. And you are—?"

"Joan, a rare breed here, a native New Yorker from Hell's Kitchen."

What beautiful teeth, she thought as he began to talk of his Tennessee roots and his love of New York City. Sitting there, they began to get to know a little of what each had in common besides a love for history. Joan mentioned the theater and growing up in Hell's Kitchen while Jason talked of his summers at his uncle's chalet in the Smokey Mountains. They ended up talking for what seemed an eternity but like all new encounters, it was just a few minutes. But those few minutes were enough. Joan was smitten and Jason knew it.

What followed was the beginning of a romance that lasted for six months with a lot of highs and lows. She needed attention. Joan was lonely, introspective and withdrawn. Jason was the perfect match. He was outgoing with many friends. They found common ground in such endeavors as Broadway musicals, dinners in small cafes along Bleecker Street, poetry recitals at Café Reggio on MacDougal and sitting under a tree, resting her head on Jason's lap. Joan became part of Jason's world.

But, after six months, a discovery would forever change Joan. It was a day that years later, teaching college, caused a lump in her throat and a longing for what could have been. She looks back on that day when, as a commuting student and not wanting to return uptown, instead she went up to Jason's dorm around the corner from the elegant Georgian townhouses, known as 'The Row' that aligned Washington Square North." Arriving unannounced to tell Jason that she had finished her finals early, she entered into his room, smelling a woman's fragrance which she recognized immediately as Elizabeth Taylor's Passion. It was a perfume she didn't use. Like most women, she knew that the smell of a different fragrance spelled trouble. She then encountered Jason in bed with another graduate student, Lois Bartley. At once, Jason let go of Lois, grabbing his pants and following Joan out of the room into the hallway of the studio on Barrow Street and into the street, shouting at her and begging her to understand. A tough product of Hell's Kitchen, she told Jason to go to hell and the next day, dropped out of college, mailing him the keys to his apartment with no note or explanation attached. She refused to open the three letters he sent, sending them back unopened. When he tried calling her, Joan's supportive mother, knowing things that only a mother knows, politely told Jason "Joan is no longer living here. She needs some time to herself." *"God forgive me for lying,* Maria Conway said to herself, *but I won't let him hurt my Joanie.*

15 years later and happily married to a local homeboy of Armenian-Italian background, Joe Gregorian, she looked back with nostalgia and regret on what happened on that November afternoon. Certain good memories with Jason never left her—the time they went to Asbury Park for the weekend and the feeling of being a kid again when eating ice cream on the boardwalk, hand in hand with Jason. But she also remembers submitting to Jason's charms and ending up with him at his studio apartment for three hours. Always careful, she found Jason irresistible and ended up getting intimate with him. He promised her all the while of his devotion to her. Joan was not used to this attention. Her family, her father proudly boasted, "came from the school of hard knocks."

Her father, Tim Conway, was a tough, hard-drinking local who, although faithful to his wife and kids, spent too much time at the bars along 9th and 10th Avenues before the advent of the yuppie invasion and gentrification of the West Side. Foul-smelling, a gruff manner complemented his sad eyes with a wrinkled brow. He always offered a "Hiya Joanie" whenever he came into the 9th Avenue walkup. Joanie was his pride and joy and he was determined to make sure she made it, sacrificing to get her into parochial school and always showing up for his daughter at school events. "She's the only one in the whole bunch who will make something of herself," he remarked one Christmas. Joan understood her father and loved him despite his distance.

Her mother, Maria Louise, a devout Catholic, was the first generation of Polish-American immigrants from Warsaw and a war bride who met her father when his battalion was assigned to assist refugees from Eastern Europe in 1945. Maria insisted that her two girls, Joan and Patricia, and her son Michael attend the local parochial school in the tough neighborhood of the 50s and 60s known for its notorious Westies gang. So, Jason was a dream come true.

He was her first real love and his unfaithfulness left her devastated. When she announced her withdrawal from NYU, her father was livid. She was, after all, the first to graduate college and make something of herself.

Joan's mother Maria, was much more sympathetic, having gone through tough times with Conway. Marrying into an Irish family was difficult enough for someone who was new to America. In fact, many of her in-laws were opposed to a 'mixed marriage' with a Polack! For Joan, it was easier to identify with her mother, who had her share of hurt and left her family and country for the man she loved. Taciturn, hurt and controlled, she refused to tell her parents of the details of three months of intimacy with Jason. Had her father and brother known the truth, she feared that they would get the locals, 'Westies' and others and set out to get Jason. Worse, as a woman scorned, she might be thrown from her home and have to fend for herself. The last thing Joan wanted to do was hurt her family. So, she retreated, took a job in the public school system after securing the necessary educational courses from Hunter College and one year later, at age 24, largely out of boredom and fear of her biological clock ever ticking, married Joseph Gregorian.

Joe Gregorian was a tall, dark-haired man with a rough exterior to match a tender side. He graduated and went on to welding school and had a decent job with a large Queens company, Myers Welding. Joan knew that this marriage would work, as Joe was loyal and respectful. Unlike Jason, who wanted Joan to live with him, Joe waited until their marriage to sleep with her. Aware of her hurt from both Jason and the circumstances surrounding her disappointment of leaving school, he was the perfect person for her at that time in her life. With his job as a welder and her teaching in the public school, they thought of owning a home in the suburbs and living out their years in suburbia.

Both worked hard, raising their two sons. Joe spent his spare time coaching the local Hell's Kitchen Pop Warner baseball team that met on 51st Street, off 10th Avenue. It was a good bonding. His sons honed their skills and, with Joe's encouragement, became star players. Joan knew she made the right decision in marrying Joe, even though Jason was always with her. It bothered her that his presence never left, but something just felt left out. She got on with her life, devoting her energy and love to her boys and Joe. Then tragedy struck in 1987.

The principal came to her classroom and said there was an urgent call for her. She had no idea of what events were to unfold. "Ms. Conway, (she found it easier to use her maiden name) something may have happened with your husband. The woman from the office, I don't know her name, asked for me to get you on the phone. She used your husband's last name. Let's go to the office." The look of fear and exasperation was evident on Joan's face. The principal, Ms. George, gave her a gentle touch as she raced to a phone in the office.

"Mrs. Gregorian?" The voice on the other end was clearly shaky.

"Yes, this is Joan Gregorian, who is this?"

"I'm the receptionist at Myers Welding. It's Marie Collins."

"Sorry, I didn't recognize your voice—is there something wrong with Joe? The secretary said there was an emergency. What happened?"

"I'm afraid there was an accident and he has been sent by ambulance to Cornell Medical Center. Can you get over there?

"My God, what happened?"

"I'm not sure, but the supervisor and some crew went to the hospital and told me to get in touch with you and for you to get to Cornell. The paramedics didn't say much—I wish I had some reassuring news."

"Oh God, do you know anything about what happened?" Joan asked.

"No, but please get someone to take you there. Please have someone take you to the emergency room now."

Joan hung up the phone and the secretary's aide, Nancy Cruz, took her hand and got her coat to shield against the March wind and headed for Cornell. Cabs were always on 9th Avenue, so they had no trouble flagging one within a few minutes. She didn't remember anything except for Ms.Cruz holding on her hand. Along the way, she had a sinking feeling, the kind of feeling one gets when one knows but can't or won't come to terms with an untenable situation.

Arriving 15 minutes from the PS #17 on 47th Street to Cornell on East 67th Street, Joan was ushered into the emergency waiting area and, when told of her arrival, three of the fellows on the job came up and embraced her. She recognized Joe's foreman, Frank Gorman. He did not look directly into her eyes. She found that unusual and scary. Gorman was a no-holds barred man who was well respected by his crew. Joan remembered Joe telling her that he was a fair and decent man.

"Where's Joey, what's going on?" she asked.

"Oh, Joan, I'm so sorry it happened."

"What? Tell me; tell me!" she shouted.

"It all happened so quick; Joe was sitting on his break and a piece of metal fell from the construction site and hit him. He was..."

"Don't even go there—is he going to make it? I need to see him now!"

"I don't know what to tell you; the ambulance driver said it didn't look good." Gorman put his hand on her shoulder as he added, "He didn't look good. He's in surgery now." Gorman then took Joan into his burly arms and held her tight, allowing the tears to flow from both the teacher and himself.

After what seemed hours but was a mere 10 minutes, a team of three doctors came out of the emergency area. One of the doctors approached Joan. She didn't like the look in his eyes. "I could see that they weren't making eye contact," she remembers. As an educator, she knew that avoiding eye contact wasn't helpful.

"Mrs. Gregorian?"

"Yes?"

"I'm Dr. Crawford. Your husband suffered irreversible brain damage. We did everything we could. I wish I had better news, but he died 10 minutes ago. I'm so very sorry."

Frank Gorman took Joan by the hand once again and she kept shaking her head, sobbing softly and saying, "Frank, he didn't deserve this. He was working overtime to buy us a house and get the kids into college. Oh why do these things happen? He was a good man, a good man. Why? Why?"

The funeral of Joseph Gregorian was well attended by members of his extended family which included his mother, three sisters and two brothers plus Joan's parents and brother, sister and many of the staff at Myers Welding, plus the staff at PS #17 and neighbors and friends. The wake was held at Buckley's on West 43rd Street followed by a Mass at Holy Cross. Holy Cross, the oldest building on 42nd Street, was beautifully decorated with flowers celebrating the 150 anniversary of a church that saw the famous Fighting 69th during World War I of Irish regiments who distinguished themselves in the French trenches and was forever immortalized with a movie and famous statue of Father Duffy in Times Square.

Joan's apartment was full of people who brought all kinds of foods, from cold cuts, such as ham and cheese for sandwiches to ethnic dishes, such as *pasta fagioli, cannoli* and *baklava.* Joe would have liked the mix of construction workers, teachers, students and Hell's Kitchen neighbors who attended his funeral. His sons were strong, but Joan, in the arms of her brother, had a rough time saying goodbye. Joe was buried in Cavalry Cemetery in Queens in the family plot that held his father and grandparents and had room for Joan. Joan's recollection of the events were murky; she was also consoled by her 14 and 12 year-old sons, Joe Jr. and Owen. Once again, like that dreadful day at NYU, Joan felt betrayed, angry and alone. Angry at herself, God and the world around her, she became more reclusive and, in the weeks after the funeral, sat for hours reading and not answering her phone.

Within five months, Joan's father died at age 67 from long years of medical neglect and over drinking. Joan's mother consoled herself with the faith that always sustained her. Both she and her daughter were recent widows. They bonded closer and Joan's dream of happiness seemed to be gone and her life was now centered on her two young sons. Occasionally, she thought of Jason and wondered what kind of life he was leading. Surely by now he had obtained a professorship at a prestigious college and was secure in the knowledge that academia provided him a comfortable niche. By now, he had either married Lois or some other woman and surely never thought of the moments they shared together. He would have long forgotten that she ever existed. Yet, even now in her grief, after 16 years, she often wondered what would have happened if she stayed, finished her PhD and married Jason.

Joan continued to work at the school until 1991 when she decided she needed to change things in her life. She took supervisory courses at Baruch and was installed as an assistant principal at her school. The additional salary plus the settlement of $150,000 from Joe's accident would help get her boys through school and college. Already, Owen was an outstanding baseball player for Chelsea High School and Joe Jr. was a history buff like his mother and scored 98% on US History Regents exam at his school, John F. Kennedy in the Bronx. Despite her loneliness, she remained a good daughter to an aging mother racked with asthma and emphysema due to years of smoking largely out of neglect from second-hand smoking by her husband. The diseases caught up with her mother who died in 1994 at age 73. Joan, at age 48, had her sons and brother and sister and yet felt very alone. Coming back from Cavalry after her mother's internment, she felt guilty for thinking about Jason and not her mother or husband. For the next few months, after cleaning out her mother's apartment, she thought again of leaving, but where would she go? "I was born in the Kitchen and I'm destined to die here, too," she said to herself.

In 2004, Joan retired from the school system after 30 years of service. Both her sons were grown—Joe Jr. had a BA from CUNY and Owen, always the History buff like his mother, was finishing his MA a U Albany. Her retirement package gave her a nice nest egg—$5000 per month pension and a chance to teach at Mercy as an adjunct at the request of her principal.

Her retirement party was attended by family and colleagues; she hadn't been involved romantically with anyone since Joe's death 17 years earlier. Despite a promise of a good life, she knew something was missing. Again, at her retirement party, she thought of Jason. At least, she would teach at leisure pace at the college and travel to Europe and possibly South America. It was time for her to do something for herself.

Students in Joan's class at Mercy found her affable, intelligent, entertaining and well-prepared. Her classes from 2004-2006 were full and the waiting list was such that the department chair, Dr. Murphy of the main Dobbs Ferry campus, asked her to teach two classes. Joan had to admit that she was enjoying her debut in academia as an adjunct professor and wondered why so many years earlier she had let her heart dictate her decision. In retrospect, she had a good life, however abbreviated, with Joe. She knew he would have approved of her stern measures in bringing up Junior and Owen. Now both were married and Joan had two granddaughters who were her pride and joy. "If only Joe had lived to see this," she lamented. Again, a vision of a young, handsome, seductive Jason came into view. Joan quickly regained her composure and began her class lecture for April 12, 2005—"The Election of FDR in 1932 and the New Deal." She did not let the date go unnoticed—it was the 60th anniversary of the death of FDR.

"In order to understand the depths of the Depression, it's necessary to see our city and the conditions that surrounded it in 1932 which led to the defeat of Hoover and the election of Franklin D. Roosevelt." Joan proceeded to play a 21 minute video from the History Channel which showed the depths of the Depression in the city—Hoovervilles in Central Park, bread lines on Wall Street, people evicted from their apartments, banks closing their doors while frantic and screaming crowds of depositors demanded to enter. The video had a profound effect on Joan's class, many of whom never had the opportunity to take a class in American history.

At the close of the video, several students' hands were raised. "Why didn't Hoover do something to stop the Depression?" "How come people were being evicted?" "If Hoover fed half the world in World War I, like you said the other day, why didn't he help his own people in the Depression?" Joan knew that she had touched a nerve with these students. The video was graphic, showing white and black New Yorkers suffering the indignities of the Depression and blamed an insensitive Hoover for the crash. Joan, ever the good teacher, threw the questions back to the class, starting a debate over the role of government in people's lives, the theory of Keynesian economics, the aura of FDR and the activism that surrounded the New Deal First 100 Days. After an hour of class discussion, she gave a series of handouts that highlighted the alphabet legislation that transformed the US. At this point, she asked students to look into their wallets and pocketbooks.

"Many of you work and you have a Social Security card. What is the concept of social security? How does it work? Why is George W. trying to dismantle the system?" The class summarized the program through the series of handouts and a few defended the Bush proposal to direct a private savings for younger people before the system goes bankrupt.

Joan knew her students were thinking when they started debating the merits of tampering not only with social security, but the social implications it had on the US.

She listened to some of the banter from Greg Armstrong and Mike Coffey—"People are living longer, we have to do something?" Armstrong said, adding "Social security should never be tampered with—it's the Bible of the New Deal, the Republicans and Bush want to get rid of any vestiges of the New Deal." "What about us and our future? Bush is right on target when he talks about saving Social Security for our generation." Coffey quickly interjected. A smiling Joan then asked the students, as the class was coming to a close, to write a reaction paper of two to three pages summarizing the major precepts of the New Deal.

After class, several students came up to the desk. One said, "Professor Conway, I really liked the video and the discussion we had today. It meant a lot to see people in suits begging for jobs and food."

Another said, "I guess we should be thankful that we have unemployment, social security and the need to help others." Joan, well aware of many of the immigrant student status, could sympathize. During her lecture, she mentioned that her own grandfather, Tim Conway, the oldest of seven children, went to Montana as member of the CCC and worked on the Missouri River flood control program. She was proud that her own family had a linkage to the lesson.

Taking on this class had been a real joy for her. Alone much of the time, except for occasional visits from her sons and their families, she spent much time preparing her interesting lectures at the NY Public Library 40th Street branch, a mere 15 minute walk from her apartment in Hell's Kitchen. She was delighted when the department chair sent Dr. Anita Rodriguez of Mercy's Graduate Center to observe, remarking, "It's not too late for you to get that PhD and be a full professor." She thanked the good professor.

"I'm not stressed out like I used to be when I was in the public school system, but thanks anyway. I'm going to focus on giving myself a much-needed vacation."

All Dr. Rodriguez said was, "You go girl!"

By late August, Joan was on a trip of a lifetime. Taking off at Newark Liberty, she checked her two bags for London on Virgin Airways Flight #2. Having flown with Joe several times to the Caribbean and Bermuda, she was not afraid of flying, but this was her first overseas tour. She boarded the flight and took her copy of *The Da Vinci Code* out for the long flight to Heathrow. She was excited and couldn't concentrate on her book.

As dinner was being served, the passenger next to her, a young male Brit, asked, "First time to the UK?"

"Yes, I've always wanted to go, but had other job and family responsibilities, you know."

"Well, I'm Jack, may I ask where you're staying in London?"

"On Russell Square at the President Hotel."

Jack quickly responded. "Oh, I know the area well; you selected a central spot."

Jack continued to tell her "I'm a 24 year-old recording artist who was in New York on business and am now returning home to my flat in the Kensington area of London."

By the time the plane landed six hours later, Joan got her fill on places to go to. *What a great kid*, she thought. *If only I were thirty years younger!*

Jack helped her board the right train to Russell Square and wished her well, reminding her to "watch her coins" as the pound was extremely strong against the dollar. Joan gave Jack a hug and she couldn't help but notice that he gave her a big thumbs up.

Riding the train into London, Joan felt free and eager to begin her adventure. Arriving at the President, she noticed a large amount of tourists from the US. Settling into her third floor room, she was struck by the room—typically wall-papered in floral pattern with a twin bed, bathroom with shower and a view of Russell Square. She was anxious to see London but hated being alone.

"If only I hadn't left that day so many years ago at NYU. I wonder where I would be today," she said to herself.

Feeling guilty for not thinking of Joe, she freshened up, had dinner in the cafeteria of the hotel and went on a three hour tour of the city that highlighted the main attractions from Trafalgar Square to Piccadilly to Buckingham Palace and St. James Park. Being the history buff, she took her guidebook and spent three hours at Westminster Abbey, finding the presence of royalty, writers, politicians and artists a great delight. After a few days, Joan's felt relaxed. A changed and happier, less brooding person. She was ready to take the chunnel to Paris for two days before ending in Rome for a three day stay.

Paris was indeed a city in which to fall in love. Taking the Bateau Moche on a night sightseeing tour, she conversed with fellow travelers from Iowa and California. She marveled at the floodlights illuminating the government buildings along the Seine, the beauty of Notre Dame and the lovers walking and publicly embracing along the riverbank. She was both enthralled and melancholy in the City of Lights. The next day, like the good tourist she was, she went for café au lait atop the Eiffel Tower and later walked along the Seine like the lovers the previous night, wondering what it would have been like for her so many years ago. Again, images of Jason poured forth. She began to weep softly, feeling alone in a city that reaches out for your embrace. After all these years, it still hurt. She noticed a tall, slender man looking at her. Feeling uncomfortable, she walked away, never bothering to see if he was still staring.

She walked back to her hotel where a group of Americans from a Methodist church in western Kansas were outlining their itinerary for the next day and Joan, ever the teacher, reminded them to make sure to spend time at the Louvre and see the Mona Lisa. "You're in for a unique experience," she told them. "Make sure you spend the day there and plan nothing else.!"

When she got to Rome the next day on the express train, her mood was much improved. She took the #64 to the Vatican, remembering to watch her valuables as this was the bus known for its notorious pickpockets of unsuspecting tourists headed for the majesty of the Vatican and the Sistine Chapel. Seeing the 'Creation' by Michaelangelo was the highlight of the Vatican tour for her.

"I must take a refresher course or seminar in Renaissance painting," she remarked to a friendly young man on line who hailed from Plattsburgh in upstate New York. The afternoon was punctuated. by a great Italian dinner along the Piazza Repubblica with a view of ancient Roman ruins and a concert beginning at 8 PM of Neapolitan songs. With her glass of Chianti and salada misto, which consisted of seafood and pasta, Joan was relaxed and grateful that she finally got to see what her fellow educators had witnessed many times before. Life was all around her from the beautiful music, to the night air, to the young lovers strolling by the fountain. Yet, she felt so alone. Her magical trip was at last coming to an end.

The next day, she boarded her Delta flight to JFK, feeling rejuvenated and at ease.

She reached home in a better state of mind. The trip lasted 11 days and was without incident. Looking over the brochures and pictures taken, she knew this trip was good therapy for her and felt that an annual ritual would be to travel to different destinations far and wide and enjoy the time left. *Maybe Australia or Rio or China next year*, she thought. She didn't mind traveling alone, but gave serious consideration as a woman approaching 60 that a traveling companion should be considered. Her best friend, Linda McNeil, a retired educator and a recent divorcee, would be perfect. She would approach the subject with her in the next couple weeks. Putting down the brochure on Paris, she decided that an appreciation course on Renaissance Art would be her next venture. "I have to get to the Met and see the Renaissance wing again. It's been too long," she said quietly. A refresher course in European history would climax her venture.

Within a few months, a request went out to retired educators interested in traveling to enroll in a two week seminar on "Effect of Renaissance and Reformation on Europe" at the University of Virginia at Charlottesville. "This will give me the opportunity to combine my knowledge of American history and architecture at Jefferson's university with a period in European history that I can relate to." The brochure promised that retired educators would enjoy an appreciation course from the best scholars in European history. Joan didn't bother to examine the entire package, as she knew the University of Virginia would offer her an opportunity to visit the DC area, Monticello and Mount Vernon as well. The course would highlight the trip and the campus of the University of Virginia would be a sight to see. She accepted the offer.

Joan took Amtrak to Washington, spending a day touring the capital and the Vietnam Veterans Wall. She knew two men from Hell's Kitchen who were killed in Vietnam and, with the aid of volunteers, was able to locate the names on the imposing wall. She also visited her favorite presidents' memorial—Jefferson, Lincoln and the new FDR memorial. *I'm glad the disabled president is depicted in a wheelchair*, she thought as she studied the New Deal accomplishments etched in stone. She went to the National Cathedral and Arlington and placed a rose on the grave of JFK. It was an emotional time for her, for the assassination occurred within a few days after she found Jason with Lois. *The memories never fade*, she thought. *That day lives with me always.*

The next day, she rented a car at Avis on Avenue K and began the two hour drive on the interstate to Charlottesville. The beautiful Greek structures were Jefferson's gift and she would play a small role in gathering some knowledge among the beauty of such a bucolic setting. She was told that the professor conducting the seminar was a prolific writer on the period and a tenured professor at Vanderbilt University in Tennessee. Joan never read much on European history, as her area of expertise was American history. She never gave it a second thought as to which lecturer would be assigned.

Arriving at classroom 604 at the scheduled time, she glanced about the classroom. It held about 30 desks and Joan, short and a bit myopic, decided to take a front row seat. The professor's back was to the board. He was, she assumed, late 50s or early 60s. He was tall, with graying hair, and wore a perfectly tailored suit. There was something about his presence that made her look up from her notebook. She began to have that feeling once again like many years ago. That gut-wrenching feeling that made her feel out of control. "Oh no, please Jesus, it can't be!"

The professor turned to the class and Joan let out an audible gasp when he said, "Welcome to our seminar on the Renaissance and Reformation. I'm Dr. Jason Scarborough."

CHAPTER 3

"Good morning, everybody!" The loud voice was magnified by the cordless microphone used by the tour director for Platte Tours, Omaha, Nebraska. Joyce Nelson had been with the group since they left Omaha for a nine day bus tour that ended in New York. Next to her was NYC tour guide, Tony Russo, who had just boarded the bus. This was her chance to introduce the step-on guide from Manhattan, Tony Russo. Tony was her favorite. She always requested him from the NYC Convention and Tourist Board. She knew that the busloads of native Midwesterners were going to enjoy the city now that Tony was here. He was a walking encyclopedia, full of facts and anecdotes and most importantly, didn't talk down to the people and seemed to enjoy the job. Joyce had been in the tour business and had seen all kinds. What she looked for in a tour guide was a person who not only knew the city, but also was a happy person who treated her busloads of seniors as people. That person was Tony. Many of the people on the bus hadn't been east of Chicago before and despite the fact that they were a senior group, they were giddy, nervous and anxious to see the city. "They're like a bunch of school kids," Joyce remarked to Tony. Joyce wanted the best and knew Tony wouldn't let her down.

Just two months ago, she had a high school group from the state capital of Lincoln and Tony, knowing his audience, took them to the Chelsea Piers and Greenwich Village's Washington Square to see the street theatrics from roller-blading to The Bahamian Tumblers. The school group itself was the Drama Club and the setting in the village was too good to pass up. Tony knew his audience. Later that evening, he was their escort to "Mama Mia," which they thoroughly enjoyed, participating in the music and dancing to the rhythm.

Tony Russo was introduced to the seniors and proceeded to give his standard greeting, which consisted of welcoming everyone to the city and asking, "How many are here for the first time?" The show of hands was overwhelming; of the 43 passengers on the bus, 32 had never been to New York before. Sizing up his audience, Tony knew that he would entertain this group by citing facts, showing them sites they had seen only in movies and TV. Tony quickly put his own cell phone on vibrate, as he was expecting a call. A very important call! Tony wanted to act as normal as possible, especially in the presence of Joyce, one of his favorites.

The bus driver, Tom Engstrom, was with the group from day one. A native Nebraskan whose roots went back to his German and Norwegian immigrant great-grandparents, he was a bit awed by the city. "Tony, just tell me where to turn and let me know when you want to stop," he said. Tony sized up Tom, a fortyish, balding, overweight man who probably took this assignment because it took him to New York and gave him a chance to see this part of the country and get away from his wife and kids.

"Are you glad you're here, Tom?" Tony couldn't resist finding out if his instincts were right. "Yeah, I was here on my honeymoon 19 years ago and want to see the changes. Gives me a chance to get away, too," Tom said as Tony smiled broadly, giving Tom a gentle pat on his right shoulder. Tony knew that Tom would be in for a real surprise because the city had changed since he was last here. Having conducted tours for over 15 years, Tony knew the rules: first establish a rapport with the driver, make him feel at ease and include him in the commentary. *Everyone wants to feel that they're important,* Tony thought as he began to outline the route for the downtown tour of Manhattan.

It was one of those bright and warm, but not muggy, days that preceded the advent of a long, hot summer. "Morning. It's the best time to work and the best time to see the city," he said to the group. Tony knew these Midwesterners would see the real New York—loud, intimidating, challenging and almost surreal in its never-ending drama. The older passengers would be able to put up with the weather, which made all the difference. Tony wore his standard attire—a short powder blue shirt and matching red tie. *This group's from Nebraska—a red state and they don't like surprises. Good Midwestern conservative values,* he thought. He knew his audience well and where to go with his commentary, so essential to getting the group's attention.

Before the bus left the Milford Plaza at 8th and 44th Street, Tony announced to the group that they would be heading down Broadway, ending at Battery Park for the 12 noon ferry to the Statue of Liberty and Ellis Island. "I see you have your cameras out, good, and I see some of you with light jackets. Today should be about 72, typical for late May in the city." He couldn't help but notice the fact that all were white, elderly and were atypical of what a New Yorker is—largely rural, Scandinavian and German surnames judging from the tags each was wearing: Lang, Sorenson, Anderson, Schmidt etc. He liked these senior, homogenous groups; they were easy to entertain, punctual and cooperative unlike some of the high school groups he had to work with who constantly wanted to know where P Diddy, Rosie O'Donnell, Tom Cruise and other celebrities lived. Seniors obeyed and were the most cooperative.

Tony's job as a tour guide was but a temporary step in his bid to act. He had been in NYC for 16 years from upstate Mechanicville in the Capital District, just 17 miles north of Albany.

After graduating, he majored in theater at Boston University and his goal was to come to NYC and make it in theater. He lived in a six-story walkup just a few blocks away on 48th and 10th Avenue. The work assignment was just a five minute walk from his Hell's Kitchen studio, a studio that was a throwback to the dumbbell apartments built for immigrants, complete with a tub in the kitchen! He knew all the tenants in the building and was always looking out for the older residents, such as 87 year-old Mrs. Clancy, for whom he always shopped. He had appeared in minor roles in off-Broadway plays and had been a SAG member for the past five years. Like most people in the arts, he worked with a larger goal in mind. "The dream is always there; never, never give up hope," Tony kept reminding himself. Tony was no quitter.

Tony's mood was euphoric, as he had just auditioned for a new sitcom entitled "Hell's Kitchen," about the myriad personalities that make up the special New York neighborhood. The line for the casting call went around the block at the Al Hirschfeld Theater on 45th Street. Tony read a three-minute segment on the character Jim Holloway, an upstart actor from Idaho trying to make it in the big city. Like Russo, the Holloway role had a goal of making it as an actor while working as a waiter at the local Greek diner on 9th Avenue, a bookstore and was taking acting classes and going on constant cast calls. The casting director, Muriel Stewart, had a smile on her face when he finished the reading. He hoped he sounded like an Idaho native.

First impressions and first readings were the meal tickets to a role. "Maybe, just maybe, this one fits me perfectly and I found my niche," he kept reassuring himself.

Before he left, Ms. Stewart's assistant, Mark Goodman, putting down his styrofoam coffee cup, remarked to him, "I liked your passion when you read. Very real, nice job." He left feeling good, but knowing the competition was fierce and this was step one in determining who would ultimately get the role. Yet, he felt something different inside. "My big break," he whispered as he walked away. He remembered that this reading, unlike others, was almost autobiographical and he hoped his identity with the character was a plus. The character, Holloway, was working in a bookstore while trying out for various parts. A neighbor, Ruth Halpern, tells him of an upcoming play based on Hell's Kitchen. She encourages Holloway to audition and within two call backs, lands a tour de force role that gives him a Tony nomination. "If only this was true," Tony kept saying after his reading at the Hirschfeld. "Who knows, maybe Holloway is me." He was, in fact, expecting a decision on the casting call today and, despite the tension, was determined to move on no matter what the decision was. *Please, people from Nebraska, bring me luck!* he thought.

"Hey, Tony," the driver shouted, "Which way?"

"Sorry, turn right on 46th Street, so we can go into Times Square." Reality had suddenly set in and he began by stating facts to get the groups' attention. "Hello and welcome to the Big Apple. Do you know that New York has more people than 38 states in the Union, that Brooklyn has more people than Philadelphia? There are more people living in Queens than Houston and the Bronx has more people than San Francisco and Boston combined." He got their attention by adding, "In addition to the 8 1/2 million people, we also have one million dogs, 800,000 cats and 17,000 psychiatrists." The laughter was enough; he knew he was on his way.

Within a few minutes, the bus entered into Times Square. "Let's see why they call it the Great White Way. Look around at the neon." As the bus proceeded down Broadway, Tony pointed out the Times Building where the ball came down on New Year's Eve. He knew the group would identify with some of these landmarks and pointed out the current running plays and could hear the group politely remarking, "All the people; look at that one with the tights, a balding, bespectacled man shouts."

Tony had been a tour guide for six years and had the routine down to a science. He looked upon each assignment as if he were performing a solo one act on Broadway. He loved the interaction with his group.

"Lord, look at these crowds!" shouted one woman in the back to no one in particular. Tony smiled as he was pointing out the current-running shows from "Sweeney Todd" to the showstopper, "Producers."

"We're at the crossroads of the world—42nd Street and Broadway. The seedy, tawdry neighborhood that once was Times Square has been replaced by ESPN bars, Disney attractions, Madame Tussaud's Museum and BB Kings, McDonalds and first rate movie theaters showing films not rated X. If you were 15 years ago, you would have run from here with all the interesting activities that went on, both legit and illegit—boy, I miss those days," he said as the group laughed.

Within five minutes traffic was flowing well on this Saturday morning and Tony knew he could get downtown with several stops for this elderly group. Passing Macys, the group remarked at the large amount of shoppers with their Macys, Conway, Old Navy and Victoria's Secret shopping bags. A police car raced through the red light, the siren overwhelming his monologue for the moment. The sight of several police cars at the corner of Broadway and 32nd Street was cause for discussion. "Are they going to jail," asked a man whose name tag said Otis Braun. Tony replied: "The police will give him and the others a ticket and they'll be fined. Most will be back tomorrow. Just trying to make it in the big town," he adds, almost apologetically. Within a few minutes, Tony and the others saw several people in custody, selling bogus DVDs and CDs.

"You must have a vendor's license, similar to my tour guide license, in order to conduct business." Tony pointed out to his license, displayed around his neck. He remembered too well the day when a young woman hit him with a $75.00 fine for not displaying his Department of Consumer Affairs license showing him to be licensed tour guide. "New York is strict when it comes to people getting ripped off and the police issue these summons for bogus Gucci, Louis Vuitton bags." He relates his own misfortune to the group. " I swear it must have been that twit's first day on the job."

"Some of us like to buy the fakes and give them as gifts," someone in the back shouted. Others join in. "Yeah, that's right." "We know they're fake, but they make good presents."

Tony explained that he too sympathized with the vendors, but the city wanted the consumer to know what they're buying. "Most of these guys are hard-working West African immigrants who send a good deal of their salaries to family back home, live in one-room apartments on 110 Street and are good workers. So, what if they're illegal!" Tony knew from experience how hard the city could be. He struggled with jobs ranging from working in markets, bookstores, restaurants and landed his tour guide job when a few fellow actors told him of the need for good guides with 35 million tourists a year to New York. Before heading to Greenwich Village, he quickly checked his cell phone, hoping for a message from Ms. Stewart. No luck.

"Is this where the Thanksgiving Day parade is?" asked a lady in the back.

"Yes," answered Tony. "5,000 Macy employees are used in the parade. We're right at the spot where the Rockettes and other celebrities are featured on TV courtesy of NBC and hosted by Dick Clark."

Within 15 minutes, the bus headed south onto 5th Avenue at 23rd Street when Tony pointed out one of his favorite buildings, the Flatiron, built in 1902. "Look at the interesting shape and you'll know why they call it the Flatiron Building. With its protruding front and beaux arts facade, it was the center of New York when Tin Pan Alley and vaudeville were in this location." "By the way, the expression '23 Skidoo' originated here when the Irish cops used to get the young boys off the streets from looking up the dresses of women, as this corner was one of the breeziest."

Arriving in Greenwich Village, Tony explained the origin of the name from Greenwich, England and recited a familiar history of the artists, writers and actors past and present who lived in this part of town. "Notice all the people eating *al fresco* at the Riviera."

"Is al fresco good?" one elderly man in a middle aisle seat asked. Tony, trying to prevent a grin and knowing that many of these visitors haven't heard cuisine talk, said to laughter, "Yes, ask the waiter, I'm sure he'll recommend it! So, be sure to order al fresco!"

The crowd was thick, a testament to the great weather and entering Soho, they came upon the Art Show. Tony pointed out that Soho stands for South of Houston and explained the gentrification of the village in the 60s led to a complete renovation of Soho, an old Italian neighborhood often used for backdrops to such movies as *Ghost, The Godfather* and TV shows like *NYPD Blue* and *Law and Order.* Tony noticed the one gray-haired woman commenting on the crowd, the art and architecture. One remarked, "You don't see big stores, a 711, a gas station or even many pickup trucks or children."

Tony couldn't resist. "This is Manhattan. The rents here are $2100 for a room with an adjoining closet—a studio. If you have a family and are middle class, you probably would live in the outer boroughs."

By the time the bus travels down Broadway towards the court area, he asked Tom to turn left onto Worth Street to see the Foley Square area. Pointing out the federal courthouse, Tony related the recent Martha Stewart trial and other notable trials in federal court, such as John Gotti's trial. He also showed the NYS Supreme Court Building and the Metropolitan Building with its ornate minarets and statue to Minerva, the Greek goddess of wisdom. "Many of you see these buildings on *NYPD Blue, Law and Order* and *The Practice.* He was always astonished at the beauty of the Metropolitan building with the minarets and ornate façade, a great segue to discussing the Brooklyn Bridge. Tony had all the tourists looking at the great promenade of the Brooklyn Bridge. He mentioned the facts, "It was finished in 1883; the first person to walk across it was the President, a former Tammany hack who became president after the assassination of Garfield, Chester A. Arthur, the 'dude president' who wore $2000 suits in 1882. This was the same Arthur who defended a black woman thrown off a street car because of her race and won a civil suit of what-was-then the enormous amount of $500.00."

Tony mentioned the best-selling book by David McCullogh which highlights the history of lower Manhattan in the 1880s. Tony worked the group by asking, "Are you enjoying the city—did you think it was this nice and clean! It doesn't smell—at least not here." He knew that this group would head home and tell of their tour.

The people on the bus noticed the crowd of mostly tourists walking towards the bridge and city hall. "This is the place where you history buffs know so well from Ticker Tape Parades to the oldest city hall in the country," he said.

Tony pointed out City Hall in its classic French Renaissance style. "Lincoln and Grant lay in state here. This is the oldest city hall in the country. Yet, we conveniently hide from you the Tweed Courthouse. Some of you who read a lot of history know that Boss Tweed ruled New York, ending up milking the city of millions of dollars before being extradited to America from Spain. Someone noticed the Nast cartoon and reported him to authorities and he ended up in jail with wall—to-wall carpeting and a manicurist every day. So much for prison conditions," he finished to laughter.

Entering into the Wall Street area, the Saturday crowds consisted of many school groups heading for Ground Zero, the site of the 911 terrorist attacks that brought down the World Trade Center. For Tony, this was a somber visit, as he was reminded of the two firemen he knew in his 47th Street firehouse and one person who worked in the souvenir shop on the 110th floor. He said little, allowing the crowd to absorb the enormity of the moment; he saw from their faces the pain and anger always visible when first-timers arrived here. 2001 was a year he would like to forget. It started off so promising when he got the lead in an off-Broadway cast called "Bermuda Dreams," about a cruise director and staff embarking on a mid-autumn cruise to Bermuda. Unfortunately, the critics didn't like the show, but Tony was given two very credible reviews in the Times and Post. If only they liked the show, it could have made it to Broadway. Two weeks after the show closed, 911 happened and his Dad died at the end of the month which caused him to miss several casting calls while comforting his mother upstate. To make matters worse,he suffered from a bout of shingles, which he attributed to the stress he endured over the year. Life hadn't been easy for him and he was determined not to let circumstances dictate his fate and would stay focused and keep his dream alive. But, with every passing year, he saw new talent and ultimately felt that he would remain one of New York's best tour guides for years to come. He checked his cell phone again. No messages.

By the time the bus arrived at Battery Park, the line of parked buses numbered over 50 and Tony knew the routine well. The weather brought out the numbers of visitors to the statue and Ellis Island. "Remember those vendors the cops were giving summons to in front of Macy's? Many of them are here with watches that say Gucci on one side and made in China on the other." As the laughter subsided, he told his group not to pay more than $20.00 for those watches. "It depends on what language you speak–French, Italian, German and Japanese are hit for $50.00, but with the bank rate in their favor, it's no problem. So only offer $20.00." Ms. Nelson smiled; she knew Tony was out to educate and look after her flock. Ms. Nelson kept quiet throughout Tony's commentary, occasionally nodding and smiling at his comments. The tour itself gave Joyce a chance to relax as well.

Within a few minutes, Tom parked the bus and the slow movement of the crowd inched closer to the ferry boats. Tony had the tickets for both the statue and Ellis Island and proceeded to take his group to a 30 minute wait for the ferry. He again checked his cell phone, but no calls. He had kept the phone on silence. He thought of putting it on vibrate, but he felt that too would be a distraction for him.

Waiting for the ferry was itself theater. Dozens of performers, hustlers, singers, vendors overwhelmed the tourists. Tony had already advised the group to buy from vendors with the Department of Consumer Affairs. "They're legit and you won't get ripped off," he told them. He liked the agile tumblers who were a spectacle to behold. Coming from Barbados, they had been written up in the city's major newspapers and even appeared on the Fox 5 morning show. The troupe consisted of six powerfully-built men who had spent hours rehearsing their routine of tumbling, jumping and gyrating that defied gravity. Tony especially like Abdul, a 6' 1" athletic man who had charmed his audience into a frenzy of shouts and buildup to a climactic human pyramid that amazed Tony time and again. The tourists were quick to take pictures and spend their wait applauding and awarding the troupe with dollars in a cap extolling 50 Cent's group—G-Unit. Abdul smiled at Tony and in a loud voice shouted, "You got a great guide here—give him some good tips!" Abdul gave Tony a high five as the group boarded the ferry to the Statue of Liberty. Tony checked his cell phone and still no calls. He looked outside the window momentarily distracted. He would wait until he got to Ellis Island before rechecking his calls.

After an hour at the statue, the group proceeded to Ellis Island. Tony always like this part of the trip; it gave him a chance to grab a bite and roam around the expanse of the island while the group watched a PBS film on the immigration at the island from 1892-1954. Tony informed the tourists to check the computers and locate their ancestors, provided they knew the date and proper name that was used as they entered America. "They're like kids when they discover their roots." He had once remarked to a fellow guide, Jerry Moore.

Tony had already given the group an extensive walking tour of the exhibits, showing this largely German and Scandinavian group pictures from the farming areas of the Dakotas and Minnesota and their state of Nebraska. Upstairs where the pictures are gave his group a chance to see the old photographs that aligned the second floor of the vast area used as a reception center for the millions of new immigrants. A few of the people recognized the towns of the Midwest where their forebears immigrated. Then, Tony showed them the website to check on their own family and gave them 30 minutes to explore. During this period, he usually ran into fellow tour guides and, like most workers, swapped stories over what group he had, how they responded and if the day was going to be a success. This was his time to chill, make calls, check his cell phone once again and get a bite to eat. As he entered the expansive cafeteria with beautiful black and white photos of arriving immigrants, he spotted Miriam Stern, a fellow guide.

Tony approached Miriam, also a struggling actress from Hell's Kitchen, who was known for her quick and sometimes risque wit.

"Tony, how's everything? You're looking great." Miriam always had a good word; he remembered a dreary, damp depressing Noreaster in which both of them had to work with a large high school group from Virginia. It was Miriam who won the day by taking them to the MTV studios in Manhattan, which was gracious enough to allow for an instant tour, complete with the sets used by rappers and other artists for the students to see.

Like a good diplomat, Miriam also got the students to purchase from the large selection of DVDs, CDs and clothing. She made Tony's day and he was grateful whenever they worked together. "A real team player," Tony said to himself.

"How's your day been?' asked Tony, noticing Miriam was wearing a print rose-colored dress with her hair tied back and shoes that nicely complemented her dress. She sipped on a bottle of Evian water. At 45, she kept herself active with yoga and, despite the rates, kept a membership at the pricey New York Sports Club.

"Not bad, T," she said. "They're a middle-aged, church group from St. Louis, complete with their own chorus. If they keep up their singing, I'll have them featured in front of the fountain at Lincoln Center. I'll get the credit, of course."

"Of course, what could I expect otherwise," he replied, laughing aloud.

"Are they singing on the bus?" asked Tony.

"Are they ever."

"I wish they'd shut up despite the good voices. They ought to save their breath as they're scheduled to sing at Antioch Baptist on 125th Street tomorrow."

"Well, we both have to be grateful. I have an elderly group from Omaha—pretty decent and the driver's very cooperative."

"Yeah, if you have a decent driver, that's 90 percent," Miriam said as she finished her bottle of water.

"Tony, did you hear anything from the casting call for 'Hell's Kitchen?'"

"Still waiting, I've checked the cell phone at least five times this morning, as Mark Goodman told me they would call back for a second reading. Why, did you hear anything?"

"No, and I don't want to foolishly get your hopes up, but

Mark told me—you know we went to LaGuardia together—that you were perfect for the role of the lead, Tim Holloway. I hope to hell I'm not sticking my neck out man. I know what a bitch it is to have your hopes dashed, but Mark is a straight shooter, like me and he's a real mensch. Maybe I shouldn't say anything—all I know is if you don't get the part, you have at least made a great impression on good old Mark and he's not chopped liver, baby! Speaking of chopped liver, you got a lot of class, not to mention a great ass!"

Miriam had a way all right. Tony's infectious smile radiated all over as he gently grabbed her hand affectionately. "You're the best, you know—you made my day."

Miriam proceeded to tell Tony that she was working extra tours as she wanted to get to Scottsdale to see her ailing mother. "She's 81 and with my dad gone five years now, my brother Seth and I have been taking turns going out there. I love the place, but not after June 30th —the heat's unbearable."

"It can't be worse than New York's humidity, can it?"

"No, you're right, nothing is worse than working in 90 degree weather with humidity. At least it's a dry heat, even if it's 103 in the shade!"

"Well," Tony remarked, "you're at least seeing your mom and being responsible." Tony didn't want to get too personal with Miriam, as he knew she was raising a teenage son after an ugly divorce.

"Got to go, T," Miriam said as she noticed her group getting up from their tables. "It was great seeing you and keep your hopes up. Otherwise we'll grow old together here and have our ashes in the Wall of Remembrance."

"That's one way they'll never get us off Ellis," Tony shouted as Miriam started walking towards her group.

"You'll be the first to know if I get a call. Thanks, take care."

If only I get a callback, Tony thought as he checked his cell phone.

Once back on Manhattan Island, Tony had the driver go through Chinatown, East Village and across 42nd Street to get back to the Milford. Along the way, Tony thought of what Miriam told him. He, like her, had turned into a hardened New Yorker who knew who was real and, as an ambassador of the city, knew how to relate to the best in people. He remembered what his late mentor Joe Briggs once said, "Everything in life is attitude. No one wants to hear a sob story, so deal with your problems and move on." Joe was right on target with the attitude. He related this to the group as they passed St. Mark's Place and a demonstration against tuition hikes at Cooper Union. "Do you know what famous speech was given here?" he asked the group. Getting no volunteers, Tony related the House Divided speech given by Abraham Lincoln in 1860, which was recently reenacted by Sam Waterson of *Law and Order.*

The bus headed north and turned onto 42nd Street, as Tony pointed out the UN, Chrysler Building and Grand Central. He reminded the group that a visit to the newly-renovated 1913 Grand Central is a real treat. "See if you can identify the different constellations when you're inside the main area." Tony checked his cell phone and still no calls. "Don't forget to go downstairs and get the best cheesecake in New York, direct from Junior's in Brooklyn. Forget the diet; you're in New York!"

As the bus passed Madame Tussaud's Wax Museum, one

woman, seeing the wax figure of Morgan Freeman, shouted, "We got to go there!" Tony explained the cost and the exhibits, telling them they would probably enjoy the "Room of Torture" most. As an aside, he couldn't resist telling Joyce to 'be sure they don't go back to Nebraska without seeing a play."

The bus finally came to a stop back at the Milford. After a minute thanking Tony and the bus driver, Joyce asked everyone to thank Tony personally as they leave the bus. Everyone on the bus thanked Tony and left him a dollar or two in his hand. Bidding goodbye to Joyce, he checked his cell phone and notices two messages—one from his mother and the other from Ms. Stewart. Tony proceeded to call Ms. Stewart and headed home. Yes, it was a good day.

"Hello, Ms. Stewart, this is Tony. I did! Yes, yes, I'll be at the theater first thing—7AM casting? Thanks, thanks very much!"

CHAPTER 4

"It's just a New York thing, a neighborhood thing," Boyd Howell remarked to his cousin Bill Faulkner visiting from Aiken, South Carolina. He pointed to the middle-aged man looking outside from his fully-opened window at every passer-by. Waving and acting as if he were a famous Hollywood celebrity or worse, an obsequious political figure, the figure in the window made sure he was noticed. "He's out here every day, like some bird of prey surveying the scene below, ready to greet the masses passing under his first floor window." What Boyd was describing was typical of old New York neighborhoods that were once an unofficial neighborhood watch, much like the wealthy patrons on the east side with their doormen and elaborate security. Known as the 'watcher' or 'keeper,' these colorful New Yorkers gave the poor parts of a growing city a sense of stability and served as unofficial cops on the block. The six story walkups were perfect niches for them. What remained on the present Westside on the side streets of the 40s and 50s blocks presented a spectacle to anyone walking the streets. It also gave the opportunity for those having the time to become unofficial watchdogs for the block and be part of the dynamic of New York. Nosy, gossipy and with an 'in your face' attitude, one would be wise to get know the 'watchman' or 'watchwomen.' They look out for you and the neighborhood. All you needed was time. Plenty of time and a pillow. It involved simply taking a pillow to rest your arms in an open window sill and watch the events of the city unfold below your perch. In the days before electronic security,

Internet and hidden cameras, there was the old neighborhood watchdog. "Some people disliked their presence, as they could gossip the comings and goings of the block. They knew who was cheating on their wives, who was out late and coming home early and who needed some counsel. But others felt it was the security blanket that was needed to protect the crime-ridden areas in the not too distant past," Boyd said. Seeing the expression on his cousin's face with his finger pointing up to the open window, added, "Oh, this guy? He holds court; he's like a neighborhood fixture."

Indeed, everyone looked up and saw a tank-topped, 57-year-old, balding, paunchy Hispanic male with eagle dark eyes named Sam Otero as he looked over his domain on West 47th Side opposite the new Starbucks coffee shop. This was his turf and the unwritten code was that Sam ruled here. Sam was there to acknowledge the waves from old and new residents alike and was always available for advice and opinions. Advice and opinions whether sought or unsought. He has become an ambassador of sorts. People of all ages and backgrounds looked up to see him and wave. He was the lord of the roost. "He's become a morning ritual that even has been written up in the local press, <u>Clinton News</u>. If he's not there by 8 AM to greet the throng going to work, people will inquire or yell up to him. He's become a neighborhood sight, symbolic of a stable and welcoming sight to the people passing below. A bit of the old adapted to new times. A very New York thing," Boyd murmured to his cousin, a slight grin evident as he surveyed the blank expression on his cousin's face. Bill looked puzzled. His cousin seemed to be enjoying his role as tour guide and commentator. "You won't find this back home in Aiken," he added, looking at the strange, contorted face of his cousin, shaking his head in agreement.

No one really knows how Sam and the other 'watchers' obtained their prestigious, unelected status. Boyd was, like most newcomers to New York, curious as to what triggered this very New York phenomenon that was repeated in most of the ethnic areas of the five boroughs. Plaques had even been attached to the main entrance, identifying watchers of many years gone by, immortalizing them as 'patron saints of the block.' One was at 48th Street between 9th and 10th Avenues. It was dedicated to a woman, Mrs. Carpenter, who was the fixture on the block for many decades. These reminders were like the plaques placed on birth sights and homes of famous writers, politicians and actors that the famous walking tours highlighted in areas of the village where O. Henry, Edna St. Vincent Millay, Mark Twain and Henry James had lived. His old and now deceased neighbor Mrs. Castro told Boyd, "We used to make sure our kids got off to school and didn't try to cut. There was always someone to make sure they got to school. That person was the 'watcher.'" To explain it further was to compare people sitting on their porch and gossiping about everyone passing by in a small mid-America town whether in Kentucky, Texas, Montana or Vermont on hot, steamy nights years ago when there was no air conditioning. Only in New York there were no porches. The stoop or the window sill was the next best thing. The stairs were too hard and people going in and out of apartment needed to get by and not be blocked. So, the stoop and the 'watcher' gained status and the block was always his domain. Soon his fame grew. Local leaders confided in him, asking him of whom to be wary, who was reliable at election time and who should be monitored. Sensing that his cousin would probably want to absorb as much information before returning to Aiken, Boyd felt the need to explain to his visiting cousin how he came to appreciate this unique New York experience.

Boyd Howell started by telling his cousin that on his first visit to New York, he couldn't understand this unique New York tradition either. He was a stranger in a big, loud and crazy city and was mesmerized by the sights, smells and sounds of New York. Boyd told of how Otero and the others Oteros of Hell's Kitchen and other neighborhoods scanned the site and witnessed an array of events that unfolded. "When I first got here, I noticed that a lot of the old, six story walkup railroad apartments seemed to have a designated person who wasn't a building superintendent, but was a lookout for whatever good or bad activities occurred below. I knew that Otero was a good observer, not a bad one. Maybe a nosy body, but there's a sense of community when you see Sam. He's there every day, except for bad weather in the winter or rainy deluges in the spring."

"What's a railroad apartment?" his cousin innocently asked. Boyd answered saying "many of the tenements built after 1879 had a dumbbell shape to allow more ventilation and consequently each floor originally had two individual apartments per floor that ran from the back to the front, like freight cars, lined up in a row."

Sam Otero had quite a few stories to tell. A fall at his job as a school custodian left him with a permanent limp and an early retirement pension in 1998. "The Board of Education forced me to retire early. They were worried I would sue, but I loved the job and the kids and teachers." Consequently, he stayed at home and eventually was mobile enough to work part time in his building with the aid of his son Freddy as an assistant to the building superintendent, his friend, Pedro Guiterrez. His building was like thousands of walkups built in the dumbbell style described by Boyd to allow more sunlight and ventilation as a result of the city's efforts to accommodate a surge of immigration coming in from southern and eastern Europe in the late nineteenth century. Consequently, the Italians, Jews, Russians, Poles, Hungarians and Greeks ended up in the tenements that aligned the avenues west of 8th along with the Irish and Germans who preceded them. Now, with Hispanics and yuppies occupying most of the old area, things had changed. So had Otero. Sam had been eyeing his audience and knew it was his time for center stage.

"Hey there, got company today?" Otero shouted to Boyd after seeing him with a strange face.

"It's my cousin from my hometown down South," Boyd casually remarked.

"A homie is always welcome." Otero's mouth was missing two upper molars.

"Want anything from Starbucks?" Boyd asked.

"No, not my kind of coffee. I'm used to Bostelo, you know, the strong Puerto Rican coffee like espresso, with lots of sugar, unlike you guys. But thanks anyway."

The aroma spilled into the street, as Otero and his wife always left a fresh perked brew on the stove for anyone bold enough to taste the eye opener.

"You're welcome." Boyd can't resist asking Sam about his perch, since his cousin is amazed by the sight of the balding man holding court for all to see, waving to everyone and knowing everyone of all ages, races and economic status by name. Bill, like most naive out-of-towners, thought everyone in the city was too absorbed in their own lives to be friendly to strangers.

"Sam, what's some of the craziest things you seen from that window?" Boyd knew that his cousin had time for a good New York story to bring back to the folks in Aiken.

"How much time do you have, my man?" Sam laughed.

"I'm all ears—by the way my cousin's name is Bill. He's from my hometown, Aiken, South Carolina."

Several people of all backgrounds—young schoolchildren, mothers, trench coat men with the daily papers under their arms, delivery men from several food purveyors that aligned both sides of 9th Avenue have all waved or given a thumps-up greeting to Otero. Indeed, this stretch of 9th Avenue is probably the most diversified street in the US. On the block adjacent to 47th Street, one can find the following: Italian-French pastries at Pozzo's, an even more, pricey upscale pastry shop at Amy's, a bike shop that prides itself as having the largest selection of foreign bikes in the city, a Laundromat, a cellular shop, two delis, one Chinese restaurant, two bars one straight and one not, a Mexican take-out that prides itself as having the 'best home-made tacos north of El Paso,' an upscale bath emporium, a Vietnamese restaurant that formerly served as a numbers joint in the backroom and a fruit stand that has served the neighborhood since 1912, still proud of its family service.

Sam looked at his admiring twosome and asked Boyd, "How long have you lived on the block?"

"Just 10 months—I used to live on the Lower East Side before I got a studio on 47th and 9th Avenue." Boyd detected a little playfulness on Otero's part, who was known to tell lurid stories of Hell's Kitchen's past and didn't want to pass up the chance and asked again,

"What's the most crazy thing that happened in the block since you been here?" He hoped to get Sam to let loose with the rich history of the block and Hell's Kitchen. The twinkle in Otero's eyes told him that a story was at hand and he was ready for his audience.

A sly smile on his face coupled with a burrowed frown that accentuated his forehead, Otero began, as he folded his hands, wiping his brow with an immaculately white handkerchief.

"This block was notorious in the 50s and 60s. I was a kid then. You have a lot of back lots that served as speakeasies during Prohibition, but were also used as whorehouses until the late 60s. Many a john got rolled; some even never made it out. The police before the Knapp Commission just turned the other way or were on the take. Good cops didn't want to get involved." Otero pointed to the Starbucks directly across the street and continued. "You see all those yuppie types today in what is Starbucks. If that place could talk, you would have a bestseller—farce, tragedy, comedy all rolled into one. That was a grocery store that served as a front for numbers and illegal card games and even illegal cock fights in the summer in the back lot. When I was a kid, I made a bundle by tipping off the owners as a lookout when the patrol cars we recognized as unfriendly went by. Those were the days. Of course, some of the cops were on the take and looked the other way. Like every place, we had good and bad. You just never hear much of the good stuff."

Boyd said to his cousin, "The Knapp Commission, which was started by the Lindsay administration in 1973, to weed out corruption within the NYPD."

"Did you ever get caught?" asked Bill.

Otero let out another of his hearty laughs and said, "Sure, probably every other month, depending on who was in office or who wanted to make a name for themselves." Otereo readjusted his pillow and looked directly at Bill and said, "This wasn't something I elected to do; I had seven brothers and sisters and I was the oldest. My parents were good, loving people. I knew right from wrong. But, this little gig put bread on the table and never hurt anyone. The hookers respected me; remember I was a 14 year old kid with an attitude. A bad attitude. I thought I was tough. Nobody could hurt Sammy Otero. I thought no one could upset me and I was out to prove myself. When I'd recognized a plainsclothes trying to entrap them, I sent them a signal." Otero put his index and middle fingers in his mouth and let out a lilting whistle to demonstrate, amusing Boyd and his cousin. "They appreciated the little favors and I would get a kickback. You know the expression: 'One hand washes the other.' Well, I was the little runt who gave a legup on things about to occur. A snitch, but a cute snitch," he said as a big smile revealed his missing front molars. Boyd thought to himself that his cousin was getting the best free entertainment of anyone right now. Otero, scratching his head, got serious. "It was hard, hard times. We were all okay, then it took over."

"What took over?" Boyd asked.

"The drugs. The drugs killed everything. Crime was up. A couple of businessmen got rolled when some of the hookers changed when pimps got them high on crack and left them without their wallets. They were too embarrassed to tell the cops and didn't want their names in the paper. One of the houses served as a 'hot-bed' hotel. What the management did was enter a fictitious name on the ledger and rent the room for an hour of fun. That same room was now registered for the night and any of the ladies who came in later with a john were able to get a 'take' as well as the clerk and management. Same room, same price, just pocket the proceeds. Great arrangement. The fact that the joint was owned by the local officials in city hall made corruption widespread. I remember there was a fire violation and the new fire commissioner wrote a citation to the Union; that was the hotel across the street. A real flea-bag joint. No one in their right mind would ever go there for the night. It served one purpose and was there for one thing only—hookers. Today, it's full of pricy studios. Some change," he laughed, shaking his head. "Anyway, the fire commissioner didn't know the deal and that the borough president was part owner. Secret part owner, known only to the locals, such as the captain of Midtown North. As you can guess, the citation was never paid because the hotel was owned on paper by an agency that was also part of one of the big Brooklyn families as well as the borough president."

"You mean the mafia?" Bill shouted.

"You catch on easy, kiddo," Sam said. "Are you surprised?" Otero took a cup of coffee from his wife, waving to a few passers-by and continued.

"Well, these places were all fronts for illegal activity that was condoned by a lot of people on the 'take' from the inspection officials, police, politicians, down to the hookers and pimps. Everyone got a piece of the action. But, like I said, once the heavy duty drugs entered and crime went up, people demanded changes and Lindsay got the Knapp Commission to enact all those reforms.

"You're too young to remember the movie *Serpico*. It made Pacino as an actor, but it sent a message." Otero was referring to the 1973 Sidney Lumet movie that highlighted the rogue cop Frankie Serpico, who refused bribes and was subsequently shot by fellow cops and living today in exile in Switzerland. Otero also told of a close call he had when two groups starting arguing over a slight fender bender. "Once the guns came out, the rest was carnage that saw three people shot dead at 4 AM on an early spring morning. The next day, the police commissioner, local councilmen and community leaders were demanding action against the illegal late night clubs."

"Do you miss the good old days?" Boyd asked.

"No, no—once the neighborhood started going downhill and I got older and wiser, I didn't want to do time upstate like a lot of friends. No, I don't miss it at all. I like you guys; I like the changes despite the out-of-whack prices for a place to live. You wouldn't have walked these streets after midnight. All the good, poor people stayed indoors. A hell of a way to live. They had no choice. We had no choice. We had to live here."

"So when did all this change?" asked Bill, as Sam's wife, Mayra, gave him a second cup of coffee and nodded to the boys.

"Once the newspapers got into the act, it was all over. No more covering up. When they had a foxy, young reporter pretending to be a hooker take her story to the _Times_, it was the last straw. This was about 1975. Also, once the drugs got hold, crime went up and a whole different bunch of characters came out of the woodwork from the pimps to drag queens and drugged up hippies. The place went downhill fast, especially in the 80s."

"Is that when you got out?" Boyd asked.

"I was older and interested in girls and didn't like what I saw. What bothered me was the pimps beating up their girls and hooking them with drugs. Look, I guess the worst and most tense situation happened when I discovered a dead hooker in the back lot in 1974. She still had the syringe in her arm. That scared even me. My mother made me go to my aunt's on Staten Island until things cooled off. I knew I wanted out." Sam's note was noticeably more somber. He shook his head, and his hand, as if to brush off his past.

Bill quietly asked, "What did you do—did you call the cops?"

"When I found that poor dead girl? Remember she wasn't much older than you guys. I had seen her before in the block—it wasn't like she was a stranger. A beautiful slim, blond blue-eyed girl from Hibbing, Minnesota—the same town that Bob Dylan's from. An all-American type. Like a lot of pretty, young and vulnerable girls, she started dancing at clubs, got mixed up with the drug scene and became a hooker because of her looks and the lure of money. Being controlled by the pimp was next. Those lousy pimps. I've seen it many times—taking a perfectly innocent young girl, getting her a job, usually dancing at some late-hour strip joint and then introducing her to the drug scene slowly at first until she's hooked and subject to the abuse of a pimp. The pimps were all abusive and if I had my way, I'd blown them away. All about control. It's not a very pretty sight to witness and I felt for these girls. Anyway, she always had a sad look on her face—a kind of distant look. I thought she was the most beautiful woman I'd seen. Don't forget I was still a kid. She was so alone and scared. Anyway, have you ever seen a person dead with her eyes and mouth open? I can still see her today looking back at me as if she were trying in her last moments to connect with someone. Death is not a pretty sight, let me tell you. Like I said, I was just a kid, a pretty scared one at that. I looked around quickly and I let out a scream and got hustled out of there by two people who grabbed me and pushed me out of the alley within a minute or two." Otero looked away, as if reliving the incident once again.

"Hey, within five minutes, the entire block was crawling with cops, sirens blowing and the neighborhood hawks trying to find out what came down. I had just come onto the scene and like I said, about 10 people were there within a few minutes. The police questioned us and took about 10 of us in for questioning. For me, it took four hours. I thought my father would kill me when they called the house and asked him to get me. They found no fingerprints of mine and knew it was a bad overdose with cheap drugs, an accident, if you want to call it that. That year there was a killer drug out there and even the news warned the junkies to be on guard. Daytop and other drug rehab programs came around with trucks and loudspeakers in English and Spanish warning the hood of the dangerous drug, I think it was called 'Spike.' I think that's what happened to her—a bad overdose of a too powerful drug. Things changed. Things definitely changed. It was a different, tense and crazy place. No longer safe for anyone. I knew it was time for me to quit the game. My parents raised no dummy."

Otero's wife came to the window and gently touched his hair, as if to put a stray hair back in place. Facing the boys, she said, "Is he telling you some big old story about the wild west side of Hell's Kitchen?" Her laugh and his smile showed the affection between these two.

In the meantime, an elderly man, complete with shirt and tie waved up to Otero with his black umbrella and said, "Sammy, want me to get a lotto ticket for you? You know it's up to $48 million tonight." This diversion allowed Otero to get back to his routine.

"Thanks, my man. Get me two quick pick cash tickets. By the way, have you been to the hospital to see Mickey?'

"Yeah, his doctor's going to let him out tomorrow. He's got to watch that cholesterol and diet. Otherwise, he'll be in trouble."

"For sure," Otero said. "By the way, these are two new friends."

The man with the umbrella was Joe Logan, a lifelong resident who always walked by Otero's window each morning.

"Good to meet you boys. I'm sure he's giving you an earful."

Bill stared at his shoes, a little embarrassed at the attention and replied, "He's telling me a lot about this area."

Logan gave another wave, smiled and was off.

Boyd could see that his cousin would have quite a story to tell his friends when he got back to Aiken. He looked at his cousin who was sizing up Otero and could see that he believed him. *You just can't make this shit up*, Boyd he thought to himself.

"Hey, Sam," shouted a loud voice from across the street.

"Leon, what's new?" Sam shouted back to a 40ish, gray-beared, middle-aged Hispanic with round, owlish glasses and a tee shirt that said: 'Bush Lied.'

"Just heading over to the clinic. Want to stay clean." Leon casually and openly related his drug problem to Frank who has known him since childhood and considered him a good friend.

"Start by taking that job Steve asked you to do for him," Sam shouted as Leon continued towards 9th Avenue.

Turning to the boys, he said, "Leon is like me. We used to call him El Gato—the Cat. Always quiet and sneaky, like a cat. He made mistakes, got in trouble but is still here and part of the hood. Leon had a lot of trouble with drugs–his father was abusive and took it out on Leon, the oldest. He joined up with the locals and starting doing drugs. When a few of the crew overdosed, he knew it was time to quit. But, still, here's a man in his forties still plagued by this mess. I've been talking up for him, trying to get him a position at the new building they're putting up on 54th and 10th. They need some help."

Looking at his new friends, he addressed his own problem.

"Now, people like me eating too much rice and beans and are now diabetic. That's a real scare for me. I've had friends who lost a leg and toes from diabetes." Sam waved to an elderly woman who had shouted hello to him.

"You see that woman who just waved to me? That's Mrs. Bridges. Her sons Hugh and Mark were friends. One of them ended up getting drafted in the army during Vietnam and made a name for himself. Got a Purple Heart, a real one. He lives somewhere in Montana on a ranch. Can you imagine that—from here to a Montana ranch? According to his mother, he took a liking to the outdoors, met a chick from there while in the army and now has a family. Mrs. Bridges has been out there, but as a tough, old New Yorker, she was bored and had to come back to stay here."

"What about the other son, what's his name, Mark?" Bill asked, almost as an afterthought.

"Mrs. Bridges don't want to talk about it." Bill smiled from the New York accent, grammatical errors and all. "I believe he's still doing time upstate for all the drug running with the Westies. Should be getting out soon. Mrs. Bridges will let me know when he's due back."

Bill was impressed with Sam's candor and matter-of-fact statements. He knew that the history of this neighborhood, like most, was a collection of happenings, good and bad that are duplicated throughout America's inner cities. He liked the democratic spirit of Hell's Kitchen. Class and social standing don't seem to matter once you embrace the neighborhood. He noticed that his own cousin, clearly a New Yorker now, speaks to everyone, from the newspaperman to the vagrant with a plastic

Dunkin Donuts cup asking for a few cents to the vested suited men who wave as they pass.

Mrs. Otero took time out from her ironing and came to the window, a large smile radiating her face.

"Is he telling more crazy stories about the old days—don't believe him, boys."

Mrs. Otero had a twinkle in her eye. She knew that her husband was loving the attention. The truth of the matter was that much of what Sam Otero told these young, impressionable boys from down South was the truth.

Bill had quite a tale to tell when he got home. How many would actually believe him? He really didn't care; he had learned a valuable lesson from a master storyteller who had walked the walk and talk the talk. He admired Otero for not only his honesty, but also for the manner in which he dignified a long dead throwaway woman who everyone probably forgot except for family. *That's the tragedy of it all*, he thought. *The city has the best and worst to offer and I got a taste of what it was like to experience what was a very difficult, unsafe and scary era.*

"Let's go over to the diner on 46th Street today," his cousin said as he pats his shoulder. "They have the best burgers and waffle fries on the Westside."

Giving a big wave to Sam Otero, the 'Storyteller of the Westside', they set off. Otero, recognizing Jane Brownelle, the elementary teacher on her way to her fourth-grade class on the next block, greets her. "Good morning, Ms. Brownelle. Make sure those brats learn something today." Blowing a kiss towards Sam, she goes on her way and a new day begins.

CHAPTER 5

"That's $42.11," the cashier at Food Emporium on West 43rd Street said to Mark without even looking up at him. It had taken him awhile to get used to the impersonal and stiff response he often got from some people in the service industry in New York. Some. Not everyone, for sure. At first, he thought he wasn't being polite enough and tried successfully a few times to get the cashier to say "Good morning," before proceeding to his checkout. *$42.01, oh great,* he thought to himself. *Why is it that every time I come here the bill ends in .01 or .06 and I get a bundle of pennies for not being smart? If I had any sense, I'd buy one of those little purses that I see people carrying loose change in. Oh well, more pennies, what else is new? I wish I were talented enough to write a play—I'd make it a comedy and entitle it 'Four More Pennies!' I'd have the main character weighted down with pennies and would get back at all those places that post their charges without including the tax, which always seems to be an extra .07 on the dollar. Oh Lord, please! It was going to be one of those days!*

Mark Andrews, a 47 year-old native of Cincinnati, had lived on West 39th Street for the last five years and was getting tired. Very tired. Tired of waiting in line at the supermarket, tired of cold people who, like him, were unhappy in their job situation, tired of his family calling only when they wanted him to come home and stay with his elderly mother and never asking how he was faring, tired of covering up for his boss's incompetence when it came to bookkeeping at the hardware shop where he worked and tired of having friends cancel dinner engagements, movie dates and workout sessions. What good was all this—living above a store in an $860.00 small studio, "a room with an adjoining closet," while pursuing a quest as a pastry chef in a new and fancy restaurant? It was a mid-life crisis and like most people with talent who had come to New York and settled in Hell's Kitchen, he was still determined to make something of himself. But the city can get to you—the tension and constant demands of city life. Now it was resonating in his old, historic neighborhood with the endless din of drilling, excavating and building of high rises aligning 42nd Street clear to the Hudson River. The dynamic and exciting real estate boom now underway in the Kitchen was evident everywhere he looked and it was also out of his financial range. He envied the fellows taking risks and buying property in the neighborhood walkups one year and, in the next, making a killing in the market.

In fact, he had just run into Willy Lyons, an Iowan native, who had recently bought an $820,000 one bedroom in the luxurious high rise next to the Times Square Post Office on 42nd Street. He admired people like Willy who were not afraid to take a chance and ended winning the game. Willy arrived in New York in 1997 after graduating at University of Iowa, landing a job with a publishing company and within two years, was in charge of his department. Now, as a junior CEO of the accounting department, he was making $150,000 a year and was on his way. His hometown paper in Dubuque featured an article on his success and he was invited to the annual state fair as one of "100 Important Iowans" in which he was to receive a plaque from Gov. Vilsack. So, people like Willy were both a source of admiration and envy and Mark knew he had to make changes soon if he ever wanted to be successful. But, what was there to do? He knew he could cook. He loved cooking. He loved the smell of lemon chicken, homemade pasta sauce and potroast. So he took out a $7000 loan from Citibank on 9th Avenue and enrolled in New York Culinary School. "My last leap at success," he told himself when he signed the loan.

He was one of the oldest students, but he didn't care. He loved the classes; earning how to measure and demonstrating his craft in front of the class and having the other students marvel at his expertise—desserts. Desserts of all kind. Cakes, brownies, cookies, pies and an assortment of goodies that complement a meal, such as finger-food snacks. He excelled and graduated at the top of his class.

Yet, today, leaving the supermarket and feeling down, he thought of real estate and Willy. But one had to have capital in order to invest. His current dilemma was, now that pastry school was finished, paying off the loan and, if his dream of getting his own little shop in Hell's Kitchen failed, he could always try for a job at the Cupcake Café on 39th and 9th or Amy's at 47th and 9th as an assistant to the pastry chef. He knew he could do it; he just needed a chance. *A chance*, he thought. *That's what life is all about—taking chances.*

His present job, a dead end at a hardware store, paid the rent, but allowed for little advancement with someone who had not completed college. His fellow coworkers included a tattooed, macho local named Chico who, in reality, was a transplanted redneck from Alabama named Chet Allen, who tried to score with Hispanic females pretending to be one of them with his fractured Spanish. Chico always made eye contact whenever a Hispanic female over 20 with a skirt came in, but learned from the boss, James Bowman, to keep his comments to himself. Millie Figueora was the opposite— a local person living a few blocks away who was engaging, helpful and assisted in translating for the large Latino clientele in Hell's Kitchen. She knew 'Chico' was a phony, but tolerated him because he tried to impress her with his gringo-accented Spanish.

"He's just a kid with a crazy dream; but who cares, as long as he works and stays out of my hair, it's ok", she once remarked to Andrews. In his own perverse way, Chico was an oddity who made the day pass. He was theater and no one took him seriously. Millie, however, was a fixture at the hardware shop, knowing the names of all the items, from the kitchen gadgets to Phillips screwdrivers, paints, lighting fixtures and Venetian blinds. Most of all, she didn't talk down to customers and maintained a touch of sanity, especially when Chico went into character.

Stepping into the cold February morning outside the Food Emporium on 43rd Street with his two plastic grocery bags, he noticed a few people running towards something at the corner intersection of 10th Avenue. The snow was still compact, testament to the brutal winter so far. His blue knit cap, handmade by his mom the previous Christmas, was over his ears and he made sure he zippered his matching parka to his neckline. The temperature was only 12 degrees, which made the freshly-fallen snow very challenging to anyone. Hard snow and ice underneath,was the worst part of being in New York in the winter. That temperature, along with the famous wind-chill off the Hudson, made the 12 degree temperature feel near zero as Mark navigated slowly lest he fall prey to the icy stretches notorious on 10th Avenue. With every step he took, his boots made that crushing sound that only a frigid layer of snow allowed. Looking up, he saw what the commotion was all about—a horrific sight— a woman lying in the street, surrounded by several passers-by, one of whom was talking frantically on his cell phone to 911. Young, thin and clutching the hand of an elderly woman, she had that distant look in her eyes, the kind that drivers often see from frightened deer frozen by the headlights on some country road. She lay still with her eyes open as several people from the adjacent deli and liquor store came out and covered her with blankets. The woman, dressed in a heavy, black puffed-up North Face parka was still, but able to talk to the woman who held her hand. She couldn't be more than 30 and from what Mark could see, had dropped what appeared to be papers on the pavement and an iPod plugged into her ears. The man from the deli, Samir Aziz, asked her name and she responded, "Rasheeda Jones. I was just walking to my accounting class at John Jay and he came out of nowhere."

"This wasn't a hit and run, was it?" asked an elderly man who had just come up to Mark, as New Yorkers often did, bonding together when an incident occurs. The desire to know what's happening sets in, much like people slowing down on the highway to view the aftermath of a crash. Regardless of where you were, people's curiosity was such that they spoke to total strangers, even in New York in the dead of winter on such a cold morning. "

I don't know; I just got out of the supermarket and noticed the commotion. I thought she may have fallen on the ice, as I don't see anything resembling an accident or a car or driver. Do you?" asked Mark of an elderly woman, appropriately dressed with a heavy coat and hat complemented by a scarf that completely covered her mouth.

Mark was not right about the accident. Within seven minutes, an EMS crew arrived and took the now-stable, garrulous woman to St. Vincent's Midtown on 52nd Street. Mark marveled at how efficient these first responders were—reassuring her that she would be okay and asking her to not to move as they placed a neck brace on her and checked her vitals—blood pressure and pulse. He especially appreciated the skill in which the technicians, identified from their name tags as Jaime Gutierrez and Karen Short, kept reassuring Rasheeda that she was talking and appeared to be okay. Short, in fact, inserting the neck brace, told her it was a mere precaution given the fact that she was probably thrown and X-rays would determine more facts. In the meantime, two patrol cars pulled up and began an investigation. One officer, Dexter Johnson, asked Mark Andrews what he saw. He explained that he arrived just after the incident, but a woman interrupted by yelling, "I saw a black Lexus speed off after they hit that poor girl. There were two men inside. I know one of them was yelling at the driver, probably pleading for him to stay, but he panicked. The man next to me, my friend, Mr. Morrison, got a New Jersey license plate for you. You wrote it down, right? You know they need this stuff."

"Yeah, I have it right here—Jersey plate XRY 324. I hope you find these idiots."

Officer Johnson and his partner Milagros Ruiz took statements from the witnesses. They were on the phone calling in Midtown North with the license plate that Frank Morrison, a middle-aged, hatless man with a white manicured moustache had given to the two officers. They were writing everything that the woman and Morrison were describing.

"Do I need to give you any other information?" asked Morrison.

Officer Johnson, clearly in charge, asked both Morrison and his female friend for their addresses and phone number if further queries were to be made.

"I hope they find the bastards who did this—there are just too many crazies out here who think they own the street," Morrison repeated. "It gets so you can't even cross these streets." The female eyewitness with Morrison, Cheryl Ladison, was on her way to work and both she and Morrison's account were given top priorities by the officers. Ladison, a tough, long-term resident of Hell's Kitchen, was an activist, having recently resigned from Community Board 4 over the board's approval of still further high rises on the Westside of 9th Avenue. Bundled against the frigid winter weather, her brown coat and matching brown leather gloves were complemented by a satin scarf to fend off the wind. Both officers wrote their addresses and phone numbers in the obvious criminal investigation that would ensure if and when the perpetrators were apprehended. In the meantime, a NYI news van arrived on the scene and took some film for their 24 hour coverage format. Andrews recognized the reporter, Laurie Laudon, who, despite the frigid wind, was hatless and kept her cool as she interviewed the angry witnesses.

Well, they'll be on the air, that's for sure, thought Mark as he watched how Laudon and her crew from NYI were able to get a story out. He admired the reporter's job and often thought it sounded like an exciting job. *The job of a roving reporter, a cop, a fireman, a teacher—each day is different from the other due to circumstances.* Both Morrison and Ladison repeated their account to the reporter who also took their numbers and addresses. Morrison clearly enjoyed the attention and kept asking the reporter if she needed any other accounts.

It was then that Mark heard another witness say, "That young girl was running across the icy street when she slipped, fell and the car hit her. As she fell, she hit her head on the snowy pavement and the car hit her." Officer Johnson made sure to get a statement from him too. He identified himself as Joseph Critten. As he did to the other witnesses, Johnson asked Critten for his address and he responded that he lived up the block on 41st

Street and was on his way to the senior citizen center for morning coffee on 9th and 44th Street. Mark knew the senior citizens' center and often passed by it and was always amazed at the number of people there despite the weather. *There must be a lot of lonely old people*, he thought. For a moment he thought of himself 20 years down the road in the same situation and quickly brushed the thought from his mind. Putting the events in perspective, it appeared that Rasheeda Jones fell and then was hit by the Lexus and it sped off.

This incident reinforced Mark's attitude towards life. "You never know what's going to happen, so be prepared. Just be prepared and don't be afraid to take a chance. I just wish something would come out of all the classes I took.

"That's it—I need to prioritize and take a chance. That woman who got hit could have been me." He made sure of his footing in the snow and hidden ice as he proceeded to his apartment. Standing 6'1", 212 lbs., he was a striking presence, a tribute to his athletic lifestyle underlined by his daily two mile run along the Hudson past the piers and a workout regimen at Mid-City which complemented his cardio workout with weight. He had also met a few workout buddies, but was, like many people in his age category, lonely and in need of female companionship. He had a few girlfriends in the city, but several were impatient with his busy work schedule that saw little material gain. "Shallow people whom I don't need. I'm better off alone, sometimes. Princesses come a dime a dozen and I can't afford one right now."

Trying to put this episode behind him, he stopped at the local deli and bought the <u>Post</u> with its sensational headline of the latest happenings in the life of Brad Pitt. "The world's going to hell with Iraq and terrorism and they worry about Brad Pitt. Just goes to show you where people's heads are and what they want to hear," he said. He couldn't get the young girl off his mind. Etched in his mind was the fear and remoteness in her look; he sometimes felt like her, a vulnerable person in need. "New York can be a lonely place." It was early and he was feeling down. He also felt a tinge of pride as a Midwestern transplant, seeing the best of his fellow citizens when someone was in need. It reminded him of the aftermath of the 9/11 tragedy and the tremendous outpouring of goodwill. Those witnesses, the officers and EMS and the local store owners and workers made him proud to be a New Yorker. That's what New York does—makes you cynical and leering, but when the chips are down and you're in need, its best side shows through. He completely forgot about the surly cashier at the supermarket.

He got home and climbed the three landings to his third floor apartment. Putting down his groceries, he needed a minute from a combination of the weather, the accident and the stress of everyday New York. Outside the wind was forcefully pushing against his window as if to defy the builders of the nearly century old walkup. The message was one of defiance and grit, challenging anyone who got in its way.

He glanced at the ice on the window. It was the kind of ice that he remembered back in Ohio when he had to scrape his father's car on cold mornings. He hated getting up on the weekends and getting the ice off the windshield while his father slept. The sound of hissing steam from the radiator was the only sound that remained a pleasant reminder of his childhood. His mother always had hot chocolate for him when he came in from the cold after shoveling snow or scraping the windshield. The hot chocolate and the warmth of the hissing radiator were good memories. Indeed, its strange sound was no longer an annoyance he had endured as a youngster, but instead was like an old, reliable and steady friend. He knew he was lonely and at times afraid of the future, but he had acquired toughness. That toughness made him ever so vigilant to finish his class at pastry school, even if it meant an entry-level $20.00 an hour job at some of the local shops. Deep down in his gut it was something he felt he had to do. This was probably his last chance at getting somewhere and he was willing to take that risk. *I'm not afraid to try. If I did, I wouldn't have been here in New York all these years*, he thought. However, his thoughts were back with the accident. He turned on the TV and poured himself a hot chocolate in the cup with his initials on it—a Christmas mug from his mom from so many years past. He glanced at the photos of his Grandma Betsy holding him at five months, the faded picture of him and his mother when he got his tricycle one long ago Christmas and his graduation photo from high school that were hung on the wall near his one, faded cushion chair. *Good memories*, he thought. *Good memories.*

His plastic grocery bag was stiff from the cold as he reached and put two containers of maple yogurt, soy milk, Oreo cookies, Cheerios, bananas and pears away. Then, the chicken he bought at the nearby meat market was put into the freezer next to two pork chops and frozen beef. He had enough to get through the next three or four days. Mark had to avoid the temptation of going out to eat. He knew his school expense and his job at the hardware shop kept him busy until the course at the culinary school ended. Now, it would mean stretching the budget.

He thought of his younger days in Cincinnati, working at a German bakery while attending high school. He thought of his 20s and his failed marriage of four years. He had a desire to break free and, upon the advice of a now deceased friend, Joe Warner, to come to New York and work with Warner in a local restaurant while sharing the apartment with him. Warner, 10 years older than Mark, was a Vietnam veteran who had alcohol and drug-related problems unknown to Mark in his Ohio days. He had no idea the extent of Warner's addiction until he moved in with him. It didn't take long for Mark to realize he had to find his own place—any place to stay and get away from the on-going conflict that evolved around Joe. Like most people, Mark tried to help, but when Warner started borrowing cash that he never paid back plus the loud shouting and cursing directed at him, he realized he wanted out. "I've already experienced a bad marriage and now I have a lunatic for a roommate," he told a friend who had called asking for him and was met with a list of obscenities from the dipsomaniac Warner. He had to leave to survive the nightmare. He found a cheap studio above a store-front that he still occupied to this day. Warner's heart eventually gave out at age 57 in 2001 and, although Mark called occasion-ally and inquired about the ongoing battle with booze and if Joe was still attending his AA meetings at the nearby Metro Baptist Church hall basement on 40th Street, his contact with him was minimal. He was told of Joe's death on another cold day—a day which he recalls very well. The phone rang at 7AM. It was Cecilia Vazquez, the super's wife. Mrs. Vasquez said that Joe was dead and his remains were already cremated and sent to his sister in Covington, Kentucky, the other side of the Ohio from Cincinnati where she lived with her family. Mark remem-bers that he wasn't surprised by the news, but felt a ting of his own mortality and decided he had to make a choice to better himself. That began the series of classes he started after 2002 at the culinary school.

It did bother him that Mrs Vazquez said Joe was dead at least two days before the people at AA called her to check on him. "We need friends and Joe needed one too," he had said to himself. His death was a wake-up call for him to pursue his dream and not look back.

Pouring more hot chocolate, he settled down in his well-worn sofa and switched the TV to channel 1—the all news station. It had been a couple of hours since the accident, but no mention was made of it yet. "It'll probably be on tonight's news, especially if they find who sped off," he said to himself.

The phone rang and a woman spoke, identifying herself as Joyce Kurtz, the owner of Amy's on 9th Avenue.

"Mr. Andrews, we had an unfortunate situation occur today. Our pastry chef, Rasheeda Jones, was hit by a car and…."

"I'm sorry, is that the woman who was hit on 43rd Street by a hit-and-run just a few hours ago?"

"Yes! How did you know about that?"

"I was there and saw her just a few minutes after the accident. The police questioned me, but they found a few eyewitnesses who were able to give a full accounting."

"That's amazing, Mr. Andrews."

"Call me Mark, please."

"I was just thinking. I called you because I got in touch with the NYC Culinary School and your professor, Martha Garrison, said you would be perfect to fill in for Rasheeda until she recuperates. It's a start and, as you know, we have opportunities for full employment. Can I ask you to come in and see me at our 9th Avenue shop? I know it's short notice and the weather is horrible but…."

"Oh no, I live right down the street and I'll be there. Is Ms. Jones going to be ok?"

"Yes, she's very special to us. The doctors at St. Vincent's Midtown told her family she sustained lacerations on her legs and bruises, but luckily no broken bones. But, I'm sure she'll need some rest. They're already talking about some physical therapy for her that will last a few months. She's very special to us," she repeated, lest her opinion go unnoticed.

Mark realized that fate worked in his favor. He spoke to Joyce for a few more minutes, finalizing the time to meet and what identification was necessary to file the proper forms, such as W-2 and insurance preference. Joyce was very personable and he felt a tinge of mixed emotions, knowing he was the recipient of a twist of fate. Rasheeda Jones' accident opened up his chance to fulfill the start of his dream in obtaining a very stable and lucrative profession that was sure to grow, given the reputation of Amy's.

As he hung up the phone, the local news station showed footage of the hit-and-run. He saw himself in the background as EMS and the police were attending to their duties. He recognized the eyewitnesses, Morrison and Ladison speaking with the reporter Laurie Laudon. The updated news, now two and a half hours later, showed Officers Ruiz and Johnson escorting two male suspects in Midtown North precinct.

"I'm glad they caught those guys," he said. He knew that he was part of the scenario, having been on the scene and witnessing the events unfold and the surprise connection with the job offer as a result of Ms. Jones' injuries. He listened to the report which indicated that the Lexus was stolen the night before in a New Jersey mall parking lot. The suspects were not only identified, but had apparently robbed the car and also fled from an armed robbery at a gas station in Fort Lee near the George Washington Bridge after having just taken the vehicle.

Mark reported to the bakery and was soon put in charge. He gave notice to the hardware store on 11th Avenue, adjacent to the Market Café that he would be leaving within the next week. His boss, Mr. Bowman, called Joyce Kurtz and assured her of his satisfaction with him as a devoted and hard-working employee for the past five years. While hating to see him go, he knew that Mark would do well in a job geared for him and would excel in his new environment. The pastry school, knowing that Mark was one of the best pastry preparers, highly recommended him to take over Amy's in the absence of Ms. Jones, a person who was written up in Gourmet and local publications as one of the New York's rising stars. Indeed, Mark found the job challenging and needed to bond and gain the respect as a boss from the 10 people working as preparers and counter people. It only took a few days before several of his fellow workers indicated that they found his knowledge of preparation of cakes, brownies and cookies to be as professional as Rasheeda Jones. His insistence on accuracy was a reflection of the expertise he gained as a student at NY Culinary. He doubled-checked recipes, making sure that the ingredients were prepared and stored properly. He held staff meetings and listened intently to suggestions from his crew. "He leads by example," one of the veteran employees said to Joyce. Soon, people used to Rasheeda's finished products were back and there were lines outside onto 9th Avenue.

One day, an EMS ambulance pulled up and walking in, Mark recognized both Guiterrez and Short. Mark told them of the unusual circumstances that brought them together a few months before and insisted that they avail themselves of any of the tempting delicacies without charge. Both Short and Guitterez were told by the counter person to try the famous fudge brownies or cupcakes. "If it smells as good this, it's got to be good," a smiling Karen Short remarked. They left, giving Mark the satisfaction that he helped in some small way to make their challenging job a little easier.

Within the next month, Ms. Jones was released from therapy as her recovery went well. The owner of Amy's, Ms. Kurtz, was so pleased with Mark that she asked him to stay on and would give Rasheeda control over her new store in SOHO, a larger and more upscale emporium. Rasheeda was pleased, as this venue was closer to her home at Stuyvesant Town on East 14th Street and also gave her the opportunity to be placed in a more challenging environment close to the clinic that provided minimal physical therapy over the next few weeks. In the meantime, Mark's classes were finishing and he would obtain his license as a full-fledged pastry chef. He was now making a salary double from the hardware store. He had made it! "It's strange how circumstances bring us together." Even stranger was the events that led to his now new status as a rising star on the New York scene. He knew he made it when his picture appeared in a column in Thursday's <u>New York Times'</u> 'Dining Out' section. In it they mentioned the "...new pastry chef, Mark Andrews at Amy's. His brownies are among the best found anywhere."

The phone rang. It was from the Metropolitan Museum of Art asking him to cater their pastry table at the upcoming showing of Van Gogh collection.

"Can we send a representative to Amy's and discuss prices and possible orders with you, Mr. Andrews?"

Dreams do come true for some. For Mark Andrews, this was his start.

CHAPTER 6

Roy Stafford knew what the doctor was going to say. "It's the weight; I know," he said. He could see the expression on his doctor's face. There was no easy way out on this one. What's worse is that, like most middle-aged men, he had let himself go and was now about to face his judge, Dr. Berman.

"Look at you—you're putting on the pounds," the doctor said.

For Roy Stafford, the 48 year-old cab driver, the news wasn't what he wanted to hear. But it wasn't a surprise. Dr. Edward Berman, cardiologist at Mt. Sinai, had just completed a stress test on Roy and gave the results to a resigned Stafford. He knew the routine and sure enough, Berman, wiping his brow with a tissue, put on his glasses and gave a momentary glance to Stafford as if to size him up as he read aloud. "Your blood pressure's up this time over last to 145/96. You're 5'9" and weigh 210lbs., about 25-30 pounds too much. While your glucose and triglycerides are normal, things need to be done and done now." Berman, putting down the chart, took off his glasses and gently put his hand on Roy's right shoulder adding once again, "Changes need to be done, now, Mr. Stafford."

Stafford, avoiding direct eye contact, stared out the eighth floor window overlooking Central Park and 5th Avenue, knowing that it wouldn't be easy. He looked at the walls in Berman's office, which showed his degrees at Colgate and New York University Medical Center. He suddenly felt like a kid in the principal's office, sent there for bad behavior, awaiting punishment. No one liked bad news and Roy wanted out of this place as soon as possible. He said to himself, "I guess I've been bad again, but this time you got no one to blame

Berman interrupted this mea- culpa. "The good news is that your arteries aren't clogged—at least not yet," he said, looking directly at Roy. "But I'm going to give you a prescription for cumaden, a blood thinner and I want you to continue to take 320 milligrams of aspirin twice each day for at least a month."

"Okay—what's the alternative?" Roy asked, almost in a whisper.

"If you continue to eat at this rate, not watching your diet, you're going to gain additional weight. Coupled with your sedentary life, I'm afraid you're headed for a serious heart condition."

Stafford turned in his chair and looking directly at the doctor for the first time said, "Food is my enemy, I...."

Dr. Berman, his voice rising, tapped his desk with his hand and interrupted by shouting, "Stop eating everything in sight. I know you drive a cab and it's eat on the run." Roy nodded as Berman continued, "Cut out hot dogs, cakes and ice cream. Start by using this menu." Berman gave Roy Stafford his diet.

"The next time you're in my office, I want to see some good results. Your diet begins today. The stress test I'll give you next time will be the exact same one as you failed today. Your diet, Mr. Stafford, begins today—are we on the same page?"

"Yes, yes doc. Sorry. I'm sure my wife will understand."

"She will or I'll have her in the office for your next visit. Any questions, you call my office. Do we have an understanding?"

"Sure, I'll make it a point to make the changes," Roy murmured as he donned his red flannel shirt, his black Docker jeans just given to him as a birthday present last week from Jean, his wife.

"We're not finished yet," Dr. Berman announced.

"What do I have to do now?" Roy asked, a look of exasperation on his face.

"Go over to the mirror and look at yourself," said Mr. Stafford.

"You're kidding, right doctor?" Roy asked.

"As I just said, go the mirror and look at the person you see. Describe him—go ahead."

Roy walked to the full-length mirror on the adjoining wall and again, asked, "Do you really want me to talk to myself or should I just tell you what I see?" Roy was uncomfortable with this procedure.

"Whatever makes you more comfortable, just do it! This is part of my therapy."

Hesitantly and with difficulty, Roy Stafford began to describe what he saw. "He's scared, 48 years old with a wife and son, who has a stressful job driving a cab and he eats on the run."

"Good," Dr. Berman interjected. "Go on now and tell us what the person in the mirror eats in a given day. Think and try to remember what you ate yesterday."

Stafford, fidgeting and looking down at his feet, was reminded by Berman to look into the mirror when speaking as he readjusted his glasses and touched his chin with his right hand and with an audible sigh, said, "For starters, I had a large, regular coffee with one, no two sugars, an egg on a roll with bacon and cheese from the deli across from the dispatcher's office, as I was running late for work. I didn't want to wake my wife, as it was my day to start the early shift at 5:30AM."

"You're doing a good job, now what else?" Berman wrote down everything he ate. "Remember we're talking about snacks and anything else you consumed." Berman was determined to get Roy to come to terms with his diet and the dangers it posed. His therapy was right on target.

Not one to let anyone off the hook, Dr. Berman persisted, and asked, "Anything before lunch?"

"Yeah, about 10:30 or 11:00, after driving for a straight four and half hours, I had another cup of regular coffee with a chocolate donut from the Dunkin Donuts on East 37th Street. Then, I made two runs to LaGuardia and stopped off at the Greek diner in Astoria about 1:00 PM before getting back on the Grand Central Parkway. Let's see, it was Thursday yesterday, so I had the pea soup at the diner with French fries and a burger and chocolate cake for dessert. The traffic was...."

"Forget the traffic and stick to the diet, you're on a roll." Roy noticed that the doctor was still writing everything that he ate down on a pad.

"And later?"

"About 4:00 PM, I had a bag of chips. When I punched out at 5:30 PM, I went home and arrived there about 6 PM. My wife had a pot roast with gravy, mashed potatoes, carrots and a salad. I drank two more cups of coffee and after dinner, while watching the Yankees lose to the Red Sox, I had a slice of pizza that was left over from the night before. I think that's about it."

"I certainly hope so," Dr. Berman said, handing a paper to Roy.

"If you keep eating at this rate, you'll not be here very long. Look at that diet."

"C'mon, doc, I know I have to make some changes," Roy said.

"More than some changes. Here are two copies of your new diet; in fact, take three. One for you, one for your wife and the third, post on the refrigerator." Roy's eyebrows were turned up, a sign of the tension he was experiencing. He waited for the next salvo from Berman.

"For the next five months, I'll see you every three weeks. We'll go through this little exercise and you'll look again and again into the mirror and describe the man facing you. We'll see good results only if you make changes in your diet and start exercising. Am I getting through to you, Mr. Stafford?"

"Loud and clear, doc." Roy managed a smile.

He scanned the menu and looked up at Berman and again sighed, releasing some of the pent-up tension by adding,

"Yes, I know I have to make changes. I want to see my kid grow up."

"And you will, but we have to start today, understood?"

"Understood."

Over the next 15 minutes, Dr. Berman had Roy Stafford review the entire daily regimen to assist him on his road to recovery, as a preventative measure to halt the progression of cardiovascular disease.

"Let's begin today. Remember to exercise—walking is a good start, but at a good pace. Take a look at page three of the regimen and look at the suggestions for exercise. What does it say in relation to exercise?"

"It says that at least 15 minutes initially and gradually up to one hour for a cardiovascular regimen." Roy continued to look at the paper, an obvious diversion from what expected Dr. Berman to say next.

"You don't have to join a gym, although you might consider it with proper personal training. What is the main concern do you think when it comes to food?"

Berman's persistence paid off and Roy said, "I think you want me to eat less, eat better foods and try to be less stressful by exercising."

"Good, I couldn't have said it better myself."

"Doc, I don't know if I have the time for all this because...."

"Look, if you have the time to sit and relax in front of that TV and watch a sports event for three or four hours, plan to have an hour to yourself. That's in the packet. You'll notice I want you to write everything you eat in a given day, what portions and what exercises you've done. Are you going to tell me that the Yankees mean more than your wife and kid?"

"No, of course not," Stafford almost shouted. "Thanks, I know you're making me come to terms with myself."

Patting him on the right shoulder with the menu still in his hand, Berman smiled and looked directly at Roy Stafford and said "Good, the first step is accepting there's a problem that is manageable before it becomes a major issue. Step over to the appointment desk. Myrna, my secretary, will make sure that you get the prescriptions and the date for your next appointment.

It's a nice day; how did you get here?"

"I took the subway."

"Well, your exercise program begins now. Walk home from here at 99th Street. Go through the park and walk down the Westside to your apartment. Can you do that and time yourself in the process?" Berman gave him a stern look, awaiting a reaction.

"Yeah, I owe that much to my wife and kid."

"Okay—I see we're making progress. Look into the mirror every day and remember, get out of that cab when working and stretch a little, even if it's a mere two or three minutes."

Myrna Adams came in with the prescriptions and gave them to Roy, as he was ushered out into the corridor.

Once outside, Roy sat on a park bench opposite the hospital and looked at the diet again. It was May and Central Park was awash in spring. A perfect pre-summer day before the onset of the oppressive humidity set in. Roy saw a father with his young son, riding a bike with trainer wheels. The boy was no more than six and Roy remembered how he helped his son in the park nearby his apartment on 51st Street. Older kids, with skateboards, were going into the park near the reservoir renamed for Jackie Onassis. Roy also saw an impromptu soccer game with a group of Mexican immigrants on 96th Street. He thought of his own dad, dying at 56 of a massive heart attack when he was just 24. His dad, a meat packer at the Washington Market on 14th Street, worked in the refrigerator room and put in long hours.

"Dr. Berman gave me a wake-up call. I'm scared. Real scared. I don't want to end up like my poor slob of a dad, working late hours, coming home to our apartment and never taking the time to give us the attention my sister and I craved because he was too damn tired and stressed out," he said to himself. Roy remembered his arthritic fingers, a testament to the long hours in the subfreezing compartments he worked. "My poor mom put up with a lot." Now, at 87, she lived downstairs from Roy. "Poor mom, I'm her only son. She needs me too. My wife and kid need me."

His thoughts drifted off momentarily as a mother and baby passed. The mother was no more than 30 and the infant daughter was in her carriage, complete with a mesh screen to ward off any insects on that fine day. A faint smile was on her face. Roy nodded as she passed.

Roy saw life all around him as he got up from the bench and headed west through the park.

The familiar tourist favorite, the horse-drawn carriage gal-loped nearby with a young couple who gave a big wave to Roy. Waving back, he thought, *Doc was right about going through the park. It gives me a chance to reflect on myself and see things a little differently.* The smells of the kiosk were evident as he neared Central Park West and 66th Street. Hot dogs and pretzels with mustard permeated the air as a group of German speaking tourists approached the vendor. Within a few minutes, he was outside the park on 59th Street, heading for 9th Avenue and his apartment.

Within three months, Stafford's determination paid off. He not only religiously adhered to the menu and life-style changes advocated by Dr. Berman but also was a changed per-son. By eating less and putting more fiber and less fat into his diet, he shed an impressive 27 pounds. He also began walking from his home on 54th Street to the dispatcher's office on 34th Street in Hell's Kitchen each morning. No longer did he stop for coffee and donuts; now, his breakfast was one of orange juice, dry cereal or oatmeal and fresh fruit. Coping with the stress of midtown traffic, he started playing New Age music with the headset his wife bought for him on sale or listened to smooth jazz on CD 101.9. No longer working 12 hours a day, he cut his shift to seven to the delight of his wife and son, Mike.

Coming home to Jean meant something new. "Money isn't everything, so I take home a few less dollars," he said to Jean one morning. He had more energy. He was a happier person and it showed. He took his wife for a long weekend to Atlantic City and was able to perform as if it were their honeymoon night. Jean noticed the change, the relaxed Roy, the new Roy and the healthier Roy. She found him more attentive, even grocery shop-ping and stopping to see a few friends long neglected.

Jean's birthday was August 10th. He was scheduled for another of Dr. Berman's stress tests, complete with the self-analysis mirror therapy. Arriving five minutes before his 10:00AM appointment, Myrna Adams greeted him and remarked, "Nice to see you Mr. Stafford. You look great."

"Thanks. I owe it to the doctor." Dr. Berman emerged from his inner office, a thumps up gesture directed at Roy as he announced,

"I see from your presence, you're continuing to stick to the menu and exercising. The hardest step is to get started and be accountable. And most of all to come to terms with your situation. You seem to have gotten the message."

"Thanks to you, doc. I'm a new man. I was telling Myrna...."

Berman interrupted and shook his head. "No, Mr. Stafford, you're the same man with a new mission for success. Like all changes, one needs adjustment. I see you have adjusted well. Keep up the fine efforts." Dr. Berman then directed Roy towards the full-length mirror and said,

"Let's do the drill. You know it by now. Look into the mirror."

Noticing the grimace on Stafford's face, he continued, "You've done it before. Don't hold back and don't be modest. Be truthful and compare the man you now see with the man who was here just three months ago. Go ahead, Roy you can do it."

Roy began, "Three months ago, a...."

"Stop!" Putting down his pen for a moment, and placing Roy's chart on the desk, Berman said, "It's my turn to do the therapy part of this session. Continue to look in the mirror." He stood and walked close to where Roy Stafford was standing. Smiling, he said,

"Three months ago a scared, middle-aged man was referred to me by his private physician. This man, 48 year-old Roy Stafford of West 54th Street, a stressed-out cab driver who was working much too hard, putting in to many hours, was a walking candidate for a coronary."

Berman, seeing the unease in Roy's face, loudly orders him to continue to look in the mirror.

"Today, we have that same Roy Stafford with us. But he is a changed individual. Like a good student, he has done his homework and has arrived to my office a changed man."

"Okay, I gave the introduction." Berman grins. "Your turn."

"Oh doc, you were doing such a good job, for a minute I was starting to like this guy too,"

Roy said and both join in laughter. A dead silence ensued and Roy knew he was center stage as he proceeded,

"Here goes. This guy got the scare of his life from his doctor, Dr. O'Conor,. His doctor sent him to Mt. Sinai to see Dr. Berman in the cardiology department on May 12th. He has a wife, a son and an elderly mother who lives just below in the same Hell's Kitchen apartment that he grew up in. He desperately wants to get well and not end up like his dad who died when he was 24. After visiting Dr. Berman, he was given the menu that gave him a new lease on life." Roy pauses, getting a little chocked up and clearing his throat before he added, "He does have a new lease on life. He's happier; he's nicer to his wife and kid and even the fellows on the job have noticed his weight loss. Last week, he bought his wife flowers just because he wanted to. It was no special occasion. No birthday or anniversary. He has cut back a lot on his work load. He walks to work, unless it's really bad out. He notices things that he didn't notice before, such as kids going to school, playing ball in the park, posters for new movies, the scent of flowers when he passes the flower stands. He watches less TV, even the Yankees, and takes a walk, sometimes with Jean, in the evening. Jean has been his biggest supporter and has made sure that he sticks to the diet. She has lost a few pounds as well ,not that she needed to. The most important thing that has changed, I guess, is his attitude towards food. I don't think I can go on further, doctor."

"No need to. That was great, really a good evaluation," Berman said with a smile.

"So I guess the bill won't be so bad, since I did so much." Roy grinned as Berman laughed aloud.

"It's good that you have a sense of humor. It is a great tonic. By the way, do you like this new Roy?"

"Yeah and so does my kid and Jean."

"Are you giving her more attention and discussing her needs?" Berman wanted Roy to discuss personal matters to determine if everything was acceptable.

"Yes, I could elaborate a bit. We spent a second honeymoon in Atlantic City two weeks ago. It was like old times. We….."

"I think I get the picture, Sir." Berman smiled, and winked from his left eye.

"One thing I want you to elaborate on is when you said you notice things that were there before and now you appreciate. Could you explain that for me?"

"I'm enjoying walking. I walk a lot. Our neighborhood has so many side streets, despite all the changes that are occurring, it still maintains that old New York neighborhood spirit. You know what I'm talking about?" Roy noticed Berman nodding and added,

"I was by the old basketball court where I used to play ball with my buddies in the old days. It's at PS15, just off 45th and 10th Avenue. Something inside me made me stop and look at the kids playing ball. It brought back such memories. I was looking at the young kids playing basketball. I was one of those kids not too long ago. I just stared, not really focusing on the game or at anyone in particular. I suddenly saw myself with my old buddies—Joe Cochran, Frankie Rotolo and Sammy Welch. All of them are dead now. Sam was killed in a car accident in Peekskill; Joe drank himself to death after his girl left. In fact, it was just last year. Cirrhosis of the liver. Sammy Welch got hooked on drugs and ended up HIV positive and died upstate in jail. So, at 48, I had to ask myself—do I really want to end up dying before I retire? So, I was watching the young kids play ball and seeing myself. As I stood there, one of the kids stared at me and I began to walk away, knowing he probably wanted his space or worse, thought I was some kind of nut or pervert. But the most extraordinary thing happened—this neighborhood kid, who I assumed had an attitude came up and asked me if I wanted to throw a few hoops. I laughed and apologized to him, telling him I was a little too old and that I used to play ball there many years ago. He told me that his father also played a lot of ball, but was dead now for five years. He then told me his name, Joey Rotolo, the son of one of my best friends! We spoke for a few minutes and I told him that I knew his dad and was sorry for the fact that he was growing up without one. He asked if I had a son and I told him yes and he said that I was fortunate to see a son growing up. He really had an impact on me, this kid. This kid and I had a common connection to his father. Finally, he just tossed the ball to me without asking and I ended up throwing a few hoops and felt great. Before I left, he asked if I were a coach, saying, 'You still throw well.' I felt great. It was just weird that these set of circumstances happened the way they did. Just weird."

"No, Mr. Stafford, it's a great story. Treasure it. I hope you go back to the court and play some ball with your son." Dr. Berman asked Roy, "Is there was anything else you can tell me.? ?"

"Sure, the point of the chance meeting with the kid of one of my friends is that I felt good to be alive," Roy answered. "I left that basketball court knowing that I touched that young man's life. But, the bigger picture is that he touched me and made me realize that my wife and son need me. Here is a kid without a father. He wanted to know everything about the games I played with his father. He didn't have the opportunity to sit down with his dad, as he was only nine when he was killed in that car crash. When I asked him if he knew my son, who is five years older than he is, he told me no. I was able to stop and appreciate a simple, neighborhood game. That kid asked me to come back and I've been back three times just to show support. The smile on that kid's face was worth it. He put a smile on my face."

"It seems that you learned a lesson in human relations. It was not just a game, but a chance encounter that made you realize the importance of life. By the way, how's your jump shot?"

"Not bad, I got my son to the court and he's pushing me."

"Just take it easy."

Roy knew that the therapy Dr. Berman implemented is working. No longer afraid to stand and look himself in the mirror, he has come to terms with himself and made some important life changes. Berman's rather unorthodox tactics seemed to resonate with astounding results. Not only was Roy able to make the important changes, but was also coming to terms, as a middle-aged man, with his mortality.

Roy kept returning to the basketball court and started to get some of the other adults who were there interested in playing a few hoops which led to him forming a team for the neighborhood. He got a few of his buddies interested in watching their diets and became a sort of guru when it came to food and exercise.

His next visit to Berman's office showed a further reduction in blood pressure and a loss of an additional 14 pounds. Standing before the mirror and knowing his role, he was ready for the Berman Treatment. Within six months, his prescription dosage was reduced and he and his wife were planning on visiting Jean's sister for a week in Michigan. He kept returning to the basketball court and, during the winter, was able to use the indoor court adjacent to the outdoor court by raising money with some of the mothers who had set up a table at the 9th Avenue Food Festival.

By the time of his next birthday, February 16th, Roy was given a clean bill of health and was

thinking of his father and wished his dad had known Dr. Berman. "It would have given mom many years more with him and I would have had a dad," he said.

CHAPTER 7

"Apartment 27K, please. My name is Kwame." Melvin Davis, security desk officer called 27K and Phyllis Kane answers. "Kwame's here to see you."

"Thanks, please send him up." The voice of Ms. Kane, a 29 year-old Savannah native and current understudy to Christina Applegate in "Sweet Charity," was clearly anxious by the presence of Kwame Jackson, her personal trainer. Tense all week, knowing that she was replacing Applegate, out with a bad cold, at tonight's sold-out Friday performance, Kwame was who she needed right now. As an understudy replacing the star Applegate, she knew the profound significance of being at her best tonight. Sipping some green tea with a teaspoon of honey, she took a deep breath and whispered, "I hope I'm all right tonight. I know I can do it, but this is my moment of truth." Indeed, this was her night to show the world that years of preparation in minor off-Broadway roles had finally paid off well. It was her time to shine and she was determined to see it through. Looking out the window of her 42nd Street apartment as she awaited Kwame's arrival, she looked at the view, soon to be obscured by the overdevelopment of the Westside. *Enjoy the view, like the show and life, it won't last forever,* she thought. However anxious, she knew and trusted Kwame and was anxious to see him.

She had met Kwame three years earlier, admired him as a person in the business who had a calming effect on her at once by his positive and caring nature. He had been there too and knew what was going on in the mind of Phyllis Kane. Kwame was ready for her too.

Jackson, tall, angular at 6' 2" and 172 lbs. was a major dancer in the original Alvin Ailey dance troupe. Now, at age 52, he made a living as a personal trainer, especially helping his fellow dancers and singers with stretching and breathing exercises that preceded performances. At a cost of $80.00 an hour, he paced his schedule, allowing no more than three clients a day, giving him the opportunity to be the professional that he was while not overtaxing himself and unwinding when he wanted. He knew that Phyllis, despite all her talent and poise, needed him to overcome stage fright and that this visit by Jackson, however brief, would be the perfect panacea for the much-anticipated event. Well-known himself in the entertainment industry, Jackson had to turn away prospective clients, recommending them to competent trainers he worked with over the years. He knew the importance of getting his clients de-stressed by the discipline he learned with the Ailey company and he applied his expertise by demanding 100% during his sessions.

"With Jackson," one of Phyllis' friends once said, "there's no mid-point. Either you do it right or you repeat it until he's happy."

The years of strenuous dance plus the preparation and intensity of getting the timing and delivery right left him with a very toned body and a calm demeanor. With Phyllis, he knew he would have an anxious and excited individual. He had been there too and was a lead with Judy Jameson on Broadway in Duke Ellington's "Sophisticated Lady."

Entering into her neat, spartan studio apartment that was typical of many single New Yorkers, he found a ready, albeit nervous, individual who had already placed the workout mat on the rugless floor. Soft music emanated from her CD player. Wearing a black Speedo workout outfit, the 5' 4", 140lb woman with hazel eyes that complemented her shoulder-length bond hair was quite a contrast to the tall, black soft-spoken middle-aged Jackson.

"Kwame, great to see you." She gave Kwame a big hug. "Want some green tea?"

"No, thanks, maybe later. You sound confident—that's a good sign. I know you. You'll be fine," Kwame said, giving Phyllis a light tap on her shoulder.

"Listen, girl, you'll be great tonight and you know I'll be there cheering you on."

"Thanks, K," she answered, using the name everyone called him.

"It's a big night and I hope I'm ready."

"Take it from one who's been there; it's only natural that you have the butterflies. It wouldn't be right if you didn't." Kwame Jackson was talking from experience. He was always the lead in several of the Alvin Ailey performances. His presence alone today was a comfort for Phyllis who knew she needed the support from people who have been in the limelight. She respected Jackson as a performer but, more importantly, for his honesty, sensitivity and sense of fair play.

"My family called from Savannah as did my agent. I'd be lying if I told you I wasn't a little nervous, but, you know, I'm ready. I'm really ready."

Jackson, smiling broadly, said, "You already sound like a star. Before long you'll have an attitude and won't even know me."

Phyllis returned the light tap. "You know my old-fashioned Southern roots won't allow that."

"Of course, not! You're talking to someone from Florence, South Carolina! Now let's get you on your way so the world will know by tomorrow who the hell Phyllis Kane is."

Phyllis, getting serious a moment, said, "You know what I'm going through. I've been in little roles both off and on Broadway, but this is the big Magila."

"All the more reason for you to strut your stuff and show them what you're all about, girl!" That's what she loved about Jackson—he could be serious one moment and, in an instant, drive his point home succinctly with such aplomb.

"Has this Southern belle become a Buddhist? What's that I smell?"

"Oh no," Phyllis said with a laugh. "That's jasmine incense—I find it relaxing."

"Whatever does the trick, I'm all for that," he said, as Phyllis gave him a high five.

Feeling much more confident with Jackson, she smiled and said, "Okay, let's go for it."

Jackson and Kane started their stretching routine and began a 45 minute session that incorporated yoga, deep Swedish massage and breathing routines to relieve pressure for the night's big performance. While they began their routine, the security desk downstairs was as busy as ever.

"Hi," said the thirtyish, balding, slender man. He had a warm smile that made Davis, the security guard, feel good. "I need apartment 30G. My name is Bernie, here to see Norma Kaufman." Davis buzzed Kaufman's apartment and Bernie thanked Davis. Bernie, after signing the security book, was let into the lobby to the large, elevator area. In a building with 46 stories, three elevators on each side greeted the visitor once going pass the myriad of mailboxes, bulletin boards and mirrors. Bernie entered elevator number four and proceeded to the 30th floor.

Norma Kaufman, a retired teacher in the New York City school system, was and had always been an activist from her early Lower East Side roots. Presently, her recent accomplishment resulted in a fair contract for the 1,000 or so tenants who occupied her building. Her constant lobbying from the local political clubs, such as the Midtown McManus Association to NYC City Council members was intensive to the point of annoyance to anyone who got in her way, earning her the affectionate nickname of "Stormin Norma" by Council member Gomez. She waited anxiously for Bernie Posner, a tenants' rights attorney to examine and cover the fine points of the draft of the negotiated contract that Kaufman would present on Tuesday at the monthly meeting. The contract, as Kaufman and the tenants association members demanded, protected stabilized apartments in accordance with NYC housing guidelines. Her attention to details in the labor-intensive atmosphere of tenants' rights was the result of that same activism she inherited from her Eastern European immigrant parents who escaped anti-Semitic pogroms in Czarist Russia in 1905, arriving at Ellis Island and settling a few blocks north on Rivington Street. She remembered her parents and the other immigrants from Poland, Italy, Hungary, Slovakia and Greece struggling to make it during the dark days of the Great Depression. So it was that her participation in struggles that got her started.

Indeed, she could recall, as a young girl, seeing her father coming home late at night, exhausted from the job he eventually obtained in the Garment District.

But she also remembered some of her friends worse off, losing even the walkup apartment and forced to move in with family or leave the city altogether. Instilled in her was a history of overcoming adversity and she was proud of the fact that, despite all the obstacles, was able to graduate from Seward Park High School and attend Hunter College, obtaining her teaching degree in history in 1944.

One of the founders of the NYC teachers' union, the UFT (United Federation of Teachers), she was elected to the delegate assembly and served on the National Education Board, representing her union at annual conventions in cities as diverse as Dallas and San Francisco. She still shuddered when she thought of the accusations made against the formation of the union at the height of the McCarthy hearings in the early 1950s. The hearings, which she always referred to as the "Witch Hunt," left her more determined to organize and agitate. Her resultant philosophy was typically Jeffersonian in nature—questioning central authority and advocating more local community control. A diehard, liberal Democrat, she stood on street corners gathering signatures for local, state and national leaders, even tredging through the New Hampshire snows in 1960 for JFK. This determination resonated well year after year when her colleagues elected her time and again to both the local and national delegate assemblies.

Posner knew that the diminutive, gray-haired grandmother who weighed no more than 105 was not to be taken lightly, but he also knew that Kaufman, while tough, was fair and he greatly admired her. Indeed, in his eight years of practice in labor law, he never came across a person with as much zeal and enthusiasm as Norma. So it was that this visit to the feisty old 5' 2" woman was out of respect and awe. He knew deep down that the Norma Kaufmans were a dying breed and he welcomed the opportunity to see her.

"Hello, Mr. Posner, come in." Posner sees in this little lady a dynamo activist he wished others in his firm shared. He liked the fact that she was still formal when addressing him.

"Can I get you something to drink or did you want something to eat or both?" Posner smiled and told Norma that his time was limited, but he appreciated the gesture. The smell of fresh coffee was apparent, making Posner at once comfortable. It's rare for him to make a home visit and even more rare to be offered some social amenities, such as a bite to eat. Kaufman was ever so special, always quick to tell Posner that he needed to slow down and enjoy life, take in a show and visit his parents.

During the three sessions he had with her, he learned that she was the youngest of eight children, shared a bed with one of her sisters growing up on the Lower East Side, worked her way through Hunter in a millenary shop where she met Mike Kaufman, an accountant. Together, they raised two children, Miriam and Joshua. Miriam lived with her husband in Roslyn, Long Island and often came into the city, stopping by her midtown Hell's Kitchen apartment. Joshua was another story. Ever rebellious, he left college during his sophomore year at Brandeis and went out West, settling in San Diego and opening a Tex-Mex restaurant with his girlfriend, Gail Gilroy. Norma and her husband, prior to his death in 1998, made it a point to help their children. Miriam, prior to her divorce, was a successful buyer with Merrill Lynch. Now having raised her son, Branson, she was a stay-at-home mom for many years who worked as a tele-marketer with Verizon. Recently, she met a fellow trader online named Sherman Hayes. Like Miriam, he was once divorced and a maven with computers. When he came over for a first date, they had at least a common topic to break the ice. Eventually, Miriam introduced him to her mother who, surprising Miriam, found Sherman much more focused and stable than her former son-in-law and despite their differences in age (she was 45 and he was 54), she encouraged her daughter to pursue the relationship, without interfering. *Who knows, maybe a marriage in the family before I die,* she thought. Norma examined the document that Posner gave her for the third time.

"It's time to sign and let me say, Ms. Kaufman, this is your baby. You've done a magnificent job—are you sure you didn't miss your calling—our law firm could use you."

"Dearie, I'm flattered, but you know me by now, I'm all for what's right. Always remember where you came from and fight the good fight and call your mother! I'll be right back."

Norma Kaufman returned out of the kitchen with a tray consisting of two cups and saucers, napkins, spoons and a dessert cake.

"It's easier if we talk over a little snack. So, sit down and relax." No more needed to be said. You don't tell Norma Kaufman what to do in her apartment.

This small and beautiful gesture reminded him of his own late grandmother. The smell of coffee, the cake, the small talk and the genuine smile on a face that had seen so much was an experience he hadn't had for years. So, he felt a special, strong bond to Kaufman, knowing she was a dying breed from the old school of hard knocks. Feisty, uncompromising and loyal, she was the personification of a true liberal, free thinker that he so admired. Indeed, a cursory look at her apartment was a repository of artifacts from trips to Europe, Israel and China. Her paintings were meticulously arranged and included still-lifes by Monet and Cezanne. Posner felt at home here and deep down felt a sadness of what would inevitably happen. Yes, he needed to call his elderly mother more often. He needed more life and more family contact. As always, Norma was right.

"Right, so right." Posner smiled with a lump in his throat, as he thought of his own late grandparents of whom Norma reminded him ever so much.

Bernie Posner noticed an array of prescription bottles on her neat table. Almost hesitantly, he asked, "Speaking of family, is everything all right with yours?"

"Not so bad, why should I complain? My son in San Diego wants me to visit him; he's opening up a third restaurant. And to think I thought he wouldn't amount to anything, leaving college and all. He has more money than all of us put together. Good for him; he's happy in what he's doing and isn't that what it's all about?"

With a broad smile Posner replied "Yes, really it's all about family."

"Yes, just don't forget it, Okay?"

"Okay."

"Well, that should do it, Ms. Kaufman."

"Again with this Ms. Kaufman. Call me Norma. You make me sound like an old lady!"

Posner laughed out loud and handed her the contract. He exited the apartment with a piece of Norma Kaufman's homemade coffee cake.

Downstairs, Melvin Davis was busy at the security desk. Davis, 34, was an ex-Marine from Knoxville, Tennessee, pursuing a degree in business administration in Queens at St. John University, taking advantage of the GI Bill and working at Manhattan Plaza's 484 West 43rd Street address. He studied individuals coming and going into the lobby—visitors, delivery boys, mail personnel, visiting nurses and off-the-street inquirers asking how to get an apartment in the complex. He also knew most of the 1,000 tenants in the 46 story building that dominated the west side of Hell's Kitchen on the corner of 42-43rd Streets and 10th Avenue.

Davis was a decorated Gulf War veteran. Married with one five year-old daughter, he supported his family by also installing Internet programs for most of the tenants in the building when off-duty at a NYC reasonable rate of $30.00 an hour. "Once you get a reputation as an able and competent technician, they will entrust you with something sensitive, like a computer." In just the last two weeks, he 'unfroze' three infected computers, installing safeguards to block further erosion via computer viruses and downloaded and reinstalled software in three resident apartments. People living in apartments 24E, 41R and 13J were happier today, knowing that they had a working computer and that Melvin was available. Always the professional, he envisioned himself operating his own small business, probably in the Kitchen, a neighborhood that was changing daily and offered a rare opportunity for any aspiring entrepreneur with a dream. "It's becoming Chelsea North," one elderly resident remarked to Davis, referring to the over-gentrified area to the south of Hell's Kitchen in an oft-handed dig.

Davis, wanting a better life for his young family, came North after his marriage. A star basketball player and captain of his team, his dream of going to college was ended when his father died when he was just 16. Forced to help his mother, as the oldest of seven children, his grades went south and he dropped out of school in his junior year, and started hanging out on street corners.

His mother, opposed to him dropping out of school, was appalled one day to see him with Kent Black, a known drug dealer in the neighborhood. She immediately put a stop to it by enrolling him in a GED night school program while making him work at the local Winn-Dixie during the day. He had always dreamed of going to Vanderbilt and playing for its team and, despite the pleas of his coach and teachers and his mother, he left school bitter and angry, blaming everyone from the doctors attending his father to God for his father's premature death from prostate cancer at age 41. After three years of struggle which saw two of his sisters marry and one brother move to Atlanta, he felt the need to grow. What resulted was an enlistment in the army where, after basics, Davis was sent to the Persian Gulf in 1991. He was assigned to training in tank transport. Part of the first tank division to cross the Iraqi desert, his unit distinguished itself and was cited by Bush at the request of General Schwarzkopf for its role in flushing out the Iraqi army from Kuwait. He had seen war up close and two of his buddies died when a landmine detonated when on patrol. Indeed, his entire unit was given the Outstanding Service Award. His unit was given not only the medal, but also was cited by the first President Bush in a White House Rose Garden ceremony that was televised nationally upon their return. He made his mother, his extended family and his country proud. But something was missing. The taste of victory left a bad taste in his mouth. He was tired of seeing blood and, despite the brevity of the war and its one-sided victory, he felt he had enough of the military. Too many disappointments caused a feeling of depression set in. He kept asking himself, "What should I do now?" He felt that he needed to explore other areas and find himself.

So, although he and his unit gained respect from the entire army, he was restless and began looking for a purpose. He thought of his wasted chances at Vanderbilt and decided he wanted out. So, instead of pursuing a military career that his commanding officers suggested, he set his sights on other ventures and began dating a young 24 year-old he met while being debriefed. They shared a common interest in basketball, albeit she was a die-hard Knicks fan. He subsequently fell in love with the fellow army veteran, Ann Doyle, marrying her in a civil ceremony at Camp Le Jeune, North Carolina in 1993, just before their mutual discharges.

They were an interracial couple. Doyle was the product of Irish-German parents from Hagerstown, Maryland. She was a petite, 5'3" blond—a contrast to the tall, 6'1" athletic and wiry Davis. Settling at first in his home town of Knoxville, they found themselves struggling in a small one-bedroom apartment.

Doyle's uncle and godfather Harry Norville, although leery of a 'mixed' couple in the family, put aside his outdated attitudes on mixed marriages by offering the couple to come to Queens with a position in his security firm that contracted with the sprawling Manhattan Plaza complex between 42-43rd Streets on the far west side. Norville needed solid, reliable and competent individuals to help maintain the company's good reputation and was very impressed by Davis' low-key, serious yet affable manner so necessary in dealing with the public. Himself a Vietnam vet, he was impressed with Davis instantly. He knew at once that Davis would be a good candidate for the security supervisor in charge of the seven people hired by his firm at the 484 West 43rd building.

The decision to move did not sit well at first.

"Why do you want to move to New York? Do you know what it's like?" asked Davis' elderly mother, Maylene. Like most aging parents, she wanted her son and grandchildren nearby. She also feared that a city the size of New York might be too overwhelming and the job too stressful. It was with a heavy heart that she finally realized that the job opportunity offered by her daughter-in-law's uncle was just too good to pass up. Also, Ann was the favorite of Norville's nieces and who could pass the opportunity to see the Knicks in person? Ann loved New York and her suggestion to move did the trick.

Within two months, Ann and Melvin had settled in another one-bedroom apartment in Elmhurst, Queens, just 35 minutes from his job site in Hell's Kitchen. Ever the optimist, he plunged into his job with both feet on the ground and became a popular figure with both the staff and the residents within a few weeks. Always curious, he made it a point to try to know as many names as possible in the 46 story building with 20 apartments on each floor. He especially bonded well with a few 'homies' from Nashville who were in theater and performing with the NY Philharmonic at Lincoln Center. He and Ann were given tickets to a performance of 'Nutcracker' at the New York State Theater, a Christmas tradition. Melvin got to enjoy his first taste of classical ballet, dance and opera just by virtue of his job and its location. "If I told some of my buddies I went to the ballet, they would give me weird looks and ask, 'What has that crazy city done to you?'" he said to Ann.

An education ensued as he got to understand the complexity of the neighborhood, its people and the dynamic that is uniquely New York. That curiosity, which sustained him as a youth in Knoxville, manifested itself in a desire to complete college and get a home for Ann and him. Indeed, Ann informed him that she was six weeks pregnant and Davis was determined to fulfill his mother's desire that he continue the education that he interrupted years before. He knew it wouldn't be easy. Night classes, papers and deadlines. Although tuition free due to his military service, he was keenly aware of the changes that would be taking place in his family soon. His dream was to finish college, obtain a real estate license and move his soon-to-be expanded family to a new venue. Yet his heart was here in the Kitchen and he knew an important part of his education was the job itself. Davis was a thorough person in that he focused on the future. He learned this lesson as a youth growing up without a father and facing the hard, cold realities of life. He owed much to his mother who molded him into a solid, strong-willed individual, who expected nothing from life without sacrifice. Now that things were going well, he needed to make a big decision about his future. But his life was about to take a different direction with just one visit to the doctor.

He remembered that he had an appointment with Dr. Frank White. "Just routine blood tests and the usual—blood pressure, heart and other vitals. I almost forgot about it. It's a yearly physical that the company demands."

Davis went for his mandatory physical that was required of all staff. What the expectant father wasn't prepared for were the results of his physical a few days later.

"Mr. Davis." The voice of Dr. White's secretary, Madeline Arroyo, sounded a little tense.

"Yes, this is Melvin Davis."

"Dr. White is scheduling you to go to St. Vincent's Midtown on 52nd Street for further blood tests. I've scheduled an appointment for you tomorrow at 5:00 PM. Will you be able to make it?"

Melvin was surprised at the urgency of such an appointment and knew that further blood tests must mean something had gone wrong.

"Okay, can I speak to the doctor? Is there something that's wrong?"

"I think he wants to go over the results of your test and conduct some more. You'll have to wait till tomorrow as he's with a patient. But he will answer all your questions—okay? If he's feels it's an emergency, he would have spoken to you. He wants you to undergo a few tests to be sure that your PSA is normal. Okay?"

"Yeah, I'll be there tomorrow right on time." *The PSA, isn't that for prostate?* he thought.

Melvin was preoccupied with the thought of the worst entering his mind for much of the ensuing day. "That's what did my Daddy in. Same age as me." Suddenly, he felt frightened and didn't know what to think or say. The dreadful thought of Ann raising a child alone—a child he didn't even know, might be the worst case scenario. He would say nothing to Ann and just pray that it wasn't too serious.

The entire night at home Ann noticed that Melvin was very antsy and not himself. Fear does that to a person. Fear of the unknown is such a powerful and encompassing force that it makes it difficult to try to cope with the normal day-to-day routines. But, it was an unknown fear. Sure, he had been afraid on the Iraqi desert, but he had known what his mission was and he worked in sync with his unit.

This, however, was different. Suddenly, nothing—not his job, his college career, even his extended family mattered—all he could think of was how Annie was going to raise a child without him around. He thought of his own mother and realized the great sacrifices she made as a young widow and knew deep down that Ann was tough. He felt bad about blaming his mother for him leaving school when it was he who dropped out, blaming others for his family misfortunes. He wanted to be there for his child and have his child remember a father. He remembered so little of his that the void still hurt to this day. He had sought refuge on Knoxville streets without a dad with people who just wanted to use him.

He prayed hard that night that it wasn't cancer. He knew African-American men suffered in greater proportions from certain cancers, among them prostate cancer. He would hold off giving any information to Ann until he heard from the urologist. Her early pregnancy needed full attention and he wouldn't let his stress transcend, at least now, to her. Nevertheless, it was a restless night. Ann kept asking him why he was so restless, but he refused to say anything to reveal his innermost fears. "Just want to make sure I'll be there for you guys," he whispered as Ann fell asleep. Noticing it was 3:15AM, he quietly went into the bathroom, put on the light,wept softly and returned to bed, falling asleep.

Melvin Davis arrived at his doctor's office on time and was ushered into his office. He immediately asked what was wrong.

"Calm down, Mr. Davis. I'm sorry if my secretary got carried away, but the blood tests show a PSA level of 5.0. That's a bit high and I want you to see a urologist who will determine where we will take this."

"Do I have cancer?"

"No, and I hope our monitoring of this situation will arrest any possible suspicions.

A biopsy will reveal if it's cancer. I believe the urologist, Dr. Marcus, at St. Vincent's will determine if we should proceed. You're smart in getting this under control now. I'm glad your company has mandatory blood tests. There are medications to bring down the PSA and have your prostate under surveillance. Let me ask you—are you urinating too much or do you experience any pain?"

"No, I'm fine. My wife just told me we're going to have a baby."

VOICES OF HELL'S KITCHEN

"Great, all the more reason for us to monitor and keep this condition under control."

Davis' biopsy revealed no cancer, but he was placed on medication. He finally told Ann, who steadfastly augmented his diet by including green tea, more fruits and vegetables and a little less red meat. In his second visit to Dr. Marcus three months later, his PSA level had dropped to 3.1. Davis was relieved to hear the news and was given a second chance at life. He continued to work at Manhattan Plaza while pursuing his goal. Ann gave birth to a 6lb.4oz boy. They named the baby after his father, Vernon James Davis.

CHAPTER 8

It wasn't that the wind was strong, gusty and cold. Early April has its share of challenging weather, but today's gales were unusually stiff and unbearable. What made it especially difficult was the manner in which it penetrated right through one's bones, making its sudden appearance to anyone who ventured outdoors to challenge the elements. Several residents stepping out were met with an early spring jolt, much like the kind of jolt one feels aboard a cruise ship when, upon stepping onto an apparently sunny and inviting deck, is suddenly thrown back by the ferocity of the wind. Gusts came and went with a vengeance, but at 60 miles an hour, this was one gale that had a mind of its own and was determined to get noticed. That April morn, the day the weather forecasters didn't get it right and, without a doubt, would be the conversation piece at the water cooler throughout New York. In the neighborhoods of Manhattan's Westside, anything not secure or tied down was subject to the wind god's sudden wrath. So it was that countless metal and plastic garbage lids were the first to fall prey, toppling over and making a very noisy but impressive racket as they rolled past the storefronts, restaurants and tenements in perfect unison. The orderly formation resulted in a most macabre yet beautifully choreographed dance for anyone within eyesight and fortunate enough to observe this free, unique, unrehearsed off-Broadway performance. Next to go was the debris—not just dust blown up in cyclonic clouds and adding to the dance, but the debris that made Manhattan notorious—all types of cardboard boxes, plastic cups and plates and an assortment of gum and candy wrappers. Adding further to the spectacle were the noisy tin cans—all kinds of cans toppled over from soda, beer and tin cans that bore the names of Goya, Del Monte, Campbell and Progresso. Refuse left out for garbage collection and now swept out of their canisters as part of the dance cast now ruled the streets and would not be stopped. Like tough New Yorkers, no one was going to tell them what to do and how to do it. They would have their own way and to hell with everything else.

Navigating his way through this newly-created obstacle course was perhaps the most important person to the assorted lot that called this part of Hell's Kitchen home—the mailman, Paul LeClerc. Everyone in the neighborhood knew Paul. He was the type of person who you would want around in an emergency. Always punctual, polite and with a face that had few lines and was pleasant at which to look, LeClerc, was a proud 10-year veteran of the US Postal Service and known on his route as 'Paulie' or just 'the mail man.' Delivering the mail along the stretch of windy streets and avenues west of 8th Avenue from 44-51st Streets, Paul's challenge today was clearly augmented by the fury mother nature directed at the entire neighborhood. *We know who's boss around here*, Paulie thought. *It's not me today.*

Indeed, a malodorous stench from uncapped receptacles, whose lids were now well into their strange dance rolled past Paul, a few hitting the side of his mailbag. If Paul were curious to know the outcome of this free entertainment, he would see it end with a thunderous climax as the assorted throwaways and debris merged and unceremoniously ended without fanfare into the wall of an abandoned auto parts shop on 11th Avenue. Knowing the challenge would be especially demanding despite the free show unfolding, Le Clerc sighed to himself, "It's going to be one of those days." He quickly resecured his mail pouch, reattaching the well-worn leather strap tightly across his precious contents, connected to wheels to hasten his rounds. Like a shell-shocked soldier reentering combat, Paul was ready to face the elements. His first stop was a typical tenement, 612.

"Any mail for 3B today?", Millie Wozniak asked LeClerc, as he placed the assorted bills, cards, letters, magazines, junk mail and statements carefully in each tenant's box at his first stop, 612 West 48th Street, just a block from the Hudson and where the surprise dance ended.

"Yes," he replied, brushing off a piece of paper trash whipped up by the wind as another tenant entered the narrow premises with noticeable difficulty, the door slamming hard behind, forcing Paul to look up.

"Sorry, I just went out to buy the paper. What a mess outside," announced Michael Gray apologetically, resident of apartment 2C.

"Tell me about it!" LeClerc shouted as Gray proceeded to pass Paul into the narrow hallway leading to the stairway walkup with its white and black tiled floors, so typical of the five and six story tenements built on the Westside for the burgeoning immigrant population explosion of the late 1800s. As Gray started his climb with his paper tucked under his left arm, Paul finished sorting out the mail.

"Here's your mail, Mrs. Wozniak."

She had been patiently standing for the past three minutes while Paul was busy putting the mail in the appropriate box. He handed her four pieces of mail. Millie, taking off her glasses and carefully placing them upon her well-manicured gray hair, scanned her precious cargo and smiled at Paul.

Too proud even at age 67 to wear bifocals, the diminutive widow, originally from Allentown, Pennsylvania, performed her own ritual daily dance with Paul. Always the same question, followed by the same movement of the glasses to make the ritual complete. By placing her glasses on her head, she was able to discern what mail was important and which ones were not and would ultimately end up in the trash heap. Like thousands of other people getting daily mail, she hoped for a surprise that seldomnly came to someone in her age bracket—a postcard from a relative enjoying a Florida vacation or a short note from a long-distance cousin living in Oregon or a card that merely said, "Hello." Mail delivery and the assured presence of Paul gave Millie a momentary excuse to abandon her lonely, dire existence. The mail, however insignificant to others, was the highlight of her day. The rest of the day she would hide behind closed doors to her apartment and the world. It would be Millie and her mail and no one else.

"Thanks, Paul; my check is here," she prayerfully whispered to LeClerc, who was too absorbed in his task to respond on this busy first day of the month.

Millie, grabbing the wooden handrail of the century-old building, began her slow ascent. With her right hand firmly placed on the handrail and the left holding the mail, she retreated to her small, immaculate one bedroom apartment on the third floor landing, still nodding and smiling appreciatively to her inattentive hero Paul. No doubt the inclement weather offered a perfect excuse to further sequester herself in her quarters, out of sight and missing out on the free spectacle with the dance of the lids.

"Take care, Mrs. Wozniak," Paul shouted as Millie approached the second floor landing. Looking up briefly, he heard

Millie's faint thanks as he resumed filling the metallic boxes. Paul felt better, knowing that Millie wanted his attention.

Paul had known Mr. Wozniak, dead now for six years. He knew that Millie had a good pension as a former transit worker, but can't help to wonder if she ever got outside much. Always a homebody, Millie cooked all her own meals, venturing occasionally to Sunday Mass or to the supermarket a few blocks away. Paul knew that his link to her was important and was glad that he was able to respond to her before she went into the safety net of her room.

The mailboxes at 612 were a microcosm of the city with names as diverse as: Wong, Sanchez, Brenner, Aiello, Cherenko, Jones and McBride. Names on mailboxes didn't reveal much except for the possibility of guessing ancestral identity. It took the local mail carrier to know that each of these mailboxes had a secret all its own. But the mail revealed so much of the secrets of people behind these closed doors. Paul, like most carriers throughout the country, knew what magazines people read, what stores they shopped at and the dates of birthdays and anniversaries. The local mailman knew when events, both good and bad, occurred by the volume of mail in the box. "There were four cards for Wong yesterday, two from San Francisco, and one each from Fresno and Seattle. It had to be her birthday," he said to himself. He wondered if she got any calls, went out to dinner or if her coworkers took her to lunch.

Paul's particular challenge today, in addition to the fury of mother nature, was exacerbated by an unexpected but inviting offer from his supervisor—the chance to relocate to a cushy, indoor assignment at an upscale, high rise on East 78th Street and 5th Avenue. With 52 floors, he would be solely in charge of all mail delivered to that address and be in charge of parcels and the expected assortment of priority and express items. No longer would he have to be an unwilling spectator to any 'Dance of the Lids' or have to endure the sorry spectacle of a motley assortment of wannabees coming home to their meager surroundings in the early morning hours from a night of carousing. He would, instead, be giving up the 'stroll,' as he commonly called his Hell's Kitchen route. He was one of thousands of underpaid, unappreciated postal employees who walked the beat like the old neighborhood cops of long ago. But Paul never complained and got no reprimands in the years he worked for the postal service. He was not surly to the people and they appreciated his presence. That was the main reason his supervisor at the main post office on 34th Street offered him this surprise just three days ago.

"You'd be crazy to pass it up, my man," Lucinda Yearwood had said, a fellow carrier and friend. Yearwood was a tough, gritty single mom originally from Gary, Indiana and now close to retirement. Her advice meant a lot to Paul, as she had a reputation as being tough but fair. If she had something to say, she would let you know. In addition, she had a quick wit with an infectious grin that complemented her 5'2" frame. The portly fellow carrier was right. She usually was right on target. Yes, the lure of a cozy, indoor job site was preferable, especially on a day as challenging as this one.

"I'll get the mail through, whether I'm on 5th or here on West 48th Street, and still get paid the same," he pondered quietly as he continued to sort out the mail at 612. "Now that I think of it, today's crazy winds are nothing compared to the biting winter we just went through."

Inclement weather such as blizzards or scorching hot summer days or torrential, cold, fall rains have all tested Paul's resolve. The cold wind off the Hudson was always a challenge to workers and residents alike and was part of the New York experience. Like the stevedores working the docks, to the deliverymen constantly going to and from their rounds to the Department of Sanitation, Paul had the grit and moxie that made all the difference. It was the tough grit he inherited from his Louisiana Cajun roots. He worked his way up North with his new wife in 1994 from Slidell and was now raising two sons, Matthew and Kent. Living in Queens, he and his wife Sandra rented a two-bedroom apartment for $1400.00 a month. It was a good life and he liked his job and was afraid of change, even if it meant a lateral switch to a new venue.

He knew his supervisor, Bruce Finley would need an answer, as others would also love the cushy job indoors at a pricy locale. A decision had to be made by the next two days. "Sooner or later, you'll have my answer," he told Bruce this morning as he grabbed a regular coffee and buttered roll from the cart outside the post office from Omar before heading on his rounds.

Placing <u>Time</u> in McBride's mailbox, <u>Cosmopolitan</u> in Sanchez's and <u>USA Today</u> in Cherenko's box, he pondered his soon-to-be decision. *I feel alive in this neighborhood. I feel good when I'm outside, even on a day like this, it's part of me and I know how to handle it. I also get to walk and talk to all kinds of people and it makes my day. I feel wanted.* Indeed, if LeClerc needed a mantra to sustain him, it was simply "Walk, walk." Paul was an emissary whether he knew it or not and could easily direct a nervous tourist towards the Intrepid on a hot, sultry, humid July day or the Circle Line boat ride. He could tell those same tourists, or anyone curious enough, that the best coffee could be found at Arnold's on 45th and 9th, the best ham and cheese sandwich at the Deluxe Deli on 46th and 10th and places to shop for uniquely New York bargains from cell phones, batteries, tee shirts displaying alluring and enticing messages to those back home and the thrift shops that lined 10th Avenue in the high 40s. Whether it was helium balloons for parties, costumes for the Greenwich Village Halloween Parade or used furniture at the Salvation Army on 46th Street for the new yet financially-challenged newcomer to the city, Paul could steer them on the right path. This indeed was his domain and for a few hours he reigned supreme. He was the 'King of Hell's Kitchen,' at least from 48 to 59th Streets.

I don't know if I'm cut out for those high brows on the Eastside. *It sounds great and I'm sure I could get used to it, but I know this hood.* Change was hard for someone who had an established niche and Paul knew it. *Got to think about it and not get stressed.*

Nearly finished with his mail distribution at 612 some five minutes later, he was overpowered by the savory aroma emanating from Adele Aiello's ground-floor apartment. *It's that homemade sauce and meatballs. Every Friday, every Friday,* he thought. *That's right, I forgot it's Friday, with this job on my mind.*

That aroma from Adele's apartment was a combination of simmering, hot olive oil, garlic, oregano and parmesan cheese used to make her meatballs. "Those fried meatballs—they're the best," he said, looking up to see if Adele would venture out to get her mail. "Maybe if I make some noise, she'll hear me." He smiled to himself.

Almost on cue, Adele emerged into the hallway, white apron stained with a few specs of her homemade red marinara sauce and a plate of two still-simmering meatballs for Paul, along with a few napkins, a fork and two neatly-sliced pieces of Italian bread.

Patting him on the shoulder, like some doting mother, she smiled, handing the plate to Paul and said, "I know you can use these hot meatballs in this brutal weather. Take a minute and *mangia!*"

Trying to looked surprised, as he did every Friday when Adele had something for him, he said, "Good morning and thanks. I appreciate these meatballs any day, but especially today." Taking the fork, he cut into the hot meatball, abandoning his assigned rounds. The meatball was laced with rich, tomato sauce. He made Adele's day, as he wiped his mouth with the napkin she handed him. "The best meatballs and sauce. The best," he said, causing her to smile.

"Don't forget the Italian bread." Adele had the two pieces of buttered, warm Italian bread in her hand.

Adele took the plate from Paul, as he wiped his hands on the other napkin Adele had for him. Paul handed over two pieces of mail to her. Unlike Mrs.Wozniak, she only received a small social security check, plus a letter from a grandniece in Dover, Delaware.

"You made my day, Mrs. Aiello."

"You say that every Friday. What would you do without me?" she asked, not expecting an answer.

"I don't know." Paul nodded, realizing that his decision would deprive him of these special minutes with Adele and the other tenants. "You're right," he said again, this time to himself as Adele headed towards her apartment.

"Well, it's the first of the month. I know you're busy with all us old folks getting pension and social security check to get by on. At least I can pay the rent now. By the way, what was that racket out there? I heard the wind; it rattled my windows as if they were coming loose."

"I was in the thick of it. Those were tin garbage can tops pried loose by the winds. They were like flying missiles—sounded like that Broadway show, 'Stomp.'"

"Like what?" Adele turned fully around, wondering what Paul was talking about. Paul briefly told the reclusive widow of the percussion off-Broadway show in the East Village. "They use garbage cans for rhythm, dancing and moves," he added, laughing at the expression on Adele's face.

"So, you're telling me people come from all over to hear noise that I can hear every day free? Tell them to come to our street and we'll make money throwing the cans around and hollering and dancing." Adele laughed aloud. Turning away from Paul, she unlocked her apartment door, mail and empty food plate in hand and said, "Crazy, paying to hear that noise."

Paul shouted back to her, "It takes all kinds; thanks again for the treat."

Adele blew him a kiss. "Take care, Paulie, stay grounded and watch that wind."

Just as Adele entered her apartment, Alexa Sanchez, a Midwest transplant from Indiana and a transvestite whose real name was Karl Brenner came into the windy hallway, brushing something from her hair.

"Good morning, Sir," she said, still cross-dressed from her previous night's job at the all-night West Village drag show.

"Any mail for Brenner or Sanchez?"

Paul, looking up, said softly: "A few pieces—here they are; I was just going to place them in your box." The comment caused Sanchez to laugh aloud and Paul, realizing the double entendre, also smiled broadly. Sanchez's mail consisted of a Visa bill, an issue of <u>Vogue,</u> and, like everyone else this first of the month, the rent bill to be mailed to the agency in New Brunswick, New Jersey that owns the building.

"Thanks—I must look like a sight for sore eyes. That wind is so bad. Look at what the wind has done to my hair," Sanchez said to Paul, expecting some sympathy. At least something positive.

"Not your fault, ma'am, like you said, it's the wind." Paul mad it a point not to get too involved in small talk when it came to personal matters, especially in this case. He knew the real goods on Sanchez/Brenner and tried to respect all of his clients. With heels, at 6'1', Sanchez stood out with her amazon appearance, topped with a jet black, straight wig and a matching sleeveless black dress and makeup with a spray of the now familiar perfume Impressions that made for a powerful fragrance. Paul had asked what fragrance Sanchez wore and surprised his wife with a bottle from Macy's, thanks to Sanchez.

"Still smells good. My wife also likes the Impressions you recommended. I'll have to buy her some more. You were a good contact."

"My pleasure, glad to be of some help. Anytime."

Sanchez towered over a bent-over Paul, still sorting out the mail. He thought to himself, *Damn, she looks better than my own wife!* Sanchez/Brenner thanked Paul and began the slow ascent to her fourth floor apartment.

The exchange with Sanchez took a mere three minutes. Just as Paul was finishing his rounds at 612, Mike McBride nearly collided with Sanchez as he came down the stairs to collect his daily mail. McBride, who lives on the fifth floor, wore a blue Yankee cap and matching dark blue Yankee jacket.

"It's a bitch out there, Paulie. The Yankees home game is next week. I hope to Christ the weather's better. I got opening tickets just behind third base. Steinbrenner can buy his team, but he still can't do a lick about the weather." McBride was a classic Westsider. Born just a few blocks away, he stayed in the neighborhood, working the docks for the last 12 years. A tough local, he got into several brawls in the nearby taverns before they changed into upscale haute cuisine to serve the newcomers. His uncle, Matt, a retired cop, bailed him out on several occasions. Now in his forties, he was calm by comparison to his younger days and living with his longtime girlfriend, Tina Langford, an aspiring actress from Tucson. Paul always thought Mike to be a real, engaging sort who should have gone into show business instead of his girl.

Responding to Mike's observation about the weather, he asked, "Have you been out yet?"

"No, but I heard the racket with those damn garbage cans. They woke me up at 5:30 and I couldn't get back to sleep."

"Don't I know it," said Paul, handing the mail to McBride and added, "Hope it's good."

"You kidding! Bills, bills and more bills. Even Tina wants me to lay off going to the games. But that's one area where she has no say. I'm a New Yorker tried and true."

"Yeah, I can understand," Paul said, noticing the frown on Mike's face as he opened an envelope that was obviously not welcomed.

"It's my child support payment to my former wife and kid in Illinois," Mike said.

"Sorry, don't mean to pry, but I didn't know you lived in the Midwest."

"Never did, that's where she went after meeting this guy Pete and headed out there to Moline."

"Thanks anyway, Paul. The kid is good; he's 16 and in just two more years, he…." His voice trailed off upon realizing that Paul probably didn't need to know any other information.

Paul noticed the Verizon bill, plus the rent, child support notice and a copy of <u>Sports Illustrated,</u> with Alex Rodriguez on the cover.

"Here A-Rod is, flashing the cover with his smiling face. Let's hope he's worth the millions they're paying him" McBride adds.

McBride grabbed his mail, tightly putting the contents under his arm, as he wrestled to open the door outside, shouting to Paul, "Take care; see you tomorrow."

Paul smiled and locked the mailboxes. George Wong and Anna Cherenko were at work and the new tenant, Lloyd Bannister, was getting mail forwarded from his previous Dallas address. 612's mail was finished for the day. Looking at just this one building, Paul realized that even a small, sixth story walkup was representative of the city in general. A composite of the city with young and old, natives and newcomers, eccentrics trying to make it, lonely, happy, angry, optimists and realists. It represented life and like the dance outside had its own performance in the journey of life.

Paul was ready to face the challenging wind. He journeyed towards the next building, 610, a duplicate of 612. It too had its own character with all the different personalities living there. It too had its share of good and bad, happy and sad.

The gale-force winds hadn't abated one iota and a few more garbage cans and debris joined the troupe, hoping to make their debut like their counterparts before them. Rolling down the street and making a less-than-spectacular racket, these understudies would nevertheless make their presence known to anyone within earshot. Paul, looking at the sight, smiled and wondered what other place would offer such a managerie of sorts except for Hell's Kitchen.

"Do I really want to change to a comfortable, neat and steady job that is routine and every day is the same?" he asked himself "Where else but here can I play therapist with Mrs. Wozniak, enjoy the savory delicacies of Mrs. Aiello's home cooking, shmooze with Mike McBride and let him vent and be entertained by the ever-changing erstwhile Sanchez/Brenner?" He knew his decision would be welcomed by the person next in line to transfer. An enclosed environment, away from the blizzards, winds, heat, rain and queries from tourists sounded inviting. But it wasn't him. However alluring, it could never match a day to day event, such as today's encounter at 612. Drama, food, dance, entertainment and analysis of the upcoming baseball season were on his agenda and that was just one building.

Smiling broadly, he took a deep breath from the wind and entered into number 610 to continue the drama.

CHAPTER 9

The third Saturday of the month always brought the same routine—up by 7:00AM, a quick shower, shave and light breakfast, usually Cheerios and orange juice, then catch the #42 crosstown bus from 10th Avenue and 42nd Street to Grand Central for the 7:51 to Beacon and Fishkill Correctional Facility. Getting an off-peak ticket for $22 round trip, heading for the now familiar track #34, Marcus first stopped at the newsstand and picked up the Post, a pack of Winterfresh gum and a copy of People.

"That comes to $4.98, Sir," the cashier said.

The name tag read Sindra Singh. She was a young, attractive Indian wearing a colorful sari. He murmured to himself, "These people work; you got to hand it to them. I bet she was up at 4:00 and on the E train from Queens to get here."

He had been to Elmhurst and Flushing, two of the newest 'melting pots,' which was the old term used for the European neighborhoods of the Lower East Side, but now was used to describe a Queens full of the scents of Indian, Chinese and Colombian restaurants.

Glancing at the clock above the information booth, he had 10 minutes before boarding to use the restroom located at the other end of the cavernous station. Saturday morning at the busy terminal was devoid of the crowds and Marcus was able to exit the restroom with six minutes to spare. The morning whiffs of coffee coming from Zaro's and the additional smell of fresh croissants, bagels and cakes gave the north end of the terminal more of a market appearance than the busiest train terminal in New York.

Settling in the old, leather-beaten seat that was used for off-peak travel, he made sure he sat on the left—the view of the Hudson was spectacular and the late May day was bright and cloudless. *I'll probably see some sailboats, yachts and small crafts as we get closer to the Tappan Zee*, he thought, wishing he could be on one of those crafts on such an alluring, cloudless day. It was that time of year that the weather allowed all the stored-up light crafts to make their yearly entry into the waters of the majestic Hudson. His favorite spot to pass was West Point. A history buff, he wondered what the Point was like when Lee, Grant, MacArthur and Eisenhower were there.

He paid no particular attention to his fellow passengers, who numbered about 35. The train started up on time. Glancing at the tabloid <u>Post,</u> he saw the bold headline: "**Gotti Jr. Makes It Home.**"

"Seems appropriate today, since I'm going to up the river to Fishkill."

"Ticket, please," a female conductor announced in a loud voice, almost as if to interrupt his thoughts. Coming to Marcus, she punched his ticket, as she did with each passenger. She handed it back to him with a quick, "Thank you." He had seen this conductor before, a petite black woman with a gap between her front molars. A bit overweight but jovial, she patted the child seated with his mother across the aisle from Marcus. She smiled and said, "Up early, sweetheart?"

Within 10 minutes, the train aimed north, stopping first in East Harlem at 125th Street Station. A large crowd of mostly adult women and children boarded and Marcus saw some of the same faces he had seen on previous trips upriver for the past three years. The women, carrying bags of food and gifts were pipeline to the males incarcerated in the medium prison at Fishkill, located in the city of Beacon in Southern Dutchess County.

"These precious women, girls and boys are like angels to the men," he had been told by his cousin, Omar King, whom Marcus was going to visit. He had a shopping bag of goods for Omar—two copies of National Geographic, which his neighbor, Mr. Gray, the teacher at Park West, always gave him. He also had the newest edition of Flex, featuring an enormous juiced-up Mr. Olympia, Ronnie Coleman, on the cover wearing a pair of plain, red workout pants and sweat shirt just like those allowed by the prison. He knew his cousin had been working out in the yard and saw the results from the constant regimen of cardio and weights. Ronnie Coleman was one of Omar's favorite idols.

His cousin had buffed up his body to the point that he competed in an amateur bodybuilding contest at Fishkill and placed third in the middle-weight division.

"I guess it's positive, given the atmosphere and the people he has come in contact with. Some of these guys, tattooed and stern-looking, give me the creeps." But, during his last visit, he noticed that Omar garnered respect by the constant high fives and backslapping gesture of affection from the inmates and some C.O.s as well. "I just hope to hell he stays focused and gets paroled and puts this behind him," he said almost aloud. "It would be a bitch if he actually likes the joint."

Marcus' mind wanders back to a better time before the incident in 2002 that put Omar in jail. "If only I could have stopped him from going to work that day and confronting Dwayne, he wouldn't be there now." The incident that put his cousin in prison was always on his mind.

The train left Yonkers, a city proudly displaying its new downtown waterfront area with new condos and a beautiful new library. Again, as in New York City, more people entered with bags, no doubt headed for Fishkill or the adjoining institutions along the Hudson, either the infamous Sing Sing or Downstate Correctional, which were also located in Beacon. Leaving Yonkers, the Hudson now converged near the Point, where during the Revolution, Washington was able to fight off a British attempt to control the river and stave off the British advance.

As the train pulled into Peekskill, he saw a beautiful thirtyish blonde with matching blue blouse and pants that complemented a round face with a similarly colored Hermes scarf. Putting her small Louis Vuitton bag in the overhead section, she called someone on her cell phone to arrange for her pickup in Poughkeepsie, just one hour away. Her presence was unnoticed by anyone except Marcus. He visualized himself to be on the other end of the phone, an anxious and excited chain of events for a weekend about to unfold in his ear. He recognized the perfume she was wearing, Elizabeth Taylor's 'Red Door,' a gift he had often given to his ex-wife for Christmas and birthdays. She was indeed an anomaly in this crowd, giving Marcus a chance to fantasize. He found himself getting aroused and wondered what a night with her would be like. Reality set in when he heard her hang up after saying, "Yes Uncle Nick, it should be a nice surprise. My husband has the car waiting." He then noticed the diamond and wedding band.

Well, it was worth the fantasy, he thought, gazing back to the river and trying to forget his fantasy.

One fleeting moment of imaginary nocturnal delight with a stranger on the train who in actuality was going to a party for a relative! Yet, she was so different from the passengers around him, like himself and the others about to go to Beacon. Marcus noticed she was a woman of class—designer shades, a real gold pendant, no doubt from her wordly travels, perhaps to Europe or the Far East. He imagined striking up a conversation and finding her to be a lonely, unhappy, sex-starved and vulnerable person—similar to himself. He had been alone too long. *Oh, well, I can always dream. What would she want from a person between jobs with a high school education like myself, with a ton of debts to pay off like me. But it's been a long season without rain!*

He glanced at the other side of the aisle, not wanting to further arouse himself with the idea of an unattainable goal. The woman and two children opposite him were carrying a shopping bag of what looked like groceries and non-perishable items allowed by the authorities at Fishkill. *No doubt, her son gave a list of items he wants.* The woman, Hispanic and in her 40s, wore an immaculate white dress more suitable for Sunday Mass than today. Realizing this was the only opportunity she had to show her sense of fashion, Marcus thought, *Here is a woman who cares enough to don her best to see her son. That says something about her sense of loyalty and pride in herself—I like that.*

In front of him sat a middle-aged black woman with a Macy's bag. *Someone else will be greeted with a beautifully wrapped gift; maybe it's his birthday.*

Marcus glanced at the Hudson and saw a hawk soaring as the river was now at its widest point as the train approached the Tappan Zee Bridge. The river was always constant—whatever the season. The river always allowed him a sense of peace and the looming Catskills, rising higher as the train meandered along the river as it approached Beacon, gave him a good reality check. *I've learned a lot from the river and these trips—take it slow, don't let yourself get absorbed in details and accept the reality of events.*

Yes, the river was a good friend. And Marcus needed a good friend. Just past his 41st birthday, he was still living in the Kitchen in a walkup he grew up in. All the old timers—neighbors, parents and old friends had all gone. The' hood' was different—walkups that used to be just $200.00 were now being retrofitted and rented for $1600.00. Life around him was changing; the old bodegas had given way to health stores, the mom and pop shops where he played the numbers as a kid and was nearly arrested were now nouveau cuisine bistros, art galleries and video stores. The river, however, was steady and always there—a friend to him. *Even if Omar makes parole, I'll take a trip upriver.*

He loved the train and the constant rumble on these lazy Saturdays. A faint smile came over his face. *My family—my family is Omar, Omar's mother, Evelyn and his own daughter.* Now that his wife had left him some three ago, he no longer kept the anger of abandonment visible. His daughter moved to Charlotte with a truck driver she met at some Chelsea dive, fell in love with him and followed him down south to Charlotte, North Carolina. Marcia, his daughter, called to tell him that he would be a grandfather by November and should come south to see her and her husband, Stan. She had gone down to visit her mother, Marcus's former wife and met Stan, a cable repairman living in Richmond, who was in Charlotte on a family visit. *Maybe, but I'll only be in the way,* he thought as the train passed a barely noticeable tiny waterfall made by the runoff from the heavy spring rainfall. Marcus noticed the natural, fleeting beauty of the water cascading down and, wishing he could hear the pleasant roar of the falls, thought of how ideal a trip to the Rockies or even Niagara Falls would be. He suddenly felt very alone. "Dreams keep men alive. If only I could find a job!" he said quietly. The train was about to reach Beacon.

Arriving on time, Marcus joined the procession of visitors to an awaiting van, where for $6.00 a round-trip will take them to the Visitors Center of the state medium institution a mile away and isolated from the town. The van was always filled to capacity, thus ensuring a profitable run. Marcus was greeted by a tall, slender man with a distinct West Indian accent. He was one of many van drivers, transporting visitors to the two mile run from the train station to the correctional facility. Ever the observant one, he noticed the picture of Haile Selassie on the dash and the reggae music of Zoe Marley emanating from the tapedeck.

Within ten minutes, the van arrived at the prison. Entering first into the trailer that serves as the visitors' center, knowing the routine so well, he placed his wallet, cell phone and belt in a locker that charged 25 cents. He then approached the line to register himself and within five minutes, was asked to fill-out information on Omar while producing a photo id of himself.

Omar's number was #02A1212. "I never knew that the first two numbers meant the year he was arrested and the 'a' meant that he was an adult when arrested." The third line of the form was to register the items he purchased, which would be inspected and sent to Omar's cell during the visit. The last hurdle was the security check—he took off his shoes, eyeglasses, and handkerchief for inspection and passed through an electronic screen familiar to all airport travelers. After a quick stamp of iridescent light on his left hand, he was led to a series of barred passages, buzzed in and finally arrived in the vast cafeteria and is assigned to desk K-4.

Looking around the room, he saw pictures from Family Day, replete with photos of children with their fathers and wives and girlfriends. Omar appeared, smiling with a hardy handshake and sat down.

"How's everything M?" Omar said, using the old street nickname.

"I'm fine; I wanted to get here early, so you can tell me what's on your mind."

"I see you looking at the pictures. My daughter was up with my mom. They let me take good pictures .It's the one time of year we try to get the loneliest guys in the joint to participate." Marcus was a good listener; he knew much of the visit was therapeutic for Omar, a one-term prisoner who was up for parole on attempted assault this spring.

"O, when are you scheduled to go the parole board?" The question gave Omar a chance to get serious and he was quick to let his cousin know that it "would be within the next month.'

"What's the process? How do we get you out of here?"

"God, this is the second time I'm going to the board and I hope the last time I have to do time. I'll admit that you're 100% right; I shouldn't have settled that score while I was so pissed—a weak moment and the next thing I know I'm busted by a hostile group of people who claim I was to blame when I was trying to defend my ass. So much for the judicial system." A quick tap on the shoulder by Marcus sent a message that "It's OK, I'm here." Marcus knew that Omar felt he was set up and had tried to let the incident that landed him here die. But the pain was in his face—he knew he agonized over this in his head time and again. One moment of acting irrationally and he ended up here. Marcus repeatedly told Omar to be a visionary and not look back. Yet, he knew the present environment was a constant reminder of one stupid mistake he has regretted for the last three years. Omar was a realist and recognized that he needed his cousin as he would be tagged as an ex-inmate with a record.

Marcus tried very hard to get his court-appointed lawyer to get the charges dropped, but it was an election year and the voters wanted to see crime become a priority issue. Forget the fact that the accuser, Malcolm Fields, had a long criminal record and had repeatedly threatened Omar at his job on more than one occasion. Fields, a loose cannon, lacked the courage to confront Omar over erroneous allegations, telling the supervisor, Fred Thurson, that he was often late because of family problems. Omar had to pick up the slack at the auto parts shop on 10th Avenue and 49th Street on three occasions. As a result, Omar ended up working later hours. When he confronted Fields about this, he picked a fight with Omar and tried to ridicule him publicly on the job when Omar asked why he was "often so damn late.". He pushed Omar hard at lunch, insulting him and challenging him with dire results. Pushed to the limit one time too many, Omar grabbed a wrench, striking Fields hard on his head. The DA's office wanted to press for an aggravated assault charge. Luckily, despite the lies perpetuated by the 'so called-witnesses', the charges were greatly reduced to attempted assault, as no one was injured. His court-appointed defense attorney, Miriam Hernandez, a young fresh-out-of law school graduate was overwhelmed by pressure from her superiors and talked Omar into avoiding trial by copping a plea of attempted assault and a mandatory five to 10 year sentence. Marcus wanted a trial, but Hernandez felt that the witnesses would be too credible, as they were friends of Malcolm and indicated that they didn't want to get involved and got Omar to plea. He had now served a full four years and was eligible with good time for an early release.

"Just be yourself and tell the truth. Be a visionary, don't look back—you can't change what happened. Be positive, tell them of your involvement with the anger-management group, with the children's group and completion of your GED. That's what they want to hear—don't dwell on the past and tell them you were shafted and never intended to hurt Fields, only defend yourself, which is what really happened. They want you to sound remorseful. You *are* sorry this happened?"

"Hell, yes! I have learned from this nightmare to think before I act, to be a man and settle differences without the fist or a weapon. We grew up on the Westside when it was bad and we had to fend for ourselves. You remember what it was like—but you're right. With my father gone and my daughter needing me, I need to grow up. This place, lousy as it is, has been a learning experience. I've seen drug use here, sexual exploits and shakedowns and harassment. But, guess what, I've also seen some real human experiences. Just last week, a cellie's mother passed and when he returned, I noticed the C.O.s came up and not only said sorry, but everyone on the block gave him a hug and made him feel that at least they knew what he'd been through."

Yes, Marcus was a good listener. His presence was good therapy for his cousin. It was also a learning experience for him. Regardless of how bad things were in his life, Omar had to bear the consequences of a record and the stigma attached to it. In spite of it all, he saw in Omar a changed individual— a grown-up, stand-up guy who was learning a cruel lesson of life. Omar no longer felt sorry for himself. Marcus wondered if he could cope under these circumstances. Suddenly his troubles paled in comparison to his cousin's.

Changing the subject, Marcus got Omar to talk of the Christmas pageant and what role he played. Omar apparently didn't realize he had some acting ability and when approached by one of the teachers in his GED program to participate in a Christmas reading, he at first refused, and then, getting renewed confidence, read Clement Moore's classic "A Visit from St. Nicholas" to the children and parents. As he rehearsed for the reading, the inmates and teachers who were part of the cast remarked that his sonorous voice projected well and that he should use this experience to consider some of the neighborhood theater groups that surrounded his Hell's Kitchen home when he got released.

He laughed it off and later, when encouraged by his GED professor from nearby SUNY New Paltz, Dr. David Weiss, he got the confidence to not only perform well but also be a catalyst in the formation of an ad hoc actors group, which Omar named Fishkill Repertory Group. So the pictures on the wall were a testament to his success and tapped into a talent unknown and unexplored to date. He nearly whispered to his cousin, "The Lord works in mysterious ways, I guess."

"That's what you need to tell the parole board. Have Weiss and others who you know write letters to NYS Parole Board. Your former boss, Joe Santiago, will also go to bat for you.

Don't forget your daughter; Daisy needs a father. I can see a lot of good coming this way, O."

"I was scared facing that huge audience, but I got through it and enjoyed it and met some people in here that are determined to make it, like myself," he said..

"So, what's new with you M?"

"Well, at least you're promised a job when you're out. My job situation is not what you call good by any means." Marcus was reluctant to discuss his dilemma with his cousin. Indeed, in the last few weeks he had been pounding the pavement and looking for work in the new restaurants cropping up along 9th Avenue. "The offers that were there fell through. I stay up nights worrying about it, but I have a gut feeling something's got to give. I'll be honest—jobs are tight, even with the experience of a short-order cook and janitor services that I've done. Maybe I need a guardian angel-any ideas?"

"Man, you come every month to see me—I wish I could do something. If it's any consolation, you can stay with my mom and Daisy if you have to."

"Don't even go there—thanks, but you know I won't give up the apartment on 46ᵗʰ. The rent is still only $300.00—the yuppies moving downstairs have a renovated apartment and are paying $1200.00 No way in hell I can do that."

Now it's Omar's turn to be positive. "Check out the local new restaurants, the Greek diners, the new 9ᵗʰ Avenue stores you always tell me about. Something's gotta give. Don't give up." Marcus knew that the visit was for Omar and he quickly returned to the subject of his upcoming parole board. Omar assured him that his counselor, Dr. Weiss, the Repertory theater group and the childrens' group are all pluses and he's confident that he will get a just hearing. "You know that new DA Hernandez wanted a win and got me to cop a plea; it was the wrong thing to do, but with a weapon in my hand, she scared me into a class B felony. I hope I can get over this."

After spending two hours at the table, the inmates and visitors could walk outside in the yard or share lunch at 2:00 PM in the visitors' section. Marcus always liked the informality of this medium, laid-back atmosphere and the opportunity it gave him to speak to both inmates and visitors alike. He was struck by the volume of visitors that day; the cafeteria was full and the line long.

Marcus bought a Coke, turkey sandwich, french fries and a piece of cake. Omar was more the physical specimen—the regimen of prison allowed him to build his form into an impressive, sculptured body. He ordered a green salad, Diet Coke and carrot cake. "I need this food to maintain myself, though I like your choice a whole lot better!"

"I should follow your diet—it's probably better for me, to say nothing of the stress," Marcus said as he paid a total of $9.87 for the meal.

"You shouldn't pay—I can eat at the commissary, you know." Omar was well aware of the cost of the trip plus the round trip van rate and now lunch.

"Hey, don't worry, if you ate at the commissary, I couldn't be there and would have to leave. Where do I have to go?"

Omar knew that his cousin was a decent, sensitive and up-standing individual and he felt for him and didn't let on that he was worried about his job search.

Sitting down at a round table that seated seven people, Omar and Marcus were joined by two friends of Omar, Jeffrey Howell and his girlfriend, Melissa Graves. Jeff was a tall, slender and toothy guy who walked with a slight limp, testament to an injury he sustained in a fight with a belligerent inmate named Nico a few months ago. Melissa was a regular visitor and the mother of one of Jeff's two kids. She had jet-black hair tied in a bun and wore a matching set of red pants and blouse. Jeff was scheduled for parole, as all inmates in this medium institution were, in 2006. Omar and Jeff exchanged high fives and introductions were made for Marcus and Melissa. Small talk ensued; Jeff was an avid Knicks fan and now that the playoffs in the NBA were taking place, it became a source of conversation for the four. Marcus was no fanatic fan, but understood the importance of the visit and contributed his knowledge of the game and the chances for the Knicks.

While eating, several of the kids came by and gave Omar big hugs. He was, after all, one of the founders of the nursery area, where kids were entertained while their parents visited. "You're quite a hit, Omar. I've seen the room, the great pictures on the wall and the toys donated. You guys have a lot of heart." Omar smiled while looking down, not knowing what to say to such accolades.

Following lunch, Omar and his cousin went to the yard where the weights were in an enclosed area. "This is where I got big."

"Big? You're enormous," Marcus said. "I remember a little runt cousin that I used to pick on and now, you put me to shame. I got to hand it to you—I would want to be big here after I saw some of these characters."

"This place is nothing compared to the Big Houses—Sing Sing and Attica, just to name two."

Looking around the yard, Marcus observed an array of physical activity going on—from the weight-lifting to basketball to jogging around the track. "I still don't know how you can keep your sanity here."

Marcus' mind was preoccupied with his fears of losing his apartment once again. He wished he could find something to at least allow an income as the unemployment would dry up in a week, but he never lost sight that this visit was for his cousin. He knew deep down it was therapeutic for him to get away from the Kitchen and forget his problems for just a bit. He thought of the river and the trip back and smiled.

"Well, coz, I'd better get ready if I want to make it by 7:00 PM to Grand Central."

Omar felt that Marcus was preoccupied with something and dared not ask. In the time spent behind bars, he knew how important little things like turf, attitude and a mere look could start a confrontation. Just yesterday, one of the cellies on his block got into a verbal spat with someone who tried to get ahead on the cafeteria line. What resulted was a reprimand and a reprimand in this place means that the little freedom afforded was further eroded—such as no mail for a month, no visits or packages. Omar had learned from the system and wasn't about to challenge anyone, as he knew his time was fast approaching for parole. But his cousin had a sad and almost fearful look in his eye that made him ask, "Is there anything wrong—I know you too well and can see something's on your mind."

"It's nothing, really. But if you have to know, I was actually fired at the diner six months ago because I refused to water down some of the meals. I've been a short-order chef in Greek, Italian and fast-food restaurants. This yuppie place on 9th Avenue and 38th Street wanted to cut corners and I wouldn't do it, so they let me go. I told you the place closed, but that's not the truth. I have to tell you, though, some of the people who were regulars see me on the street and tell me it's not the same there."

"Man, I'm sorry. It must be a burden for you to spend the Metro fare."

"Don't even go there, man!" Marcus blurted out. "I come here to see you. I've been out before and I'll get back. It's my problem. I want you to focus on your situation, okay?"

"Sure, I just feel for you." Omar knew that his cousin only had a high school education like himself, with little disposable income and hoped that he understood is sympathy.

"Seriously, I'll make it and yo, don't let my problems become yours." Marcus was aware that his cousin was concerned and he knew he was the only one whom he could call family.

Walking back to the main desk, Omar gave his cousin a big hug. "You know; you're real." With that he walked slowly back to his designated area labeled Section B. Marcus walked towards the exit. He arrived at the gate and showed the left hand with the iridescent light, reminding him of how the clubs used to grant reentry to club goers in the 80s. He went through one gate, then outside and entered into a caged area that buzzed him to the visitors' section. He was free to look for his van to take him to Beacon station. Within a few minutes, he joined the hangers-on who stayed late and were about to go the station.

The 7:05 PM train arrived right on time. Entering into the car, he noticed how crowded it was. "Saturday night, all the people from the burbs are coming into Manhattan for a night on the town." Marcus walked the entire length of the car and found a seat adjacent to a woman on the river side of the track. The woman looked familiar and it took just a few moments for him to realize the woman sitting next to him was the same one who was on the train this morning. She glanced at him and smiled, saying, "Pretty crowded, isn't it?"

Marcus asked, "Excuse me, but weren't you on the train this morning?"

"Yes, I went to my husband's grandfather's party in Wappingers Falls, outside Poughkeepsie. He was 90 today." Marcus felt a bit uneasy at her friendly manner as she continued. "My car is being serviced and my husband was in Manhattan, so the train was the next best thing. Besides, it gave me a chance to enjoy the river."

"Yeah, I can stare at the river and lose myself," Marcus said.

Marcus saw that this was small talk, banter and she was probably in a good mood from the tone of her demeanor and desire to chat. *Maybe she had a few drinks in her and is loosening up,* he hoped. He noticed her gold chain with the initials "H" and remembered the silk Hermes scarf and matching jacket and pants. *She looks so out of place on this train with this crew.*

"Congratulations on having a 90 year-old grandfather-in-law. I only remember my grandmother on my mother's side. She died when I was nine, but at least I have good memories."

"Yes, that's ultimately what we're left with. By the way, my name is Harriet Bradley."

"I'm Marcus Martin."

"Marcus Martin," she responded.

"What a beautiful name." Marcus didn't respond, a little too embarrassed.

"Going into Manhattan?" she asked.

"Yes, in Hell's Kitchen on West 46th Street. The neighborhood is sure changing, but it's home."

"You do have a beautiful name. Real classic. By the way, my husband is working on the new hotel on West 42nd Street. Do you know the new Marriott on 10th Avenue and 42nd Street?"

"Oh sure, that's a beauty—41 stories just a few blocks from my house.

Is your husband in construction?"

"No, he's in management with Marriott. He's as busy as ever. We're currently conducting a job search for the hotel. May I ask, what do you do?"

Marcus was afraid to discuss his bleak job situation, but blurted out, "I'm between jobs. Actually, I was working at a trendy bistro on 9th Avenue as a cook, but they let me go. I just wouldn't shortchange and add fillers to meat and overall just didn't like the management. Sorry."

"No, no, I'm sorry. Sounds like you got a real rotten deal for your convictions. That took a lot of courage. It's a shame they didn't listen to you. Why don't you take my husband's business card? They're going to need several chefs and I'm sure he'll be happy to talk to you. As far as I know, there'll be at least two or three restaurants."

"You're kidding!"

"No, Marcus, I know he'll need help." A faint smile revealed a mouth full of beautifully capped teeth, neatly arranged and as white as any teeth he'd ever seen.

"Oh, that's great. I must tell you, I was about to give up looking for work. The unemployment is about to go out. It's so hard to get a job that you're happy with, like the people you work with and can give 100%."

"I'm glad you sat down here, Marcus!"

"No, I'm the one who's thankful." He couldn't believe this was happening to him. *Maybe, just maybe there is a God who's out to prove He's still in charge.*

The train conductor announced the next step was Peekskill in two minutes. "That's my stop," she said. "Now, don't forget to call. It was a pleasure talking to you. I feel good about this."

"The pleasure was all mine," Marcus wanted to shout.

As Harriet stood up, she looked out at the river, retrieving a packet from the overhead rack and said, "The river is just so beautiful this time of year, isn't it? I can just sit and watch it for hours. I could have ordered car service, but I just wanted to relax and see the river. I'm originally from rural Wisconsin and growing up there, we didn't have the beauty of the Hudson Valley. My husband is from here. He worked his way through college, and we met at a hotel convention in Milwaukee. We don't have a Hudson like this in the wooded area of Northern Wisconsin. The river is just so peaceful."

"Yes, the river is like a good friend," Marcus said.

Harriet left and gave Marcus a faint smile and wave as she departed for the platform.

Marcus settled back and looked at the card for the first time. "Mr. William Bradley, Marketing Manager, Marriott Hotels, NYC," he read. A broad smile radiated from Marcus' lined face. Holding the card tightly that could be his mealticket, he tried not to tear up too much lest others see him in what might be misunderstood as weakness on his part. As he looked at the river, now getting wider with the Manhattan skyline in the distance, a tear fell down his smiling face.

"Wow, this guy is big. I just hope this is real. I'm going to call first thing Monday." Looking at the river as it approached the Bronx, he beamed, knowing that this ride was worth it today.

"Yes, thanks to the river who delivered my guardian angel today."

CHAPTER 10

Mid-City Gym prided itself as the 'oldest pumping iron gym in the city.' This bold statement appeared on all the literature with the famous and not-so-famous photos as promo for prospective clients. Open from 5 AM-11 PM, the brochure offered any potential bodybuilder the luxury of free weights, the best in machines, running tracks and locker area.

Entering into the gym meant descending a flight down to the basement. One veteran called it not a gym, but a "cellar with weights." Unpretentious with no sauna, carpeting or tiled walls, one was welcomed with the dedicated men and women working out to the sound of rap or R and B, mirrors everywhere to assess their progress and a small counter serving supplements and health drinks with soy-based protein shakes.

Don Miller, a 36 year-old long-hair veteran worked the morning shift. A visit to Mid-City was not complete unless one took the time to hear from Miller what the latest was on such subjects as theater, fashion, art and music. Don was at once a welcome face and philosopher to all who entered. This particular morning was no exception. "Did you see in the paper that they closed the Gaiety?" He was referring to the male-strip joint down the street next to Howard Johnson's in Times Square. Before one could answer whether they ever heard of such a place, Don continued, "Many of the dancers are Brazilian guys who used to pay top dollar here for a day's workout, buy a lot of shakes and take supplements to the hotel. I'm going to miss them."

"Are you sure you're not missing more than the money you made with them?" asked Tony, just arriving and listening to the daily 'morning take' from Don.

"C'mon, you know I only work here."

"Yeah," Tony replied, "and I'm just a weightlifter and Ali was just a boxer!"

Don Miller was a composite of the 21st century 'well-rounded guy.' Living in a walkup on West 51st Street, he was a well-known fixture in the neighborhood, ever ready to give his advice whether solicited or not. Today was no exception. He used the article in the <u>Daily News</u> on the Gaiety closing as a pretext to instruct anyone in earsight of the gentrification of the West Side. "We're doomed unless we pull together and stop all these high-rises with $3000 rent for a done-over walkup."

Most of the clients that were at the gym in the AM could relate to Don. Many of the men and women were struggling artists working part-time and using the gym both for the necessary workout and the latest news relative to theater, training and jobs in the service industry in the many hotels and restaurants that aligned the Theater District. Miller was a pro when it came to dishing out the dirt—he told you what important figure was at the gym the night before, whether ABC was in need of extras for their upcoming sitcom, told you when a few diesel bodybuilders should hang around as the people from Conde Nast and the myriad of magazines needed a backdrop with natural body hunks to complement their latest product on the market. Don Miller was the person to contact if you wanted to get places. He himself had appeared as a cop in full uniform in porn movies, but always reminded everyone that he kept his clothes on and just executed a few arrests. No one believed him, of course, but it was worth a good laugh.

Miller was in an unusually good mood today. Last week a reporter for <u>Muscle and Fitness,</u> the premiere Joe Weider publication, asked him questions about the gym and its members. Miller, a fixture for the last seven years, had seen many individuals come and go and told the reporter, Cindy Marsh of Los Angeles, some juicy stories.

Assured of a few pictures in the feature publication, Miller began by telling her of the many personalities he'd encountered and the resulting events in people's lives that centered around Mid-City.

Jose Matos, a former WWF contender, came up to the counter to see Miller. Jose was from the 'old school,' 34 years of age, 234 lbs., all natural, he was a local kid who almost got to the pros as a heavyweight. Because of his size, he was affectionately called 'El Oso' (The Bear) by everyone who knew him. Jose was a star wrestler at Park West High School on 50th Street and won the New York State championship wrestling team in his weight class in 1999. Destined for fame, he suffered a serious knee injury in a car crash, which, in effect, ended his chances of going pro. Riding home with his friend Larry Santana, Jose was hospitalized at St. Vincent's Midtown on 52nd Street for four days. "You have torn ligaments," Dr. Mara Lowen told him. Yet he remained an optimist and was a big asset to Mid-City. He was very aware of the steroid growth in just the last few years. Jose was now a security guard with Metropolitan Museum of Art. "It pays the rent, plus I've got to appreciate the art work," he said, half in jest and sarcasm. Concerning the steroid use, Jose was angered. "We never juiced like these guys to get ahead; it sets the wrong example for my kids and others." Don told Marsh that Jose, who lived in a railroad flat on 10th Avenue, had a lot to vent and suggested that she interview veterans of the gym from the neighborhood who have seen changes in the people who frequented the gym. "In the old days, we had tough thugs and neighborhood punks plus serious ones who wanted to get big and look tough. Today, everybody's in a hurry to get big fast and you have serious, natural bodybuilders who can't come near the pros, like Ronnie Coleman and Kevin Levrone." Jose nodded and before resuming his workout, purchased a bottle of water and told Marsh that Mid-City was a good place to find information relative to the changes in the 'workout world.' Cindy admired his candor and told Jose that she would mention him in the upcoming November publication. Marsh can relate to Jose. She was born in South Central LA, was the only one in her family to go to college and the first female black reporter that M and F hired right after graduating with honors at U.S.C. Davis. This trip to New York was her first. She specifically insisted on staying in the Hell's Kitchen area and was staying at the Belvedere, a renovated hotel close by on 48th Street. She loved the freedom of New York and this, her second full day, was already momentous with breakfast at the Galaxy, a Greek restaurant whose clientele ranged from soap box stars to the average Jersey day tripper in for a Broadway show. Her visit to Mid-City was her assignment—it was fast becoming a microcosm of the people of the Westside.

Within a few minutes, Sandra Norwood entered the gym. Norwood was a designer with DKNY and at 5'2", 123 lbs. with piercing blue eyes to complement her blond hair, she was at once noticed whenever she entered a room, giving a scent of her favorite perfume, Exotica.' Offering a radiant smile to Don, she had her ID ready to scan when Cindy asked, "Do you have time for a few questions? I'm writing an article for a fitness magazine and want to get a composite of an urban gym setting." Sandra, a native of Colorado and very sociable, told Marsh that she had a few minutes before she began her cardio workout.

Asking her why she came to Mid-City instead of the pricey, more intimate clubs that she can obviously afford, her response was instantaneous. "I've been to these trendy spots, but I'm here because of my trainer, Scott. Not only is he aware of the conditioning I need, but he is also a doll and can give me sound advice about weight control and nutrition. At the other spas, the trainers are good but with Scott I feel I have a person who really cares. He takes the time out to measure my progress. Plus I like the laid-back atmosphere here. There's no BS!" That said, she shook hands with Cindy and went into the locker area to prepare for her scheduled session with Scott.

Turning to Miller, Marsh remarked, "This gym has really got a homey atmosphere. Everyone seems to be friendly, yet they seem to focus on the workout and enjoy it. Yes, that's it Don, I see the people here and they seem to like being here."

"You got it right, girl!" Don blurted out as two males in their mid-30s entered and scanned their IDs for Miller. "How you doing?" Miller said to Tim Rafferty and his friend, Al Franco. Both were coworkers nearby for a law firm as entertainment lawyers and were there for a quick workout with the weights at lunchtime.

Noticing Marsh summing up the facts from the previous interview, they exchanged greetings and Cindy asked if they could spare a few minutes for her article. "Sure, I always have time for notoriety," Franco declared. He and Rafferty sit as Cindy asked why they chose Mid-City and of what their workouts consist.

Al Franco, a Massachusetts native and graduate of Brooklyn Law School, is 6'2", 204 lbs. of solid muscle, a throwback to his running back days with Holy Cross, where he got recognized and nearly made it to the NFL. His deep dark eyes and thick hair made Franco very appealing to Cindy. Before she got too excited, she noticed the wedding band and asked the familiar questions about Mid-City.

"I come here because of its accessibility. Other gyms have more to offer with machines and saunas, but I still like the loose weights here. Look around and see the area along the mirrored wall. Most other gyms have dumbbells and loose weights, but this is history alive. It's the real thing. In fact, sometimes Tim and I take clients here for a no nonsense cardio workout."

At that Rafferty, smiling about Al's description added, "Like Al, I have the resources to pay a lot for a large gym, but the people here motivate you. You get everything from the thugs from the streets to the most-intense workout clientele. Take a look at the pictures of some of the icons from the bodybuilding world and you'll know what I'm talking about."

Marsh liked the chemistry between the two lawyers. Rafferty, 35, 5' 11", 187 lbs. told Cindy that his father, a former Republican state senator from Connecticut, encouraged him to go to Fordham Law. He had his heart set on music and upon graduation, joined the law firm of Stern, Micaela and Lowler that specialized in entertainment contracts. Working in the area just off Broadway, their firm had signed contracts with 50 Cent, Jay Z and Mariah Carey. Both Franco and Rafferty loved their jobs and told Cindy to stop by the law firm.

"Tim's really into the music and always gets tickets to concerts, so we'll see what we can do for you to make your stay enjoyable," Franco said. "He digs the rap music."

"You guys are great!" Cindy shouted.

"Oh, but there's a catch-remember we're lawyers!" said Raffety. He and Franco asked if she would mention the law firm in her piece.

"I'll see what I can do; once the editors take a look, they're bound to make changes," Cindy said.

Turning to Miller, she exclaimed "God, this place is great!" Making sure Cindy was heard over the rap music she turned to Miller smiling, "This is real theater."

Within five minutes, Cindy saw a tall, handsome twentyish African American swipe his card after greeting Don. "Do you have a minute to spare, brother?" Cindy asked.

"Well, that depends on what you want, sister."

"I'm Cindy Marsh, a writer on assignment for <u>Muscle and Fitness.</u> I'm interviewing some of the patrons at the gym, as this is the oldest bodybuilding gym in New York. Okay to ask a few questions?"

"Fire away; I got some time." Looking at the screen once his card was swiped, Cindy noticed the name of Clifton Ivey.

"To begin with, why do come here and not to another gym?"

"I'm in my last year at John Jay," Clifton explained. "My major is criminal justice and I want to work for the FBI. Therefore, I need to stay in prime shape and be focused. We have a gym at Jay, but it's nothing like this—Mid-City motivates you. Take a walk on the floor and you'll see what I mean." Cindy liked the directness coming from Ivey and saw a sadness in his eyes that she used to see in people in South-Central LA.

"Have you contacted the FBI?"

Ivey explained that the agency had seminars at schools, like John Jay, which specialized in careers in criminal justice. He told Cindy "Two of my uncles were cops and my father, dead since I was seven, always wanted me to graduate college. At least, that what my mom says." Clifton then asked, "Is this article you're writing a composite of some of the personalities that come and go here at Mid-City?"

"Yes, but I want to get a feel of a gym that is nationally known where young people like Schwarzenegger and others worked out."

"Well, you came to the right place.

Perhaps we'll talk later, if you don't mind," Clifton said nonchalantly as he headed to the locker area with a wink of the eye.

Miller asked Cindy if she would like to try one of his specialty drinks and suggested that she try his low-carb, "Rocko's Choco."

"You won't be disappointed, guaranteed!" said Don as he gave Cindy a copy of the brochure that showed a combination of the following ingredients: non-fat milk with creatine, choice of banana or strawberries and two scoops of chocolate whey protein.

"I'm sure a California girl like you wants the strawberries instead of the banana, right?"

"Okay, let's go with the strawberries," Cindy responded as a balding, fiftyish man swiped his card and gave both Don and Cindy a faint smile.

As Don prepared Cindy's drink, she asked the newcomer, whose name was Daniel Shano, "Would you mind answering a few questions for my magazine assignment.?"

"Sure," said Shano. At 6'1", 198lbs and 48 years of age, he was the oldest person to come through thus far. "Will I get a free subscription?" he laughed.

"Well, I can get you a free copy of the edition that the interview is in. OK?"

"Why not," Shano. "Ask me anything—well almost anything?"

"For starters," Cindy asked, "Why do you come here to work out?"

Daniel Shano explained to Cindy that he had been coming to Mid-City for all of 12 years and found the gym to be exactly what he wanted. Citing the now familiar litany of it being a real gym with no frills, Shano added a personal dynamic to it.

"This gym saved my life. I was 238 lbs. with high cholesterol and elevated blood pressure. My doctor suggested to me at age 37 to begin a physical regimen that would help reduce the chances of cardiovascular disease. Thank God for Anthony, my trainer. He kept pushing me, to the point that I didn't want to see his face. But, you know, he got me back in shape and monitored what I ate and looked at the suggested diet my cardiologist prepared. As I said, the man and this gym helped save my life."

"I guess it worked for you, as you look to be in great shape," Cindy said almost apologetically.

"Thanks, the truth be known, I must tell you that the drinking, smoking and running the streets were all part of it. When you're young, you think you're going to live forever and suddenly you get a reality check. Mine came in 1993 when I had chest pains and was on the verge of a heart attack. Thank God for the old St. Clare's Hospital and emergency staff. They were able to perform a stent that unclogged my arteries and I avoided a bypass. After that episode, I was determined to grow up and do something positive. When Dr. Janice Overton, my cardiologist, suggested that I begin to exercise by walking, using weights and watching my diet, I was a convert. I also knew that heredity played a part in my wake up. My grandfather and father both died in their early fifties and they didn't have the medical knowledge or opportunity to come here. Both of them were hard-working, tough neighborhood people here on 10th Avenue and worked on the docks in the most unbearable conditions. As for myself, in the past few years, everything is okay—cholesterol, blood pressure and weight. That's why I say that Mid-City is a God-given gift to me. Besides we have some great people here that you, no doubt, have probably already spoke to."

"Dan, thanks so much; your story is so compelling that I would like to mention you as an inspiration to others. Really, great to talk to you and keep up these fine efforts."

"Thanks, just be careful with Miller, he has a soft spot for beautiful women from out-of -town."

Don smiled as Shano proceeded to the locker area.

"Nice guy," Cindy said to Miller, sipping from the drink that Miller had just poured.

"Yeah, he's one of our regulars now.

How's the drink?"

"Great, and the strawberries are fine, even if they're not from California."

Cindy couldn't suppress her inquisitive nature and finally asked Miller, "Is this your permanent job?"

"At the moment. It pays the rent. But I have an associate degree from LaGuardia Community College in Queens and want to go to Baruch for a business degree."

"Have you thought of doing what I'm doing—writing, traveling and meeting all kinds of people?"

"I'm no writer like you, but I like to take pictures My hobby was always getting the right focus and zooming in on the right angle."

"Well, Don, there's always the chance that you could get a

job in photography. Why not consider that as a major in your
business classes?"

"It's something I've already thought about. I just got to
make up my mind and go to classes after work, but I can do
it."

"No doubt." Cindy smiled as she finished the last of her
protein shake.

"Well, I've got to focus and get on with it. You've inspired
me," added Miller.

Just as Cindy and Don were sharing small talk, Marion
Cooper swiped her card and greeted Don as she casually glanced
at Cindy. At 32, 5'2", 108 lbs., she was dressed with a red bandana that complemented her print blue and matching blue den-
ims. Her Hugo Boss designer glasses were propped on her head,
just above the bandana that sent a message of someone who
knew her way around.

Cindy couldn't pass up the chance to strike up a conversation.

"Hi, I'm Cindy Marsh, do you have a few minutes for an
interview?" Cindy had just finished some notes from her interview with Dan Shano.

"Is this for a fitness article?" Marion asked.

"Yes, I'm from LA and I'm writing a piece on the gym."

"Sure, my name is Marion. Is this for a newspaper article?"

"Actually, I'm here on assignment to write a piece on Mid-
City for Muscle and Fitness.

Let me start by asking, why did you choose this gym?"

"I just like the fact that you can work out and nobody
bothers you."

"You don't get hit upon?" asked Cindy, sensing an honesty about Marion that at once made her comfortable.

"Unless you want to," Marion said. "There are serious guys working out, some gay, most not and they're here, like me, to get in shape."

"Have you been to other gyms?"

Marion nodded. "Sure, the cutesy gyms are all over New York. You find gyms in all neighborhoods in this town. I come from a small North Carolina town and I appreciate being left alone while working out. If I want action, I know where to find it, in the clubs like Roxy's and such. Don't misunderstand me, I like a good time, but here it's all business."

"May I ask what you do as a career?" Cindy needed some information, as she felt that Marion and she were on the same wave length.

"I was a drama major at North Carolina State and here, while I'm a SAG member, I need to pay the rent, so at present I work for New York Life Insurance on 23rd Street in payroll. I always had a knack for figures, so the payroll department is fine for the moment and the benefits are good."

"Have you done anything to foster your career?" Cindy asked, hoping that Marion had at least a few shows under her belt.

"Yes, I appeared on 'Law and Order' and other walk-on roles, but I'm taking some acting classes at present. This gym is good therapy for me while I pursue my dream in life. You can also make good contacts here, as a lot of the guys are in theater. One of the guys here dances for the Paul Taylor Dance Company. He has given me some nice leads."

"Good luck, you seem to at least have the incentive not to give up."

Marion frowned and with a sigh blurted out, "It's harder than hell to really make it. I'm tough and at 32, I still feel I can do it, but the agents are always looking for fresh meat and reality checks in before long. I can deal with it for a few more years. Thank God, New York Life, like I said, has good benefits and I know my job, but, as they say, hope springs eternal."

Cindy shook her hand as Marion left for her locker. Cindy knew how tough it was to make a dent. Her job was frowned upon because, as a female, most of the staff at M and F felt that she didn't know enough about bodybuilding. It took persistence and several requests for an interview before Mr. Knowles, the CEO at <u>Muscle and Fitness,</u> realized that a reporter like Marsh would add to the dynamic by putting a personal touch to the magazines. Her visit to Mid-City was certainly vindication of the greater struggles that people have, herself no exception. Struggles were always part of growing up in the 'hood' in South Central. She herself witnessed several drive-by shootings and knew that she would eventually have to leave. Hurt and confused by her former live-in boyfriend, Keith Reynolds, she had known his lack of support would only hinder her from her goal. The best, albeit most painful, decision was to leave him and ask for assignments such as this while traveling throughout the US. This visit to New York was, like Marion's at Mid-City, good therapy from a most painfully unpleasant and hurting situation. Keith had promised her the world, but only on his terms. Worse, he decided that if she elected to take the job as a reporter instead of working in a downtown LA office off Willshire and submit to his control, he would consider it an insult and leave. Cindy took the first step by not only taking the job, but also leaving within four days. She, like Marion, was strong and not going to let circumstances get in her way. *I guess what my grandma taught me is true, there really is a thin line between love and hate,* she thought a few years back

While she didn't hate Keith, she came to the conclusion that the relationship was not in her best interests.

Steadfast and determined, Cindy had already proven to her family, the staff at the magazine and, most importantly, to herself that she was worth it. This visit, as others throughout the country would see, only reinforced the human spirit within to conquer fears. She had a good feel for Marion and felt inspired by their chat. Deep down in her gut, she knew Marion had what it took. Like her, she was a survivor.

Don was preparing another of his classic protein drinks for a veteran member, Joe Salerno. Salerno epitomized the drink he ordered: the "Vanilla Gorilla," which consisted of vanilla latte, non-fat milk with a hearty portion of weight gainer and non-fat yogurt. At 43, 6'2", he had grayish hair with a chiseled face that Michelangelo would have loved to carve into immortality. He was a survivor from Ladder 15 on September 11th. The dark Sicilian eyes gave away a sense of foreboding and pain. He lived 9/11 every day and the hour workout here was a relief from a world that saw so much. Ready to retire in four months, he knew that each day was a gift and when Cindy asked him for an interview, he respectfully declined.

Miller, once Salerno headed out the door, told Cindy of his situation which brought tears to her eyes when told that six of his closest buddies never came out of the towers. She at once knew that some situations were too painful, personal and private upon which to trespass. Suddenly, her own breakup with Keith didn't seem as ominous after all. She knew coming to New York was a lifetime experience. What she didn't know that it was also a reflective time for her and a powerful learning experience.

Miller, changing the subject, asked Cindy what she planned to do with her extra time. "We have several members that are professional tour guides and I can hook you up with one of the best," he said.

Cindy said that she had taken the Greyline 'hop-on, hop-off,' tour the previous day and especially enjoyed Harlem and Battery Park. She mentioned to Miller that the Apollo Theater was a must and spent an additional hour and half on a guided tour with the local theater director.

"Looking at the stage where Nat King Cole, Sarah Vaughn, Lena Horne and the rappers of today got started made my day. I took some great photos at the Apollo and the statue of Adam Clayton Powell and went to 122 Street to see Hale House. My only regret is that I didn't have a chance to dine at Sylvia's."

"Well, we can arrange for a great dining experience. But, I must tell you we have a great soulfood restaurant patronized by stars like Vin Diesel, Denzel Washington and Halle Berry and it's right in our Hell's Kitchen area. It's called Jezebel and it's located on 9th Avenue and 45th Street, within walking distance of the Belvedere. If you think Sylvia's is good, Jezebel's is just as great. Whatever you want, broiled, baked or fried, you can't go wrong. I'm not just saying this to impress you; I was there for an anniversary and it was the best—mark my words."

"Thanks Don. You're a doll."

"No, I just want you to enjoy yourself while you're here."

Cindy, almost sheepishly asked "Do you like Broadway shows?"

"What's not to like? Of course, did you want to get tickets? What show?"

"Actually, I have two orchestra seats for tonight's performance of 'Wicked' at the Gershwin Theater. Have you seen it?"

"No, but I hear it's a great show." I hope she's leading to something.

"Are you free to go tonight?" Don knew his charm was still working!

"Yes, very free to go, thanks."
Marsh would have quite a story to tell!

CHAPTER II

"That price of $32.00 per day includes the discount you asked about," the attendant, Heather Smalls of Enterprise Car Rental on 11th Avenue announced to James Hodges of nearby West 40th Street. Hodges could do the math, after all he was an accountant, and when totaled, with taxes, liability insurance, unlimited mileage and drop-off facility in Connecticut, he found that the daily amount far exceeded what he thought he should pay.

He knew it was busy. He was on hold for 12 minutes, tapping into the canned music as he looked out the window of his studio apartment at nothing in particular. *A back view gives you solitude,* he thought. But, the last thing he wanted to do was to stare at the unpainted, old and now vacant building adjoining his which was slated for demolition within the next few months. This being New York he knew that the rumors of yet another high rise on the spot would certainly further block any sunlight coming into his already dark space. "No need to buy any new plants, that's for sure," he said into the phone. James decided that there was one other option and it was close by. He decided to take the bus instead.

Since he had a ride back from Mystic, his destination, he politely hung up the phone and proceeded to Port Authority and Greyhound to buy the one way bus ticket to Mystic. The lines at the bus terminal would be long, but he was ready to get out of town. The fare the bus quoted, $31.00 one way was far cheaper than Amtrak's $54.00. He decided to take the bus. It should be a good weekend, as two of his friends were in summer stock production of "My Fair Lady". Besides, the city was too oppressive in this weather. Glad to have a ticket out of the hot city, he was told that the next bus would be leaving within 15 minutes, downstairs at platform 32.

I just need to get out of this oppressive city heat with 96 degrees today, he thought. Indeed, the heat wave was one of the worst on record—seven straight days of 90 or plus degrees. Con Edison, New York's utility source, asked everyone to cut back on energy use during peak hours by not washing clothes, not using the dishwasher and shutting off air-conditioners when not home. These so-called 'non-essentials' were vital to averting the famous brown-outs the city experienced in recent years, 2003 and the previous ones in 1977 and 1965. None of these measures affected Hodges—he had no dishwasher, not even a small air conditioner in his one-room studio above Esposito's Butcher Shop on 9th Avenue. A visit to his studio would reveal a small, oscillating fan with a twin bed propped up against the wall, a drop-leaf table with two old chairs and well-worn secondhand sofa. The only valuable merchandise he possessed was his Dell computer atop his table and a small 17" SONY TV without cable access.

So, getting away from the cocoon-like status of his apartment was especially welcomed on this hot July day for the tall, lanky Arkansas native. Living on the fourth floor without an elevator in a building that dated back to 1889, Hodges' apartment was facing the back and always darker, thus giving his apartment a constant need for lighting and a larger Con Ed bill. Yet, he wouldn't give up his rent-controlled $486.00 a month apartment despite pleas from his landlord to vacate and join the movement of gentrification of the Westside.

Hodges, a resident for seven years, originally from Little Rock was now steadily employed, despite the downsizing of his company, as an accountant for the New York Public Library branch on 42nd Street. Despite the recent downsizing, his job was secure and gave him good medical and dental benefits. In his spare time, he was active in a neighborhood repertory theater group, often directing new plays in the off-Broadway venue. He didn't want to give up his dream—to direct a long running play, off or on Broadway. He always used his drama coach's advice from his alma mater, the University of Arkansas: "Get your feet wet! Don't just talk of doing something and later regret not doing it. Get up and get started." That simple advice got him to New York and there was no turning back, regardless of weather and dismal job prospects. Too tired to travel to Arkansas for a family reunion that would last a clear four days, he jumped at the chance of getting out of the torrid city and took the three hour ride up to the historic whaling village of Mystic on Long Island Sound. Purchasing a ticket at Port Authority, he boarded a bus that was ultimately destined for Providence, Rhode Island, and Cape Cod, happy to get out of the city for a few days. "It's worth the hassle, at least I'm getting out of here and seeing grass and ocean and watching a performance," he said almost aloud.

As expected, the line at platform 32 was crowded. One person, a teenaged male Johnny Depp look-a-like, complete with mascara and bandana around a tightly cropped black 'do' stuck out above the others. Spotting a few loud, giggly teenagers clad in shorts, he wondered if the decision to abandon the car rental was a wise one. Resigned to his fate, he gave his ticket in the depot reeking of gasoline fuel and awaited his fate.

Boarding the bus, he noticed his fellow passengers—an assortment of all ages and races. So typical of New York, so typical of Greyhound passengers—mothers with young kids, young college aged students with backpacks, a few people speaking Spanish and an assortment of nondescript individuals who would otherwise remain anonymous. The driver, a tall, slender fortyish gray-haired man was very patient with the children, taking the tickets and saying, "Good morning" to each person boarding the bus. The name tag on his freshly-tailored uniform revealed him to be Joe Templeton.

"At least the driver's decent, without an attitude, like a lot of New Yorkers," James said to himself.

Arriving just six minutes before departure, he found a seat in the back of the crowded bus. *Everyone had the same idea I had,* he thought. carrying a small overnight bag and a diet Snapple drink. Finding the only window seat available, he placed his small leather overnight in the overhead rack. A young female passenger across the way, in an attempt to be helpful, said, "I think those are empty seats. Sorry, they're in the back."

Giving her a nod and noticing a copy of <u>People</u> magazine in her hand, he said in a whisper, "Thanks, you sometimes don't have a choice."

The young lady was right; within a few minutes, prior to the 9 AM departure, the bus filled up, with just one seat remaining, the aisle seat next to him. A tall, slender man, no more than 35, smiled faintly and asked, "Excuse me, is this aisle seat taken?" James assured him that it was available, and the passenger placed his bag in the overhead rack and sat down, ready for the trip that would wind along I-95 through cities such as Stamford, Bridgeport and New Haven before arriving at Mystic. Glancing briefly at his seat partner, James noticed he was an olive-skinned man, with a pencil moustache and tight, thickly-cropped wavy black hair. He wore neatly pleated white pants more common in the Hamptons and a pink Polo shirt, the collar slightly protruding.

Looks almost like a model, what is he doing with us peasants on this bus? James thought.

Unable to resist the temptation, he had to glance at his shoes and, sure enough, the beautiful Cole-Hahn loafers told him this was no ordinary passenger.

"Had to get out of town, too damn hot," he casually remarked to James. "The flights to Boston were all booked and the Amtrak was sold out as well, including the Acela," he added, as if to vindicate to James his presence. Hodges was amazed at his openness and matter-of-fact attitude and found it refreshing from such an individual.

"I normally rent a Hertz or an Avis, but they were all sold out this weekend too," James said, almost in a whisper, wanting to feel somewhat equal to his social status. Always trying to impress, he had cut his way up the corporate ladder, never looking back to see what damage he may have done to his fellow workers. He wanted to succeed even if it meant lying to get ahead.

"Yeah, I can't take the heat when it hits 95 with that brutal humidity. Are you headed to the Cape?" he asked. James was aware that his fellow passenger was no doubt headed for a resort out on Cape Cod.

"No, I'm going to visit a friend performing at Mystic."

"Good choice, some very decent restaurants and golf courses there. What is your friend performing in?"

Feeling at ease, James explained as the bus pulled out of the depot that he needed to get away and the opportunity to visit his friend perform in "My Fair Lady" was a real treat.

"Sounds good. I get to Mystic once or twice a year, usually just for some quick r and r. I'm headed for Hyannis to stay at my girl's family's summer home. I don't like buses, but this was better than waiting around. I called and went online for the car rentals and got the same hassle as you. What we're left with is the old, reliable dog—Greyhound." The stranger at least would make the ride go by fast and was not one of those crazies or cell phone fanatics who never knew when to shut up.

Feeling confident with his new seat partner, Hodges reached out his hand. "By the way, the name's James."

"I'm Ed Harper. I used to live in this neighborhood," he remarked to James as the bus began to go up 11th Avenue.

"I live here, just a few blocks from the terminal," James said as Ed smiled

"I lived here for three years in a small, walkup studio just off 9th Avenue in the 40s," commented Ed.

"Sounds like me now," James responded. "I live right on 9th and 40th—do you know the address 427 West 40th?"

"This is nuts—that's the exact building I lived in! Apartment 3B, to be exact."

"You're pulling my chain—that's my apartment!" The female passenger in the adjacent seat casually glanced over, a faint smile on her face, evidently hearing James' voice getting louder by this sudden coincidental news. James, looking at the expression on Ed's face, pulled out his wallet, and feeling the need to verify his address, showed his New York driver's license with his photo to prove his claim.

Harper examined the wallet and blurted out, "It's like an episode of the 'Twilight Zone.'"

Shaking his head incredulously, Harper smiled and added, "I thought you were pulling my chain. What are the odds of two people meeting on a bus and having the same exact address at one time in this town?"

The female passenger, no more than 20, looked at them. Putting down her newspaper, she casually remarked, "Excuse me guys, but that's one hell of a coincidence."

"Like I said, it's nuts," James said, smiling at the young woman. He placed his wallet in his hip pocket and asked,

"When did you leave that apartment?"

"It was in 1997," Harper answered, his voice rising as he squirmed in his seat, directly facing James. "I had lived there from 1989 and got a better job and was able to move on. The rent was decent."

"It isn't now," James interjected. "Like most of Hell's Kitchen, it's like the new Chelsea, with all those yuppies and upstarts moving in. As the old folks die or others move out, they're retrofitting the apartments and getting $1700.00 for a renovated studio."

Feeling a little uncomfortable at bringing in the rents, James got the feeling that his new acquaintance wanted to find out more information about his old building. Fate brought them together; there had to be some logic to this crazy chance encounter.

James, looking at the finely-manicured nails and neat haircut on Harper, couldn't help but feel that he didn't fit the prototype of a former resident of an old tenement. Sensing a need to explain his situation, Harper related the good luck that enabled him to escape from the hovel in which he was once a resident.

"I moved out in early 1997. I got a promotion from the advertising firm that I was working with at Cosmopolitan. It was time to make a move. I admit I miss the old neighborhood and get over to it from my current place on the Eastside. There's nothing like the bakeries, delis, restaurants and the vitality of the Kitchen. Tell me, I was only paying $320.00 when I left my, I mean, our apartment," he said as both laugh. "What are they doing there anyway?"

Hodges was eager to tell him of the changes in the building from new plumbing, wiring, intercom system and newly-tiled floors and new mailboxes. He told former tenant Ed Harper that renovating an apartment only occurred whenever there was a vacancy due to death or moving.

"Just like the rest of the city." Harper paused. A strange look came over his face, causing James to feel uncomfortable, as if he were going to ask him something very personal, but was hesitating to do so. A silence ensued that seemed to last for minutes, but, in actuality, was but a few seconds. James was staring out the window when Ed gave him a bolt of information that nearly caused him to jump up and hit his head on the overhead rack.

"Tell me James, you do know that a murder occurred in our building in 1979?"

"What!" James turned completely around in his seat, forgetting the Connecticut countryside as Ed, feeling the need to fill in the gaps, explained.

"It was a long time ago, before either of us were in New York. I'm originally from Colorado." He told James that upon his arrival in 1989, he got the apartment at 427, fresh out of college, despite pleas not to go to the big, bad city from his parents, conservative Fundamentalist Christians who were sure the city would ruin him.

"Forgive me for giving you my history, but…."

"No, no, I want to know what the hell happened in 79," James almost shouted.

"I was pounding the pavement when I first arrived. I had $200.00 and a ticket back to Denver and Greeley, my hometown. By bus, ironically," he laughed. "Anyway, despite the heat then too, I was mesmerized by the city and wanted desperately to stay. I saw a 'For Rent' sign on the ground floor super's apartment, 1B."

"Oh yeah," James interrupted. "It's still the super's."

"His name was Ernie."

"Guess what, he's still the super. If it's the same Ernie Cordero. Short guy with a round face and always a coke in his hand."

"Same dude. Same dude," Harper laughed. "Anyway, he talked to me for a few minutes. Gave me the management office number on Lexington Avenue and before I knew it, I had an apartment with no job."

"How did you get in there with no job?" James was more curious about Ed Harper by the minute.

"I lied and said I was a full-time student. I guess in those days, they didn't check their sources too well. Lucky for me, I did get a job within a few weeks. My parents, old-fashioned, conservative types that they are, thought I was nuts, but I took my chances and the rest is history."

Hodges wanted to find out about the 1979 murder, but couldn't resist asking, "Okay to ask where you started work?"

"Sure. I got a position as a proofreader at <u>Newsweek</u> when they were located at 444 Madison, just a few blocks from St. Patrick's. It was great. I walked to work. I was a young, naive man in the big city and starting meeting people. By 1997, <u>Cosmopolitan</u> was looking for an advertising position and I took my chances and got a big salary jump, took the job and moved. I'm on this bus because my girl's family, not mine like I said, has a summer home on the Cape. What do you do, if you don't mind me prying?"

Hodges didn't want to talk about anything except information on the murder that took place in his building. Regardless of long ago it occurred, he still had to know. Since Ed asked him about his life, he took a deep breath and began to explain. "I'm one of those Hell's Kitchen guys whose object is to get into theater and eventually direct an off-Broadway production. Had a little bit of success last year in summer stock, of all things. I was in Bucks County, Pennsylvania, with a production of 'Sweeney Todd.' But, I have to pay the rent every month, so my steady job is with the New York Public Library."

"Not a bad place to network," Ed said. "Do you work at the main branch?"

"Yes, the 42nd Street Library." James, clearly antsy, couldn't wait any longer.

"Tell me about the murder that occurred in 1979." He didn't want to change the subject any more.

Ed Harper knew that he had to explain the circumstances of 1979.

"Let me get back to your—I mean our, apartment. Cordero, the super, has never told me of any problems in the past. We don't talk about that anyway. The old timers, like Mrs. Cortez and Mr. McMillan on the second floor have lived there forever—I bet they know."

"Is McMillan—Andy—the white-haired guy always smoking a pipe who lives alone on the second floor still alive?"

"Yeah, he must be 90 if he's a day," James quickly said,, getting a nod from Ed.

"That's right. Mrs. Cortez is directly across the McMillan's apartment in 2A. Her daughter, I think her name is Gladys, it really doesn't matter what her name is, anyway. Gladys is usually there. She does the things that daughters do for an aging parent, like taking her to the Ryan Clinic on 46th Street, buying her groceries."

"These people are still alive and doing those things—look, if it's painful for you to tell me about a murder that occurred some 30 years ago before either of us were living there, it's okay. I apologize if I pushed your buttons."

Ed Harper laughed out loud. The two were interrupted by the bus driver announcing that they were now in New Haven and would have a 10 minute rest stop. Harper asked James if he needed to get off to use the rest room. Assured that he was okay, he began to disclose a murder in their building that captured the headlines.

"From the information, I got, two drinking buddies starting arguing over something with a guy named Anthony Vaccaro. Something petty in a neighborhood bar, long gone now. One of them arguing was named Barry McIntyre who was a recently returned Vietnam vet. Anyway, McIntyre, from what was told to me, came back a stoned addict and totally shell-shocked. Not too unusual. I knew some people from Colorado like that too. Apparently, McIntyre had seen a few of his buddies die in front of him and would argue with anyone who questioned the war. To him, it was very personal. It was some god-forsaken hour like 3 AM on a hot July night. Vaccaro left in a huff, telling McIntyre the war was over and forget the past—that kind of thing. Something like, 'You're a low life drunk, why the hell should we even listen to this crap.' McIntyre didn't like what he perceived to be a major dis from Vaccaro on his character and his military service, from his sometimes drinking buddy. Apparently, McIntyre couldn't get the war out of his mind and ended up pounding on the apartment door of his former friend, Anthony Vaccaro, who lived in 2B. McIntyre was stone drunk after that argument in the bar and wouldn't stop shouting and continued pounding on Vaccaro's door. Cordero, the then and now super, threatened to call the cops. McIntyre left yelling and cursing at Cordero, telling him he'd be back. Cordero misread McIntyre—remember he was an addict, and went back to bed, thinking that he had diffused a potentially violent encounter.

"To cut to the chase, McIntyre returned with a buddy, Dennis Carpenter, a real low-life with a long rap sheet and known as a bully in the Westies gang who kept egging on McIntyre to settle the score. Vaccaro was still out on that hot night; he didn't have air-conditioning like most of the tenants and wasn't home when McIntyre first went to his place. As they neared the building, they spotted Vaccaro just entering into the lobby. They rushed the door and confronted Vaccaro, getting louder and uglier by the second. They started fighting, waking the tenants, who had by now called the police, but like most people, shouted to the guys to stop without opening their doors. From what I remember Cordero telling me, he heard McIntyre shouting obscenities at Vaccaro and then a loud thud, as he plunged a knife into Vaccaro. The screams from the dying Anthony Vaccaro were, according to Cordero, like nothing he had ever heard. In fact, Cordero said he peeked through the keyhole and saw McIntyre, with Vaccaro's blood all over his white tank top. They raced out of the building, but the police were already pulling up to the building with sirens blaring. They managed to capture both of them. Easy arrest with eyewitnesses and blood on McIntyre."

"That's crazy. Did they get the knife, too?" James was riveted.

"Yes, it was still on the floor. Vaccaro managed to climb to his apartment and died in a pool of blood just inside his open door, his body lying face down and his feet protruding from his apartment."

"How did you get Cordero to tell you all this and, by the way, what was the motive, if there was any?"

"I was sitting on the stoop one afternoon and Cordero told me the whole story. They sent both McIntyre and Carpenter upstate. Carpenter was released after five or six years, since he was an accessory, even though he was the one who probably encouraged McIntyre. I believe McIntyre is still alive and now out too."

"Jesus, that's some story. But why did they have to kill him? They knew each other."

As the bus was leaving New Haven, James noticed the lady in the adjacent aisle seat had turned off her Ipod and from the body language, was listening to Harper while reading her paper and this bizarre murder.

Knowing that James needed more information, Ed asked, "Have you heard of the Westies?"

"Yeah, I know they were a powerful Irish gang, like the Mafia, that controlled the Westside and shook down a lot of businesses."

"From the information that Cordero relayed to me, Vaccaro, an Italian, had 'dissed' one of the Westies at a bar a few nights earlier on 10th Avenue where the Clinton Grille is today."

"That would be 45th and 10th, right?"

"Right. Vaccaro, drinking too much, had gotten into a heated argument with McIntyre's younger brother, Keith, three nights previous over some inane remark that was made and a fight ensued, in which both were thrown out. When word got back to McIntyre, a leader of the Westies, it was another motive to settle the score. You know, the war and the dissing." "Some score. Vaccaro never had a chance, right?" James asked.

"No, I heard McIntyre just lunged the blade into Anthony Vaccaro, who let out that bloodcurdling scream and fell dead in his apartment after climbing the stairs." Harper saw the woman who was looking and listening to the conversation.

"You never told me what apartment Vaccaro died in," James said.

"Okay—ready for this?" Harper saw the anxiety in Hodges' eyes.

"He lived in apartment 2B!"

"What! You mean I live in an apartment where a horrible crime took place?" James' eyes were wide open.

"It appears so, my good man," Harper said. "Relax. So did I, closer to the date of the crime, too. It appears that the actual crime took place in the lobby and Vaccaro staggered up to his place with a fatal wound. He would have died anywhere. It just so happens that he made it up to his apartment. He was probably drunk; after all, it was a hot night and he was out till way past 3 AM."

"It's still an incredible story. You're not lying or trying to get over on me, are you? You gave me quite a jolt. And to think that I thought I was going to have a boring ride up here." James noticed that the girl across from them had a smile on her face as well.

The young female passenger couldn't contain herself and said, "One of you guys got to write about this, because no one will believe it." All three laughed.

The bus was nearing Mystic, after a nearly three hour ride from Port Authority in New York. James Hodges never realized until now what fate had in store for him or anyone else. What were the chances of meeting someone who not only lived in his present building at one time, but also in the same apartment and had information that would alter forever his perception of their mutual environment? The old tenants, knowing the dark secrets of the building, never disclosed them to James, including the now silver-haired super, Cordero. Maybe the old tenants wanted to forget that fateful July night long ago or were too nice or too scared to tell him. It took a perfect stranger, sitting alongside him on a routine bus ride to disclose the past

Cordero, he now realized, never entered his apartment when repairs were needed or a fresh coat of painting was needed. He always sent his son, Junior, or the management handyman, Lorenzo Banks to finish a job needed. Looking through the window, he could see the tranquility of the Sound and the leaves of the trees blowing. He reflected upon some very strange behavioral events that have transpired in his building, casting them off as lifestyles of eccentric New Yorkers. Now things were starting to make sense to him. The unusual way his sixtyish neighbor, Grace Quillian, of always blessed herself when passing his apartment, as if going into church. Or Mrs. Cortez, who rushed past his door, despite her advanced age. It made sense, now. Those old twits were there when Vaccaro was slain and they relived this event. That one, hot, sultry July night changed a lot of people in the building and now three decades later had an impact upon James Hodges. An ordinary run up to Mystic became a life-altering event. No longer would he look upon his apartment the same. He was now destined to know all he could about this case and, as the bus stopped at Mystic, he bade farewell to Ed Harper, knowing he would have quite a story to tell his friends.

The anonymous female, gave a big thumbs up gesture to James, clearly enjoyed the bizarre encounter and had quite a story to tell her friends in Providence, where she was headed for a family weekend barbecue at Newport.

CHAPTER 12

"I'll miss Ronald. He was always there every Sunday passing the basket at 9:00 AM mass," Father Donald Cummings
said at the funeral of Ronald Anderson, who died three days
earlier at age 64 at Sloan Kettering from a brave battle with
prostate cancer. Father Cummings added, "Just look around this
church, and you'll see his mark everywhere. There is an over-
flow of people from his loving family and friends and colleagues
to the young people whose lives he touched. Life is a series of
choices and Ronald seemed to have made all the right ones. I
look at his wife, Caroline, his children, Ronald Jr. and Kathy
Phillips and his two grandchildren, Marcia and Brandon and his
two sisters, Maureen Cavanaugh and Phyllis Greene, and I want
you to know that you had in Ronald a devoted husband, father,
grandfather and brother. I could go on, but let me share a story
about Ronald that set him apart."

Father Cummings, 59, had given many eulogies over his
33 years as a parish priest from his early days in rural, northern
Minnesota to the inner city of Detroit and now here at New
York's Holy Cross Church, the oldest building on 42nd Street.
He was always there whenever a crisis arose. "It's my job, be it
good or bad times," he once said casually when asked where he
got his strength after the funeral of a 17 year-old boy, a victim
of random and senseless violence during the 70s in a Detroit
drive-by shooting. Yet he seemed to rise to the occasion at funerals because he personalized the individual in a way that made

the sendoff less somber and more joyous. As family and friends mourned, regardless of the age, Father Cummings always had the strength to get through to the family.

"He has that special quality; it's like Reagan or Clinton, you are mesmerized by the message," said one parishioner after his homily, attending Holy Cross for the first time at Christmas in 1999. Today, at the funeral of the popular coach, father and friend, he asked each participant to look around the church, freshly painted with the brilliant July sun making the stained glass windows of Saints Anthony, Jude and Joseph and the passages from the Bible radiant, and be happy for a person who had gone home to God. The smell of incense permeated the air, forming a small cloud as it ascended to the high ceiling with its frescos of a risen Christ. "This is Ronald's home, he wants us to smile and he wants us to know that we have to finish the job he started." Father Cummings then asked those whose lives were touched by Ronald Anderson to come forward and say a few words following communion distribution.

Making his way to the altar rail in front of the liturgical white-draped coffin of the former Vietnam veteran to distribute communion, Father Cummings first had his widow and children receive the sacrament, followed by the throng of other family and friends. He noticed the tears in the eyes, especially of the young men that Ronald touched—for some this was the only strong male figure they had. He was reminded of Ronald's love of his baseball team and Cummings touched upon it when he reiterated his commitment to a sense of fair play and team spirit. Summing up the Mass before the traditional blessing sendoff and scheduled speakers, he couldn't resist telling those gathered, "Ron made a bet that if he went before me, I would have to tell you that the Hell's Kitchen Chargers, that he founded, would have to go to the playoffs again this year in the All-City Semi-

Pro Baseball Series. Well, they have made it to the all-city play-offs." The congregation applauded. "We welcome you to come forward to speak about Ron."

He recognized some of the faces of those present and past ball players who were touched by Ron—Frank Pedrillo, Ron Acosta, Mike McLean, Omar Fletcher and Mike Hennessy. Each of them had his own stories about Ron and each was asked to reminisce about his coach. Also, scheduled to say a few words were Councilwoman Gail Larson and Community Board 4 President, Sybil Sawyer.

First to step up to the lectern was Frank Pedrillo, a successful Wall Street investment banker, aged 41, balding, 5'11" who when at age 14, was running with the wrong crowd until Ron stepped in at the request of a nervous mother. "I owe a lot of the discipline I surely needed from Ron—he was the surrogate father for me." Taking a handkerchief from his dark vested suit, he wiped his brow and continued. "My dad died when I was just three, leaving Mom to raise me and my two older sisters. With no strong males around, Ron filled the void left by my dad's death. Ron knew that my mother had her hands full and would often be seen climbing the three flights to our tenement on West 44th Street, a bagful of groceries in hand, ready to start dinner when the leftovers were gone. Many times I saw him carrying a bag full of groceries that I assumed mom had bought, when, in reality, he had paid for them. He was the one who told me that I was someone and encouraged me to play baseball and excel. The experience of playing for him transformed a young, rebellious man into a mature, disciplined and focused individual. Thanks to him I learned to be humble and work with my teammates. Thanks to Ron's connections, I got a baseball scholarship to

Marist College and was able to pursue a career which would have been merely a dream. He brought me back. He brought a scared, scrawny 14 year-old the attention he so needed. He brought confidence and hope and ultimately a dream. I wouldn't be the person I am today if Ron hadn't intervened. We all like to think we have guardian angels. I was fortunate to know one up close and personal.

"But, let me share another side of Ron—he could be unpredictable and funny. One afternoon, I remember it was one of those hot, steamy days similar to today. I was in the barber's chair at Tony's—everybody knew Tony's on 9th Avenue. All of us went there, the floors were full of all shades of cut hair, the smell of Brill cream ever present and the radio tuned to, what else, the sports channel all the time with pictures on the wall of Yogi Berra, Mantle, Maris and Ruth—a real Yankee repository of sorts. Well, Ron spotted me that hot day and came into the shop, almost tripping on the floor rug. ' I'm safe,' he announced to the four or five of us in the shop and proceeded to tell Tony to make sure my cut was short. You see, I was his first baseman and, in one play a few days earlier, my Beatles-style haircut covered my eyes whenever a strong gust of wind came through, getting in the way, causing me to miss the catch at first and allowing the guy on third to score and we ultimately lost the game by one run. Ron never forgave me for it and told me to get a haircut pronto. To this day, I think he stalked me for those two days before mom gave me the $5 for a cut, knowing my every move. When he went into Tony's to make sure it wasn't just a trim, I knew this was some kind of sinister plot. Get the haircut or leave the team. Sure enough, in the next game, with a much shorter cut, I was extra vigilant with that shorter hair which didn't obscure my eyes and consequently I didn't make the same error. Maybe he knew something I didn't when it came to tonsorial pursuits. So, I was on the outs with short hair and got fewer looks from the girls, but Ron got his just due and, yes, we made it to the playoffs that year of 1978. Thanks, Ron for making me the person I am today."

Raul Acosta, a 37 year-old construction worker, was next to speak. His jet-black hair complemented his 6'2" frame and immaculate summer charcoal-gray suit with matching blue shirt and burgundy tie. He came up to the pulpit and began. "Unlike my friend Frank, I wasn't a favorite of Ronnie's." The congregation laughed. "In fact, I probably caused him to have more gray hairs. I was late for practice, late for my first game, late for my physical and finally I was told by Ron not to show up for practice until I got a sense of responsibility. It was no surprise that he began calling me the 'late Raul.' Boy, did I get a quick lesson in growing up. My parents were loving, hard-working people and I was one of eight children in a four story walkup on 49th Street. They couldn't always keep track of us, especially the boys as we started hanging out at the 48th Street playground. But, it was Ronnie who gave me the attention I needed when he disciplined a young, street-oriented 14 year-old who thought he could 'get over.' He showed me that responsibility and self-respect go hand in hand. I learned the hard way that in order to succeed you have to be accountable. Since Frank has told you a story abut Ron, let me also tell you a very personal side of Ron that made me what I am today.

"I remember one day when my mother was having trouble with my brother Carlos and me, arguing over who knows what. Much to my surprise, Ron was at my door with our baseball schedule. Who knows what possessed him to be there—at the right time at the right place, but I remember him telling mom, 'I'll straighten them out if you wish.' Since mom's English wasn't the best, I translated word for word and could see the smile on her face. I realized that Ron cared, cared very much and it showed me that one person can make a big difference. I love you Ronnie babe—thanks for making a street thug into a man."

After a sustained applause, the next person to speak was 42 year-old Mike McLean, a retired New York police officer, living now in the bedroom suburb of Hastings-on-Hudson with his wife and two daughters, all of whom were at Holy Cross today. Opposite of Raul, the paunchy, slightly overweight and sandy-haired 5'9" former officer shook hands with Ron's widow and began, "I want to add to the uniqueness of this man. Raul still lives in the hood and, although I may not live in the Kitchen anymore, I owe my life to it. It's where I grew up. When I parked the car today at the lot on 45th Street, I could still smell the bread coming from Colasso's Bakery. As a kid, we would go to the pizzeria with coach and stuff ourselves silly on Carlo's pepperoni pizza with extra cheese. When my wife Sherry and I met, it was here in Hell's Kitchen at the Clinton Grill on 9th Avenue, watching the Giants get beat by the Dallas Cowboys. I think the score was 19-3. And we were married right here at Holy Cross. Since I was a spoiled, only child, I had to think of who would be my best man. I had a lot of buddies and a few cousins, but I really wanted someone special for such a special day. I didn't have to look too far—I asked Ronnie. Everyone up here has a story and I guess I'm no exception. When I asked Ronnie to be my best man, I think I caught him off guard—something unusual indeed. He asked, 'Why not one of your buddies or a cousin? I'm a little too old to be a best man.' I assured him that he was the major focus in my life from ages 14 to 17. He taught me team spirit and the sense of fair play and the importance of working as a unit. In large part, because of this discipline, I entered the police academy at his urging. So, when it came time for my wedding, I told him, 'I get to pick who I want and it's you. Final. This is one time that I'm telling you what plays, not the other way around.'

"Ronnie never liked to show his soft side, but I saw tears well up in his eyes as he said, 'You sure about this—you talked this over with Sherry and your family?' I again told him it was my game and I was in charge and wouldn't have it any other way. We were married on June 15, 1994 and every anniversary, we got a card and a phone call from Ron. Since he was the seminal New Yorker, he didn't own a car and every summer he and the kids would take Metro North to our home in Hastings for a barbeque. Ron was always a giving person and I think I made his day for all he did for me. Although Sherry pleaded with his wife, he would bring the best Italian pastries from Pozzo's on 9th Avenue. He brought a little of the neighborhood into the suburbs. My daughter Melissa and, of course, Sherry have been enriched by his presence as well as his goddaughter and my oldest, Caitlin, who are here today. He made me what I am today and I'm grateful to God for having him in my life."

When Mike sat down, Omar Fletcher came up nervously to the pulpit and began, "I'm not much of a speaker and my life hasn't always been stellar, but I had to be here today and tell everyone present about my brother Ronnie Anderson. Fletcher, a 43 year-old drug counselor at Samaritan Village on 43rd Street, was a 6'2" slim, balding African American who was Ronnie's shortstop and speed runner. Fletcher looked around at his audience and smiled, took a deep breath and began. "He was something else. Am I right? What he did was no less than miraculous to a misguided, gang member who probably would have been doing time upstate if it weren't for his intervention. Let me tell you about the Ronnie Anderson I know. Everyone who has preceded me has said the truth and how they were touched and blessed by Ronnie's presence in their lives. For me, it was salvation. You see, I was arrested in 1978 for cocaine possession. Yes, a crazy 16 year-old who thought he could do what he wanted. It was Ronnie who came down to the precinct with my mom and not only stayed with me, but also bailed me out and made sure I got the right legal counsel and subsequently had charges dropped. It was Ronnie who redirected my life and changed it more than any teacher or pastor—excuse me Father Cummings." He was met by laughter. "He made sure that I was on the right track by taking me and a few of the other crazies in the Kitchen up to Otisville to listen to the Scared Straight program. It was exactly that. I was scared and I got straight! I promised Ronnie if I could get the chance to play short stop, I would make him proud. Well, that season, I knew I had to prove myself and I did. Our team lost one game and we went to the finals, only to lose by one run in the last game. The team provided a safety valve and a family. I went on, thanks to Ronnie's constant pushing to City College and, with his help, got a job in a drug rehab program of which I am now supervisor." His friends applaud vigorously. "Today is a happy day for me. My pastor at AME Zion tells me that I should feel good and triumphant as Ronnie is bound for glory. All that is true, I'm sure, but without him, I don't know if I would be here today to share in my hero's life. Thank you, Ronnie."

Next to speak for a minute was local pub owner, Mike Hennessy. Hennessy's, located on West 51st Street, was a neighborhood fixture. Ownership had been handed down to Mike from his father, Mike Sr., in 2002. Everyone knew that Hen-

nessy's provided an annual fundraiser begun by Mike's late father in 1992 for uniforms for Ron's team. Stepping up to the
podium, Mike was a bit of an anomaly from the rest: attired in
casual Polo blue shirt with a matching summer pants, his casual
gait defied a tough interior inside. At 6'1" and 230 lbs., he was
no match for any weekend warriors bent on creating trouble.

Hennessy's was a repository of the old Hell's Kitchen with
pictures of past luminaries such as the late Senator Moynihan,
raised a few blocks from here to sports figures who stopped with
autographed pictures aligning the left wall. Among those sports
figures were Mike Piazza, Bobby Bonilla and Roger Maris. The
opposite wall, stained by years of cigar and cigarette smoke, had
pictures of the Kitchen from the 1930s, including the push carts
that lined 39th Street and some of the anonymous and now long-
gone people who made up the Westside. As Hennessy passed the
coffin of his old friend, he gently touched the liturgical drape
covering it which is traditional in Catholic funeral Masses, replacing the black mournful colors of pre-Vatican II and thus
celebrating life.

Hennessy began, "Ron and I go back many years. I only
have a few minutes to sum up my recollections and let you know
the Ron I knew. This is a man who would never say no to someone in need. He was persistent and kept hounding you until he
got his way. Sometimes when I saw him coming into the bar, I
felt the urge to close it, depending on what state of mind I was
in." The church echoed with laughter. "It was Ron with some
issue or another. But Ronnie got his way. I recall one bitter cold
January night when the hangers-on were sitting at the bar—what
we call the regulars. This was the time before we stopped smoking, so the air was thick with smoke and my night bartender,
Marty, was gently nudging a few of the gents to go home, as the
hour was rapidly approaching closing time. Who steps in with

four of his buddies but Ronnie, who had just returned from the Garden where the Knicks had beaten San Antonio in overtime. Only Ronnie could pull off what happened next by announcing over the din of the jukebox, the chatter at the bar and noise from the pool table. 'I got a few of the players coming by for a nightcap and they should be here as soon as they shower and dress.' I asked Ronnie what was it he was smoking, but he refused to back down. Within 15 minutes, Patrick Ewing, coach Bill Riley and their wives came into the bar to the amazement of everyone. I asked Ronnie, 'How did you do it?' It appears that Riley and Ron got to talking and he mentioned that he was a coach, albeit a baseball one in a semi-pro status. Riley and Ewing were interested in just relaxing and getting a burger and a beer. After that night, Ronnie was the talk of the Westside. Guys would come up and ask, 'How's your friend, Coach Riley? Can you give me a ticket to the Knicks playoffs? Is Ewing coming back?' As fate would have it, Ewing signed a picture autograph to Ron, which he gave me and hangs on our wall of sports figures. Ron was a person of his word. He would go places where others never ventured to tread. My wife reminded me to say that Ronnie always played Santa every Christmas at PS17 for needy kids in the neighborhood. I was proud that we at Hennessy's were able to contribute and give something to this worthy cause. I'll miss Ronnie. I'll miss seeing him on the street, going up to the ballpark on 51st Street. I'll miss that infectious smile and that hearty laugh. I'll miss the wonderful stories that he told me of his years in the service of his country to the formation of his team. Yes, I'll even miss his constant nagging to get me to contribute to the team's uniform. But, I'm a better person for knowing you, Ron. Thank you, dear friend and God bless."

Throughout the church, the silence was deafening. A few dapped at their handkerchiefs, as Hennessy stopped by the first row to acknowledge his wife Caroline and her family. With-in a few minutes, the local councilwoman from city hall, Gail Larson came up to speak. Larson, a transplant from Medford, Oregon, held a PhD in child psychology from the University of Oregon and was an administrator at NYU's Child Trauma Center, helping with mentally challenged children from the ages of 3 to 9. As she came up to speak, she nodded in the direction of the family and spoke.

"I just want to share something special about a special man. Ron Anderson's legacy will live on. What he left us is a chal-lenge for us to continue to work with young people, continue to show interest in this neighborhood and continue to complete our mission of helping others. Mrs. Anderson and the Anderson family and everyone present, I have introduced legislation to the City Council of New York to rename the 51st Street ballfield the 'Ron Anderson Ball Park.'" The church thundered with ap-plause. "Thank you. I want you to know that I've spoken to the mayor's chief of staff and, once the bill is passed and signed by his honor, we will set aside a day for the name change with a ceremony that I hope all here will attend. The New York Parks Department will have the sign ready and I'll ask Mrs. Anderson and her family to perform the unveiling.

"Let me close by saying, sometimes we politicians have to be updated on issues germane to our particular districts. With Ron, I always got support when needed, praise when he felt it was warranted and, you guessed it, criticism if he felt I was not moving fast enough on some issues, such as the installation of floodlights for night games at the ballpark. So, I too thank Ron-nie for making me aware and educating me when I got ahead of myself. We need more

Ronald Andersons in this world. Thank you, Ron. Perfect or imperfect."

The next person to speak briefly was Sybil Sawyer, the petite, blond President of Community Board 4, the local governing body in the neighborhood. Community boards were set up to make it easier for the individual to attend open meetings and raise issues on a number of subjects, such as rerouting bus lines, giving permits to sidewalk restaurants, sending letters and petitions to city council to act on noise abatement, etc. Sawyer, a tough Westsider, was a retired executive secretary for Merrill Lynch and a native of Beaumont, Texas. She was squeaky clean, conservative in fiscal matters and the type of person the liberal Westside needed as a watchdog. She had a great fondness for Ron Anderson, whom she worked with on the community board. Ron always complimented her for her attire and today he would be equally proud as she was dressed 'to the nines' with a von Furstenberg blue business suit, highlighted by a pendant in shape of the cross. As she approached his bier, she gently touched the liturgical cloth covering his coffin and began, "Our councilwoman has done exactly what we expected. The members of Community Board 4 proposed the name change and we were delighted that Ms. Larson has acted so quickly. The board, if any of you have ever been to any of the meetings, is not a place for the faint of heart. We get committed community residents concerned about the quality of life and we try to be the watchdog for the city council. Ron Anderson served on the board for three years and was one of the most persuasive and caring voices I've ever heard. We may have not agreed on all issues, but I deeply respected Ron's love of this community, his zest for life and his commitment to the young people of our beloved Hell's Kitchen. Allow me to digress and tell you how special Ron was to me.

About three years ago I was with my sister at the 9th Avenue Food Festival and visited the table Ron set up for his team. If you ever had the chance to visit the stand he set up, it was full of goodies such as homemade brownies, chocolate chip cookies and pies, all made by moms and girlfriends of the team. As you can imagine, all these goodies were spread out in a neatly organized row with the prices clearly marked. The sign above his stand said it all: 'Support your local baseball team or we won't have one!' My sister Samantha, up from Atlanta, met Ron and was being educated on what living on the Westside was all about. Ron and Samantha hit it off well, discussing baseball stats and what chances the Yankees had to reach the pennant. Last year, Samantha passed away from a bout of cancer and the first message on my answering machine and email when I returned from her funeral was from Ron, telling me how delighted he was to have met my older sister. I had forgotten that Ron had taken a picture of Sam and me and you can imagine how moved I was when he stopped by the apartment just a day later with a framed picture of my sister and me on taken at his stand that day at the 9th Avenue Food Festival. That's the memory I'll always cherish. So, you see, I have a personal recollection that will endure. But, I'm also here today representing the board and I am pleased to read the following proclamation passed unanimously last night at our meeting. I have the honor of presenting to Caroline Anderson a proclamation that reads as follows:

'Whereas Ronald Anderson, former community board member and civic activist and founder

of Hell's Kitchen Chargers

Whereas Ronald Anderson spokesperson for youth groups and tireless proponent of youth

programs that benefitted all segments of the community

Whereas Ronald Anderson organizer and catalyst for 9th Avenue Food Festival

Be it resolved, that we, members of Community Board 4 of Manhattan on this 12 July

2005, do deem that the said baseball facility on 51st Street and 11th Avenue should from

this day forward be called

"Ronald Anderson Ballpark."

Community Board 4'

After a few moments of tumultuous applause, Caroline Anderson was given the plaque that recommended the name change to city council.

Speaking for the family, his son, Ron Jr., slowly made his way up to the pulpit and began by telling the crowd that his family was grateful to all who assisted them during the five months that his father was hospitalized and taken in for chemotherapy and subsequent visits. He started, "My dad wasn't larger than life. He was our dad and we loved him for that. Like a good parent, he made sure that we got what we needed, although I still feel he was softer on my sister and let her get away with a lot. He was there for his family, my grandparents and his team. He always delighted in telling us how he met mom at a Christmas party for NBC employees. My father's cousin, Mike McAvoy, invited him to the Rainbow Room and within 15 minutes was smitten by a perky, long-legged brunette named Caroline from Toledo, Ohio. When dad asked her if she wanted to go the Radio City Christmas show, imagine the surprise he got when mom told him she went everyday—she was a Rockette! Thus began a tradition with us—like tourists from near and far we went to the Christmas show every year, free of charge thanks to mom, and attended the Rainbow Room Holiday Party. It was a good way to see some of mom's old friends plus give dad a chance to relive that special moment in his life. Even these past difficult few years when he was diagnosed with a fatal and fourth term cancer, he was grace under fire. No one is immune to the ravages of disease, illness and hardships. Dad was able to accept the final chapter in his life with the dignity, grace and faith that sustained him from birth. He fought his final battle as he asked his team to do—with all their heart and effort, regardless of the outcome. So, he was still the coach telling us to hang tough and be strong and not give up. For this, I am eternally grateful that I was blessed to be his son. This church was also his refuge, for he was baptized and married in this very church and felt at home here. As Father Cummings and the other speakers said, he was first and foremost a person who took responsible action and made a series of good decisions that impacted upon others. But, the person I called Dad was also the person every Christmas Eve would tell us to leave not cookies and milk for Santa, but a shot of blackberry brandy." Friends of Ron laughed tearfully. "'Santa will be cold and will need something that feels good in his belly. By the time he comes to our apartment, he has his belly full of cookies and he needs something better.'

"He was also the one who showed up at all of my sister's and my school activities from Christmas pageants to my basketball games. Yes, he was a devoted father and husband and coach. But, you didn't want to be around him if the Yankees or Knicks lost! Everything stopped when the game was on—mom would prepare dinner based on the schedule. The phone went into answering machine mode for the duration.

"He was also active here at church and at his job at the various construction sites throughout this city. One time mom asked me to take him some lunch at the construction of the

Victory, located just down the street on 10th Avenue. When I arrived, I saw dad directing a huge crane that was sending steel girders up to the upper floors of this 52 story building. He always told us it takes a special person to work on as a construction worker—overcoming the fear of heights, working outdoors in all kinds of weather and not being afraid to operate large and dangerous machines. When I saw him and his men in action, I realized what my mom always meant when he left the door for work by saying, take care and get home in one piece. It takes a special person to work in such an environment and I knew then how important his job was.

"When my sister started dating Frank who became her husband, I felt for the guy. Pop was tough. Very tough and protective. The first time he came into the house, my dad sat him down and asked him what he wanted to do with his life. He won by dad over when, without batting an eyelash, said, 'I'm not sure, I just want to be a good provider, like my father is to me.' That did it—Frank, my brother-in law from Morgantown, West Virginia, was able to smooth talk dad and within six months, they were married—here at Holy Cross. So, on behalf of my mother and sister and our extended family, thank you for being here for our special dad. Thanks for the wonderful tributes today, especially the renaming of the ballpark on 51st Street. I know deep down in my gut that he's happy about that, even though he never liked to be praised."

The final blessing was given and the congregation made its way out of church. Outside a large component of the police force and neighborhood people watched in silence in tribute to the man who had touched their lives. Father Cummings uttered, "One person does make a difference—look at this tribute."

For Father Cummings this sendoff was a time of celebration of life. Father Cummings felt good today and knew he had Ron Anderson to thank him for it. New York was a city of neighborhoods linked inextricably together by a common yet basic fiber of life—to interact and come together as one family whenever the occasion arose. Ron Anderson's funeral was a reaffirmation to Father Cummings that his long life was not in vain, that he had been touched by others like Anderson and hopefully he had reached out and saved others from a perilous fate. A church knocked to its knees with sex scandals in recent years that saw dwindling attendance at Mass, a Church asking its members to embrace traditional Catholic teaching in the most liberal city in America; a Church that thwarted social changes demanded in the area of women's rights, gay rights, married priests, celibacy and divorce and yet, the Church endured. Father Cummings, time and again, knew that the real church were the Ron Andersons who practiced tolerance, gave of themselves and asked nothing in return, but merely a chance to be heard. *Call them cafeteria Catholics or as Robin Williams referred to them, "Catholic Lite," they are nevertheless, the soul of the church without whom it would no longer be viable,* Father Cummings thought as he saw the throng leaving the sanctuary. Yes, today was another wake up call for Father Cummings to advance his social agenda in the variegated landscape of New York and knew deep in his heart that his parish, despite all the negativity in the press, would endure. "The pain is sometimes overbearing, but we'll get through this," he told Mrs. Costello, a devout parishioner, a year ago. She was there today for Ron, as were many people from all walks of life. It was a wake-up call for the church, as well. He said a silent prayer and, with a smile on his face, got into the front seat of the hearse to take Ron to his much desired rest at St. Raymond's in the Bronx.

CHAPTER 13

Rosie Valnick walked dogs. All kinds of dogs—poodles, schnauzers, collies, big dogs, little dogs, cute dogs, ugly dogs. The neighborhood referred to her as 'Rosie the Dogwalker,' but she preferred to be known as a 'canine custodial supervisor.' Rosie was a rarity, a native New Yorker, living all her 46 years in Hell's Kitchen. "I was in a tenement on 44th and 9th and moved to 43rd and 10th and have never left," she proudly boasted to anyone within earshot. For the past 10 years, she has been walking dogs, allowing them to get exercise, relieve themselves and returning them to the safety of their owners. "And they don't talk back!"

"It all started when my neighbor, Adele Rose, had to go to her nephew's wedding in Philly—she asked me if I could walk her dog twice a day for $20.00." Rosie's response was quick, "Why not? It's $20.00 I don't have. Besides, I liked the mutt." Ms. Rose, a theatrical agent with an extensive network of friends and colleagues, soon recommended Rosie as a competent and affable person, replacing Stan, a mercurial and temperamental sort who had occasionally walked her precious dog, yelling obscenities and embarrassing the hell out of Ms. Rose. Soon the word was out, that Rosie was the real deal. "She's a doll. She walked my dogs, got my mail, watered my plants and left me a nice note when I returned," Adele told everyone. Adele's appreciation transformed Rosie into the "Dogwalker of Hell's Kitchen." Soon, calls came from the adjoining condo complexes, such as the Strand, the Victory at 40th and the huge rental, Manhattan

Plaza. By performing a little more than expected and going the extra mile, Rosie's fate was sealed. Like it or not, she was now, "Rosie the Dogwalker."

The demand for her services went up and soon she was easily recognizable, despite her petite 5'3' frame, each morning walking up to seven dogs at a time.

Within one short year, she had two shifts—one beginning at 7 AM, followed quickly an hour later and finally, an evening walk at 5 PM. By her third year, she was walking an average of nine dogs per walk in the mornings and six in the afternoon. Rosie's reputation as the Dogwalker was undeniable. She had what it took and people noticed.

Dogwalking, like babysitting, was a fixture of a neighborhood, like Hell's Kitchen, in transition. People, all kinds of people, from the maintenance staff at the new high rises to the coffee cart workers to the sanitation men, spotted Rosie and marveled at her agility of collecting her charges, cleaning up and smiling to the passers-by.

"She makes dog-walking an art," said Ross Bennett, a thirtyish Mississippi transplant whose meteoric rise at Citibank bank made him of the top new executives. "I look at dear Rosie maneuvering not only my Pomeranian, but also the big dogs and marvel at her control. I only wish I could get the same respect and cooperation from our loan department heads!" True to form, a walk with Rosie was not just a walk, but theater played out for all to see, free of charge. Like much of New York, Rosie had her daily audience and was a reliable, fun sight to behold.

By the fifth year, she had to turn away prospective clients, referring them to younger people who needed the extra cash, like actors and college students whom she trained at no cost.

"I'm doing well now, at least financially, and so I gave the names of a few people I know who are very reliable." Several people tried to emulate Rosie to no avail, failing miserably. "They don't understand that the first thing you need is patience. The second thing is love and respect for the dogs. Dogs are too smart and will know if you don't have your heart in it." Rosie had the walk down to a science to the point that schoolchildren, waiting for buses, would give her a big high five and passing delivery trucks would toot their horn. Like it or not, she had become an institution in the neighborhood. She always seemed happy, but deep inside Rosie had a deep, dark secret. That secret haunted her, obsessed her with fear and wonder. She let no one know that this very controlled and programmed person had issues. One particular issue that refused to go away was the feeling of hurt whenever a baby carriage was near.

Her day began at 6 AM in her small, one bedroom apartment on West 38th Street and 9th Avenue. Depending on the weather, she had now established her 'Dog Walk Routine,' as she aptly called it. First, she checked the all news radio station, WINS 1010 to see what surprises, if any, were in store for today. Putting on the coffee machine, she showered followed by a quick check on her answering machine and cell phone before a light breakfast of either a toasted buttered bagel or cereal, usually Quaker Minute Oatmeal and a cup of black coffee. "If I eat too much, I'll be irregular. The last thing I need on a job like this one is to be irregular, believe me," she told one of her clients, who had invited her one morning to join her in a bacon, eggs and grit breakfast. The smell of the brewing coffee always kept her going and she usually took a smaller, second cup. Then, the routine took hold. "Out to take my children for a walk," she often said to herself.

Rosie's first stop was at 400 West 43rd Street—apartments 21K, 31B and 40A. The three dogs were just the beginning of her day. She then entered the 10th Avenue building at 484 West 43rd Street where she picked up dogs at 14C, 24L and 40B. With these six, she crossed the busy, noisy avenue to the large condo, the Strand at 500 West 43rd, where the dogs, on cue, were waiting with the doorman at precisely 7:04 AM by owners of apartment 11A, 24E and 36Q. "Now the fun begins," she said to doorman, Jerry Wright.

Rosie called each of the dogs by name. It was her way of giving them recognition and helped her establish a rapport with each one. Rosie was always a caring person; she had nursed her aunt and mother for many months in their final days. Throughout the neighborhood, people spoke well of her, many not knowing or caring to know her murky past. "The beauty of New York," she once remarked to dog owner, Ralph Henderson, "is that you can hide yourself in all the craziness that goes on." Rosie had her secret and she wouldn't let others be privy to it. It was her secret and she valued her privacy. Yet, she was still haunted by a day many years ago.

Grabbing tightly on to Reggie, whose owner was Brandon Leach, a chef at Esca, one of the trendiest and successful restaurants in town. Reggie was always a challenge. Hamilton was the proud possession of owner and political science professor at Baruch College, Dr. Stanley Glitz. Mozart, aptly named, was a feisty and loud Pomeranian whose owner, Jack Slade, was a leading flutist with New York Metropolitan Orchestra. Chi-Chi, the antsy Chihuahua was owned by actress and choreographer Maureen McQuade. MacArthur, an irascible and stern-looking bulldog, was the proud possession of retired Judge Anne Altman of the New York State Supreme Court. DeMille, the cute schnauzer, was owned by Broadway producer, Ed Basch. Then there was Churchill, owned by British author Margaret Treachman and finally X-Ray, whose owner, the rapper, Darryl Stone, had just finished recording his third platinum rap album, "U No Y."

"Yes, these dogs and their owners are a show of themselves," Rosie responded when asked about her unique responsibility.

More than once she was asked, "Are New York dogs different?"

She always smiled and gave the same, honest, true-to-the gut New York answer, "No. Dogs are dogs and will always be dogs. New York dog owners, however, are different!"

"The owners are a breed among themselves," she replied candidly to a local newspaper, the <u>Clinton Chelsea Press,</u> in a 2005 interview entitled "Interesting Personalities of Hell's Kitchen." "I get to know the dogs, sometimes better than their busy and jaded owners, but I also get to know the owners as well." She went on to say, "You gotta love them. Sometimes I dread to think what they would do without their dogs. I've become a psychiatrist without a portfolio, a rabbi, priest, good cop, bad cop and surrogate parent all rolled into one." When pressed by the reporter, Rosie wouldn't open up about her own life. Instead, she had quite a story to tell about the owners, all the while keeping her dark secret to herself.

"You don't need to know about me, really. Walking dogs and picking up after them is not what romance novels are all about," she remarked apologetically to the reporter, Sandra Smith. "What I do is maintenance work, making sure 'my children' are attended to and properly returned to their rightful owners. What I think you'd be more interested in is what I know about the owners and what I see in their apartments, which I

have the privilege each day to see—at least the six ones I enter."
Rosie was a bit uncomfortable, but decided to give Sandra, a
non-threatening and affable young woman originally from Erie,
Pennsylvania, a good story, provided she didn't probe too much
into her own past.

"Mr. Leach, the chef at Esca's, has an impressive display
of cooking books, two of which he's written himself. On his
walls are citations as a Cordon Bleu chef at a top Parisian culinary school. If that's not impressive enough, his kitchen is to
die for! He has every, and I do mean every, conceivable stainless
steel utensil used in the art of gourmet cooking. Martha Stewart
has nothing over him! He is always a gracious man, inviting me
to his Christmas party every year and gives everyone the grand
tour of his sanctuary—his kitchen. What's the real clincher is
the homemade chocolate cake that's featured in one of his books
which he gives to his guests as presents. Both my late mother
and brother couldn't get enough of it the first time and they insisted on a piece every year since I attend his party. Mr. Leach's
dog, Reggie, at first was a hard sell—he wouldn't cooperate and
didn't like his fellow traveling companions. I soon worked out
a strategy—Reggie wanted to be addressed by his proper name
in front of the others and then he would join the ranks. Maybe
New York dogs are different!" Just like his owner, Rosie knew
this fickle collie, with his impeccably beautiful rust and white
color, wanted the recognition we all craved.

Rosie then picked up Dr. Glitz's dog, Hamilton. Before she
entered the building, a tenant came through the lobby with her
newborn, causing Rosie to momentarily sigh and think of her
past. "One day, I'll find out," she said to herself..

Dr. Stanley Glitz and his wife, Chloe, were a class act. "I love to go up to that apartment because his wife always has a smile and reminds Hamilton, every day without fail, to 'obey Rosie.' She's a real lady whose 34th floor apartment has a panoramic view that stretches from the Hudson and Jersey shore to upper Manhattan on the north and east to the Theater District." Her husband, a prolific writer of history books, was a quiet, reflective and gentlemanly sort. Rosie was always in awe of their furnishings— the walls were history lessons unto themselves. One wall had reproductions by Stuart of George Washington, plus portraits of Jefferson, Franklin at the Court of Louis XVI, and to no one's surprise, the famous Stuart portrait of Alexander Hamilton, Dr. Glitz's hero. "He took me on a tour of his pad. He has given me several of his books and he's quite a thinker, although sometimes I think he's on the lonely side. At 78, he doesn't get around too much, but his mind is sharp and he's always quick to respond. He still has that twinkle in his eye." Rosie no doubt also saw the citations from Mayor Bloomberg and one from Bill Clinton for his columns that were printed in the <u>Times</u>. Even now, he continued to write and his wife was a constant supporter, reviewing each manuscript.

"Now Jack Slade is a real piece of work. It took me awhile to warm up to him. I remember our first encounter—I was ready to tell him to get someone else and bug off with my New York attitude and all. What I thought would be an interview, friendly and sweet, turned into an interrogation, much like a trial or inquisition. He acted as if I were going to abduct his mutt, Mozart. I finally got his 'approval' when Mrs. Glitz agreed to speak to him and assure him that my intentions were worthy of his trust. Like, I said, Jack is a piece of work. Imagine him with a female!"

Slade's suspicious nature seemed to have been transferred to Mozart, who growled the first two days out with Rosie. "He was a real challenge. I don't give up easily and old Mozart was my biggest challenge," Rosie, herself a lonely, single middle-aged woman who kept her closeted secrets to herself, somehow won Mozart over by a little TLC. "I even tried that technique on his owner, the leading flutist with the New York Philharmonic. Slade and I have become friends and frankly, he's one of the few people I can confide in."

Rosie and Slade had a common need to excel in their respective areas—Slade, a virtuoso, was constantly trying innovative musical variations and was in the process of producing a new CD. Rosie and he shared a strong personality. For Rosie, life was no musical number. She kept her secret of a young teenage girl, who in 1976, spent three months at her aunt's in Homestead, Pennsylvania, as a result of getting pregnant one fateful party night. "Too much liquor, marijuana and sweet talk did it." She, like Slade and Mozart, was always a bit leery of people's intentions and didn't fully trust them until she got to know them.

Rosie was still haunted on a daily basis and heartbroken whenever she saw a newborn or a baby in a carriage. She still wondered what happened to the baby girl that was born on February 2, 1976, and was given up for adoption before her return to New York. Even now, it hurt her and she wondered what life the now 30 year-old whom she called Kate was up to. Her secret desire to meet her daughter wouldn't go away. She vowed she would one day find her daughter or at least, find out what became of her.

Her thoughts of that fateful day so long ago were interrupted when Slade asked,

"Rosie, has Mozart been good with you?"

"Oh sure, I got him under control, just like you," she said to laughter. Slade's apartment reflected his lifestyle—conservative decor with Renaissance style furnishings. Unlike the homey touch of Leach's and the tasteful style of the Glitzs,' Slade's apartment let the visitor know at once that a programmed and no-holes barred individual resided within the walls. *I get the feeling that he's lonely because I see on his neatly arranged Ethan Allen coffee table brochures for Singles Trips to the Greek Islands and even further destinations, like Tahiti,* Rosie thought. *Unlike Mrs. Glitz and Mr. Leach, I've never known him to entertain. The phone has never rang once in the three years I've been up to get Mozart and I don't believe he's done much entertaining for either friends or colleagues. But, at least we made some progress, he speaks to me and even offered coffee on my birthday!*

The next stop for Rosie the Walker was Maureen Mc-Quade's pad. "The first thing you hear is the music—her CD collections number in the hundreds with Broadway shows, many of which she appeared in. If you look at her walls, the posters, some autographed, tell a remarkable story. When I noticed the 'Oklahoma' poster with a young, handsome Gordon McCrae's autographed to 'To Maury,' she spoke about it for what seemed an eternity," Rosie said to a friend. "She mentioned that 'Gordy' was 'gorgeous with a voice that soared to the skies.' McQuade herself was a well-respected and much-noticed Tony nominee in the 1950s 60s and 70s. In fact, her Broadway credits earned her a supporting role in such musicals as: "Hello Dolly," "South Pacific," "Show Boat," and, of course, her favorite: "Oklahoma." Told by her doorman, Mr. Beattie that she liked brandy, Rosie brought the petite, aging star a bottle for Christmas with a note: "To someone who makes music." After that gesture, Rosie and McQuade got along famously.

Her dog, Chi-Chi, an aging Chihuahua, was her last vestige to hang on. Her friends were gone. Her family was scattered from Missouri to Colorado to Virginia and she didn't get out much due to her arthritic condition. Rosie remembered her own mother telling her that Maureen McQuade was a star but one whose luster had faded. Indeed, she had been through four bad marriages and now at 84, was a tired, old but still a very proud woman. Rosie felt for her. In many ways, she was able to bond with her, having been through bouts of depression and constant fear of rejection. *Maybe that's why she never calls me by name, it's always 'Love' or 'Dearie' or 'Honey.' She's someone I admire with a tinge of sadness in a long career that, while recognized by the theater community, never quite fulfilled her dream. Indeed, McQuade was like the person in an old flick who looked familiar, yet was overshadowed by the rest of the cast.*

"Now you take care dear of my Chi-Chi and don't let the other mutts get at her. She's not getting younger." Almost as an afterthought, she added, "None of us are."

Rosie felt for the old girl and, looking at Maureen and thinking of her mother, knew she was destined to be next in line and hoped that someone would take care of her.

As she leashed McQuade's dog, she spotted several young mothers getting their daughters off to school and felt that pain again. "Where is my baby? What is she doing now? Am I a grandmother at 46. I never had the joy of getting my kid off to school, never." Adjusting the leashes, she gave a big smile to the doorman and headed out the lobby to the next building and her next assignment.

In contrast to Maureen McQuade, MacArthur was aptly named for and epitomized its owner, retired New York State Court judge, Anne Altman. She was known as 'Angry Anne' by the New York tabloids after she chided two rapists and held their court-appointed attorney in contempt of court with a 30 day sentence following a vicious abduction in 1978 on the Lower East Side. To the packed courtroom, full of New York media, she sentenced the two rapists, Harvey Smalls and Alex Vasco to the maximum of 20 years after the graphic and sordid details of the abduction, rape and demands for ransom came through. The victim, Holly Allison, was the14 year-old daughter of a prominent Fortune 500 executive and, although surviving the ordeal, was scarred for life. 'Angry Anne' was applauded by both militant feminists and the public who followed the events for the three days that Holly was missing. If there had been an 'America's Most Wanted,' she would have been the Judge Judy of her day. Despite her pleas for stronger laws, Judge Altman was reprimanded by the state judiciary board for meting such a harsh sentence, but was undeterred in her quest to ensure her style of justice with lengthy sentences with each conviction. It was said that defense lawyers cringed when assigned to her courtroom. Yet the diminutive, feisty and slender dynamo with shoulder-length black hair engendered fear only to those who broke the law, displayed social commentary in her courtroom or had the nerve to challenge Angry Anne. Feared as she was by both defendant and prosecutor, the former assistant district attorney, won 80% of her cases and grabbed the attention of former Mayor Giuliani. Rudy quickly appointed her to the bench in 1995, citing the need for tough judges in a city whose crime rate was plummenting. Indeed, in her role as a prosecuter, her summations to the jury worked magic on the jury with personal diatribes, such as, "Do you really want this defendant on the street, in your neighborhood, in your apartment building, on the elevator with your child?" Her most notable case in her 12 years as DA was the successful prosecution of the notorious

'Gang of Five' in Chinatown, which involved kidnapping, racketeering and four murders within a span of five months by the Chinese mafia operating out of a basement apartment on Hester Street. With the arrest and conviction of the gang, she cracked the lucrative cocaine gang, getting warrants using Chinese plainclothes cops, resulting in the arrests. 'Angry Anne' became noticed by Giuliani and when she was tapped to the NYS Supreme Court, he said it was "by far my most notable judicial appointee." Even the liberal <u>New York Times</u> called it "a controversial albeit important choice." Giuliani, in a speech to the New York Bar Association, called it "my best appointment."

Judge Altman's apartment reflected her personality. Everything was neatly placed. Rosie noticed how even the photographs of her husband and two daughters chronicled their lives from birth to weddings with photos of bas and bar mitzvahs, high school and college graduations and finally the three grandchildren. Leather-bound bookshelves adorned an entire wall with Chinese vases from the Ming Dynasty interspersed to give balance. The judge's husband, Harvey, dabbled in oil paintings, which were displayed in the foyer, showed their seaside summer escape on Nantucket Sound.

Always polite but very direct, Rosie made sure that MacArthur was ready on time for his walk. MacArthur, like his owner, was proud, a leader of the pack, never allowing any other dog to outshine him by getting ahead. Indeed, on one occasion, MacArthur growled, and taking a cue from his owner, glared until the he got his way. "No one gets in old Mac's way," Rosie told the judge when recounting the incident to her a few days later. In a moment of levity, the judge added, "He's got his own leash on life!"

If caution and respect were the guidelines for picking up MacArthur, a visit to the apartment of Broadway producer, Ed Richette and his long-time partner Arturo Sanchez, was an absolute delight. "Come in,;come in my savior, Rosie,"said Richette, owner of Demille the schnauzer. "Have a biscotti, your favorite, dark chocolate," Arturo said, as he shoved the oblong phallus symbol into Rosie's mouth. Already loaded down with her charges, she gently tapped Arturo's check and threw a kiss to Ed. Ed introduced the new houseboy, Freddy Canfield, an aspiring actor, 24 and blond with a tattoo the length of his right bicep in the shape of barbed wire. Canfield, a native of Cape Giradeau, Missouri, extended his right hand to Rosie, remarking, "So you're the famous dogwalker of Hell's Kitchen." Unable to resist, Rosie blurted out, "You may become it, if you do mess up here!" Canfield, a student at the Arts League of New York, had impeccable manners, a tribute from his strict Mennonite upbringing. Rosie, a good judge of character, saw an innocence in his eyes and the alluring shyness so apparent in his voice and manner.

"Don't mind Rosie," Arturo said, giving a nod towards Rosie. "Rosie's a fixture here and she rules the roost with DeMille." As an afterthought, Arturo warned "Don't let DeMille get too close to the other mutts. He just got out of the vets for some shots and may have an attitude."

"Like father, like son, then," Rosie quickly interjected as Freddy laughed.

With a wry smile, Rosie exited the apartment, noticing the new sofa and matching chair sets.

"Nice, guys, business must be good. House boy, new furniture and a vet appointment for DeMille."

"Just have him back in time, sweetheart," Ed shouted.

The apartment of the prolific British-born writer, Margaret Treacham had a completely different atmosphere. True to her rigid standards, she left a daily note to Rosie concerning the care of her dog, appropriately named Churchill. The notes always started politely with a now familiar: "Good Morning, Ms. Valnick." Today's note reminded Rosie that Churchill, the very proud Irish setter, had a vet's appointment on the Eastside with Dr. Chauncey White and "therefore it would be best if he wasn't exposed to too much excitement." The note, written in beautiful script on monogrammed stationary, continued, "If you must, make sure Churchill's other 'companions' respect his space—remember, he's descended from a long line of prize-winning ancestors and has himself appeared at the Westminster Kennel Show." While many people found Lady Margaret to be overbearing and demanding, Rosie looked forward to the daily notes, so beautifully written and addressed to her personally. There was something eloquent in the manner of Lady Margaret from her writing to the accessories in her 25th floor apartment. Furnished with rich, lush tapestries from Florence and Turkey, the tapestries blended nicely with the Medieval painting of Caravaggio, Rembrandt and Holbein the Younger. Rosie once remarked to a friend who asked about the apartment, "It's like being in a mini-castle." A complete library not only displayed her 22 novels, but also housed first editions of such notable authors as Sir Arthur Conan Doyle and Dame Agatha Christie. She often told Rosie that her 'other flat' in the Mayfair section of London was a near duplication of her New York apartment. Lady Margaret, now widowed in her late 70s, still preferred the social, laid-back climate of New York to the more staid London scene. A favorite of Donald Trump and the late Malcolm Forbes, she was at once a philanthropist and belle-dame in a class by herself.

A complete contrast was the rapper SX, born Darryl Stone of South Central LA. His latest hit 'U No Y' was still number one after five weeks in all the R and B and rap stations. Just finishing his cameo debut in the new John Singleton flick, his meteoric rise to fame came just four years earlier when MTV featured upcoming talent, a prelude to "America's Next Idol." Now, with three Grammies under his belt, two Golden Globe awards, he was at the peak of his career and a favorite on the night scene with such fellow rappers as 50 Cent, LL Cool J and Jo Lo. A young millionaire at 31, his apartment was tantamount to a walk in the studio, complete with glossy photos of the Apollo Theater, autographed photos from Aretha Franklin, Jesse Jackson and a letter from Mayor Michael Bloomberg as well as the new mayor of Los Angeles, Mayor Villaragosa. Always addressing her as 'Miss Rosie,' he never failed to brighten her day with an infectious grin and beautifully capped teeth and a Yankee cap, turned back lest he be out of step with his generation. Under that Yankee cap was a shaved head. He had several tattoos on his well-defined arms. Rosie felt comfortable around him and liked that he doted on her, a tribute to his single-mother who brought him up to respect elders. A former choir member in his Baptist church, he was both polite and humorous when Rosie was around, often making up lyrics on the spot for her entertainment. Rosie loved his boyishness and manners and above all, his sincerity. SX was not afraid to ask her for advice when it came to girls and Rosie was quick to dispense with maternal pride. As he was a newcomer to wealth, she warned him of the barracudas and the golddiggers. And as a newcomer to wealth, he was always aware of the struggles he endured and encouraged young people to never give up. Rosie felt he was real, despite the hype and attention that was heaped on him. X-Ray, his five-year old cocker spaniel, was adorned with a chain, with his name prominently displayed. "He's earned his right to some bling—he brought me through some hard times when no one seemed to care," Darryl said. Leaving the apartment with X-Ray, Rosie was now about to begin her walk.

Getting off the elevator, Rosie spotted a newborn with her mother. She remembered the date so well—February 2, 1976. "That's the day my baby was taken," she said to herself. She began her walk, wondering if she would ever know where her daughter was now, what kind of life she was living, if she were married and had children.

Finishing her walk, she entered into her apartment with two messages on the answering machine. One was from Lady Margaret, thanking her for getting her precious Churchill back in one piece. The other was a message that said, "Ms. Valnick, my name is Cathy Rumford from Provo, Utah. I was born on February 2, 1976 at Roosevelt Hospital. My number is 801-999-1009. Can you call me please?" Rosie let out an audible cry and at once dialed the number.

CHAPTER 14

Thursday at the Westway Diner for Pete meant one thing—it was the day he would get his favorite—pea soup. With croutons, of course! This weekly ritual was followed a daily regimen which consisted of buying the <u>Daily News,</u> checking the lotto numbers and wondering why the Yankees couldn't get it right that year with his friend of 50 years, George Clancy. "A bunch of overgrown, overpaid men playing a high school game with attitude!" he remarked sardonically to George.

Peter Rizzo and George Clancy were a dying breed in Hell's Kitchen, two octogenarians who were born and raised within blocks of each other on 9th Avenue, drafted in World War II, participated in the D-Day invasion and came back to the neighborhood. Rizzo worked the docks in the postwar boom years of the 1950-1980s. They were eyewitnesses to what Tom Brokaw called the 'greatest generation' who saw the many changes in the socioeconomic character of the neighborhood they loved so much which kept them bonded together on these Thursdays to reflect on their past glory days. Westway was their place to reminisce and just pass time for two lonely old men. Entering into the large restaurant, they always had their favorite seat waiting for them—the third booth on the right. "Just a perfect spot," remarked Pete, "far enough away from the kitchen, but close enough to smell the coffee."

Pete, as always, dunked his croutons into the pea soup and orders a decaffeinated regular coffee. He was crippled with arthritis and using a cane for support. His gray hair was always neatly parted, a throwback to the old days before the gray hairs appeared and the cane were needed. His wife Mazie had been quick to remind him that Hollywood starlets might emerge off the great liners he had serviced on Pier 90 off 50th Street. Knowing that first impressions were important, Mazie, ever the optimist, would never fail to drive home to him the fact that passengers, famous or not, would interact with him first as he ushered them from customs to waiting taxis, cars and buses.

"Do you want their first impression of America to be a slob?" she jokingly would remind him.

So the hair was always neat, the pants pressed and the shirt starched to Mazie's satisfaction. Yet the years of working outside in all kinds of weather carrying trunks, bags and boxes had taken their toll and now, at 84, it was a chore to face each day without pain and without his dear Mazie. "She was right, always right."

Widowed three years and alone, he reminded himself that each day was special, regardless of the pain, whether imagined or real. He smiled faintly when he remembered a radiant Ava Gardner and her entourage of bags and trunks with two male aides after her arrival from Southampton in 1951 on the original Queen Mary. *Ms. Gardner had class and that face, oh boy! She had told her boys to cool it and let me handle her bags. Yes, she had class. She knew what to do the minute she saw me with my uniform and allowed me the privilege of carrying her bags. When we got to the curb, I placed her possessions in the cab we used and was given $20.00—a big tip in those days. I still remember that face, those beautiful dark eyes and her hair freely blowing in the wind and the smell of her perfume. She was a sight.*

Mazie, Gardner and all his friends were now long gone. All, that is, except for George. The Thursday meeting with George was not only a chance to get out, but also gave him a reason to continue. "I can't stay home and look at four walls; I'm too big for that." Independent, he never asked anyone for favors.

The one exception was when his doctor at Roosevelt Hospital, Dr. Raj Patel, insisted that he have a visiting nurse come by for therapy following a difficult hip replacement surgery. His nurse, Maritza Ruiz, was a godsend. She was patient, a good listener and had a great bedside manner; she insisted on getting Pete out of his depression. She almost singlehandedly helped Pete get on with his life, gain back his confidence and walk, albeit with a pronounced limp that required a cane for support. "You're not the only person in New York with pain," she often reminded him after he told her of his wife's death. Indeed, Ruiz bonded with Pete and had told him of her own journey to New York via Mexico and the long hours of work as a domestic before getting money to attend nursing school at Bellevue while raising two children. She and her husband, Fausto, lived on 10th Avenue above a noisy 24 hour bodega. Yet, she struggled, as did Fausto, who worked two jobs, to make sure that her children got an education. She showed Pete the pictures of her two children: Maria, a NYC cop and Orlando, an accountant with Citibank. Like Pete, she kept her emotions in tact but, over a period of six months with Pete, it was evident that the lonely, old man needed an outlet. Pete credits Ruiz for not only getting him up on his feet but also taking a few initiatives, such as contacting the senior citizens' group at nearby St. Malachy's on 49th Street. It was there that he renewed his bond with people like Clancy, an 81 year-old retired fireman and, like Pete, a lifelong resident of the Kitchen. Ruiz's strong loyalty to family and church resonated well with Pete who, as a product of first generation immigrants, was the needed catalyst that sparked the dormant plug he needed following Mazie's death and his subsequent health issues to get back on his feet. "I was ready to give up and then Maritza came on the scene. I wouldn't be here if it wasn't for her." Her constant and steadfast determination allowed Pete to get over his depression and face the world the way Mazie would have wanted. Maritza was indeed a godsend for him. So, the introduction to St. Malachy's senior program was a new lease on life and gave Rizzo a chance to renew his ties to the old neighborhood and his buddy, George Clancy.

Unlike most of his fellow firefighters who left the city for homes in Rockland or Nassau Counties, Clancy never married and stayed close to his Irish roots, joined the local Democratic club, Mc Manus Association on 44th Street and lived in a renovated one-bedroom apartment on 41st Street, while frequenting Bellevue Bar on 9th Avenue and 40th Street operated by his friend, Tracy West.

The Bellevue was typical of an old Hell's Kitchen establishment that was frequented by locals and a few newcomers living in the newly-renovated walkups that stretched along 9th Avenue between 35-42nd Streets. With its pool table, old jukebox vintage 1950 with music by Sinatra, Ella Fitzgerald and Tony Bennett, it was a throwback to the days that George remembered. Clancy was a steady patron, drinking just one or two drafts of Coors and bonding with the few patrons in mid-afternoon who came into the Bellevue to solve the world's problems. This old, dying neighborhood bar was one of the few remaining remnants for the natives like Clancy to talk over the news and forget the world around them. Every town and city in America had their version of a Bellevue and for Clancy, it was the last vestige he could hold on to from his youth and his highly-tense job as a firefighter.

"Yeah, it was an opportunity from years ago to get rid of all the crap from my job as a city fireman," he told anyone in earshot

The one day he'd never forget occurred when he distinguished himself when a fast-moving tenement fire in Harlem in 1965 raged out of control. Instinctively, he rushed up two floors, saving two young children. A few weeks later, he was later cited by both the fire commissioner and then mayor, Robert Wagner with a picture in the <u>Post</u> at a City Hall ceremony attended by his parents, two brothers and his girlfriend, Norma McMillan.

Now, at 6'2", 198 lbs., with thick gray hair, he was still an impressive sight and the opposite of Pete, a bald, portly 5' 6", 186 lbs. George worked out at Mid-City, completed two marathons in 1981 and 1983, loved to play baseball in the parks adjoining 11th Avenue and walked at least two miles a day. Now, however, like his friend Pete, he felt the need for friendship, as most of his family including his parents, two brothers and oldest sister had passed. Norma, his girlfriend, had wanted to marry and have a family. George kept waiting and one day, Norma, saying she waited long enough, abruptly left his apartment and moved in with someone she met on the job. In Rizzo, he found a good and loyal individual who, like himself, had few friends left and was in need of bonding. Thus, their Thursday meeting at Westway was a special event.

So it was at Westway, which prided itself as 'the best diner on the Westside,' that the Thursday ritual took place.

Always meeting in front at 11:45, they sat in the same booth where they would be serviced by the doting Monica Shannon. Shannon, 34, mother of three young children, worked the morning shift from 9 AM–4 PM, giving her enough time to get to Holy Cross School on 43rd Street to pick up her kids. Her children, aged 10, 8, and 5 were all enrolled in the same school, making it accessible for her to gather her kids without hiring a babysitter. A tall, bleached-blond blue-eyed who stood 5'2', she was an attractive presence who took a no nonsense approach to her job and was quick to give her opinion on a range of subjects from politics, sexism to religion without being asked. She was a tough Hell's Kitchen product and it showed. "I've had enough bullshit in my life without having to put up with it here," she once remarked to Pete. Seeing her old buddies approach for their weekly repast, she knew the scenario that would ensue.

"Morning, boys, how's the handsomest men in New York today?"

Clancy laughed and said, "Well, you're in the right mood."

"Naw, she's just looking for her big tip," Pete chimed in.

"Well, I'd better assign this table to Jose, he's in need of great tips. I'll just remind him that he can pay the rent after serving you two!"

Pete and George loved the banter with Monica and which was part of the fun.

"Okay," Pete said. "Let's start with the pea soup for me and egg salad on white toast."

"And, I guess you're like your buddy with the soup, but a tuna on rye toasted or as we say in the business on 'whiskey down', right?" Monica asked.

"You got it; that's why we sit here, Monnie," George answered, adding, "One day we'll fool you and order something different."

"That's when I'll leave," Monica quickly said..

"I doubt it; it hasn't happened in the two years you been coming here, so why spoil a good thing?" She was right, of course. People like Monica knew her customers. She also knew that Clancy and Rizzo would give her no flax and humor her when needed.

"We're just regular guys from the neighborhood and she appreciates us being here, you get that George?" Pete said to his friend.

"Of course, she's had it tough too." George went on to tell Pete that stressful jobs like fighting fires made you more aware of your surroundings. "Pete, in fires there was always that element of danger. No two fires are alike and every day on the job was different with me. I hated to bring my stress home, but the hardest thing is to lose someone because it's too late. One fire in the winter of 83, I think it was, was especially brutal. We lost three young kids in a quick walkup apartment fire on 123 Street. I can still see the look of utter horror and despair on that poor father's face. He just grabbed me and wouldn't let go when we took the kids out. Even today, if I go the movies or any big, crowded event, I make sure I check out the exits to see if they're working. It's in my blood and part of me, man. I think the stress was too much for Norma, too. She always told me to cool it and not talk shop when I was home, but it's part of my life. We played ball with the guys from the ladder, went to events like first communions, weddings and funerals. We ate together and we bonded. Norma just couldn't take it. I can't blame her, I guess. I just wish I wasn't such a jerk."

"Hey, don't be so hard on yourself. We're all jerks at one time or another. All right, maybe you more so."

"Quit while you're ahead, Pete," George shouted.

"Jesus, I don't know how you guys do it. I thought working on the docks was hard, but compared to what you've witnessed and what we saw when the Towers were hit, it's a walk in the park," Pete said as Monica approached with two large bowls of pea soup and a plate of croutons. She also put down two beverages—a decaffeinated regular for Pete and a diet coke with a twist of lemon for George.

"No need to tell her what we're drinking—by the way, how's the kids?," George asks.

Monica's expression changed from a smile to a frown and proceeded to tell the two that her youngest, Christopher, had an argument with another student and that the principal, Sister Laura called her in for a conference, causing her to lose two hours of work.

"Did you resolve it?" asked George, knowing that as a single, divorced mom, Monica had much to shoulder.

"We discussed the reasons—I'm glad he didn't fight because he takes after his father—very short-tempered and little self-control. I bust my chops working here; someday they'll thank me."

Not wanting to pry further into the cause of the argument, George, nevertheless, knew that this situation could escalate and wanted to intervene. He told Monica that he can identify with her son. He too was a problem child at Public School #17 on 47th Street and had to put up with gangs, constant abuses both verbally and physically at home with a father who spent too much time in the bars and by the bullies at school. One day, he just snapped and broke a kid's nose, causing him to be relocated to a notorious 600 school for troubled youths. He remained there for a semester before returning to a normal public school.

"Don't forget you're talking to a kid who's a graduate of the school of hard knocks," George said, then sipped his soup.

The pace picked up as several new tables were occupied by German tourists and a group of seniors in for the day from the burbs.

Monica excused herself and as she attended to the table of three, middle-aged German tourists. "She has a very stressful job. At least we had unions and good benefits. Here's someone who's busting her ass struggling with her kids and what does she get for it?" Pete remarked to George.

Both knew that Monica's husband Stan, a sanitation worker, left her for a 29 year-old he met while working in SoHo and ran off with her to Delaware. They were now living in a trailer park somewhere in West Virginia. Monica had started divorce proceedings.

"Speaking of jerks, her husband tops them all. She's an angel and that asshole leaves his kids behind…." Pete shook his head and sipped his coffee.

"She may get child support once all this is over, but it's a mess for her and the kids. Now they're reacting to it all. You got to feel for her. It's hard to lose someone through death, but this is a bitch." Pete got a reassuring nod from George.

Pete knew how difficult the first few months without Mazie were like. Losing Mazie to breast cancer after a six month battle just three years ago, Pete needed a network of friends to get through his grief. An inseparable couple, Mazie and Pete had a good marriage devoid of rancor and strife. Their one child, John, was their pride and joy, graduating from SUNY New Paltz where he met his future wife, Kathleen Rogers. Now living in suburban Rochester, they were teachers in the local public school system. John called his dad every few days, always inviting him up to see his two granddaughters, Frances Marie and Stephanie Rose. But John and Pete knew that the old man would return to the city after a few days, ready to resume his daily routines with his friend, George. *It's a different world up there and I'm treated beautifully, but it's not here,* he thought. Having a reliable, decent and caring friend like George was the most important part of Pete's life right now. *It's not New York and they have their own lives to lead. Besides, the winters are a bitch up there.*

Monica returned with the two sandwiches and placed them on the table, saying, "Boys, my Chris is unpredictable. I was hoping that the parochial school would keep him out of trouble, but I really think he needs a male figure who is tough." Pete glanced at George, knowing that Monica's family was scattered, most living in New Jersey and in Rhode Island. Pete remembered his own situation. His dad, a Neapolitan immigrant, died when he was six. He recalled his mother wearing the traditional black dresses that were common among Italian immigrant women in mourning. *She never took off her black dresses until I was 16 and ready to enlist in the navy. That's just the way it was in those days. It was taboo to remarry and she was stuck raising us kids alone.* Pete felt for Monica and finally reassured her by saying "You like a couple of old, tough neighborhood geezers like us to talk to Chris?"

"Thanks loads, but I feel I need to handle this myself. I'm a tough broad from the 'hood too, you know. Besides, I work here and put up with this nonsense from some of these crazies we get, what else could be so hard?. Besides, I put with you two, don't I?" she said as the two laughed.

Monica was one of thousands of young, single moms working to make it right for her kids. Scattered throughout the country, the Monicas of Westway could be duplicated in small-town America as well as in the heart of New York. Working in the service industries, they were the ones who waited on tables, cleaned the streets, delivered the mail, washed the bedpans in the hospitals, delivered the packages by FedEx and were the counter boys at the local bodegas. Monica was no exception. While her job got her to work in a large, 24 hour diner on the fringe of the Theater District, she was one of those nondescript people who worked at nondescript jobs, largely going unrecognized. Her situation was multiplied throughout America by a working class who struggled to maintain their mortgages or rent, worked two jobs, sent their kids to schools and college and tried to pay for health care that was out of range for most. So, George and Pete were a comfort, relief and an opportunity to let loose with the stress of her challenging existence. They came to see her and cared about her. She represented the Hell's Kitchen of their youth. She was sympathetic of many people, now mostly Hispanic and Asian immigrants maintaining dignity as they genuinely believed in the American dream. Putting on a smiling face while hurting inside, she catered to patrons from near and far who never really looked at her as a person, but more an instrument to get a quick meal before theater or to avoid the drudgery of cooking.

Pete and George understood her pain. George remembered Monica telling him of a couple arriving late for dinner due to congestion in the Lincoln tunnel on a heavily congested Wednesday matinee afternoon and, when not getting their dinner fast enough, they stormed out, leaving Monica with a plateful of brisket and a tuna salad special. Her boss, Greek-born Spiro Papadoulos just shook his head, knowing that the pre-theater crowd was always the craziest. Coming up to Monica, Spiro reassured her that she handled things perfectly. Spiro had seen it before and, in fact, tried to get his staff to push the specials, thus ensuring faster service. Coming to America from his native Greece, Spriro made a real effort to hire those in need—a quick look at his staff was evident that he had succeeded in hiring natives like Monica to Mexican busboys, Polish-born waitresses and chefs from the Dominican Republic and Ecuador.

George bit into his sandwich and noticed the German couple next to him. "I'll bet they'll order a hamburger and fries. I've seen many tourists from all over coming in here over the years when I worked the docks. They were wined and dined royally on the ship, but when they came to the city, it was pizza, hamburgers, bagels or hot dogs. You'd be surprised how many of those first-class passengers bigwigs would ask me where Nathan's was." Within a few minutes, Monica approached the adjoining table of tourists and, true to Pete's predictions, was overheard saying, "Who has the well-done, medium and the deluxe?"

"What did I tell you, Georgie?"

George smiled and finally asked Pete something that had been on his mind for God knew how long.

"Pete, all those years working on the docks—did you ever go on one of those cruises to the Caribbean with Mazie?"

"Hell no, she hated the thought of being marooned at sea and looking out at water with no land in sight. Sure, I could have taken her a dozen times on a cruise to the Bahamas or Canada or even a trans-Atlantic, but we had to settle for vacation places like the Poconos or Cape Cod. Before she got sick in 1999, I almost got her to say yes to a Bermuda cruise. So, our vacations were to see our son and his family upstate. But, I'll tell ya—working all those years and unloading all that cargo, I still got the bug to travel."

"Well, let's do it!"

"Do what—you're nuts, man!"

George stated, "You mentioned Ava Gardner on the old Queen Mary—why not fly to London and come back on the new Queen Mary?"

"You're crazy—what would I do?"

Monica approached the table as Pete was finishing his egg-salad, She asked, "What are you two plotting now?"

"George thinks we should fly to England, stay a bit and come back on the Queen Mary."

George said, "That's right; if anyone needs a vacation, it's Pete."

"Hey guys, go—you two make a great pair!" Monica laughed as she removed their plates and placed the check on the table. As she picked up the plates, she said, "Pete go for it—they have lifeboats. Besides, I hear they have a lot of old, rich ladies that might want you." Monica rushed away.

"All right." Pete faces reddens as he added, "It's just not going happen, but I'll show you two—I make you a wager—fair enough?"

"I got to hear this," George said.

George couldn't believe that Pete was actually giving his proposal some thought.

"Well, what's the wager?"

"Let's ask Monica if she ever had a vacation. Her boys are going up to her sister's home in Rhode Island for three weeks, right?"

"Yeah." George now had a smile as he added, "Let's not be selfish. We both have a few bucks. Why not bring her along for the ride."

"Are you sure about her sister taking in the boys?"

Pete recalled the last time they had lunch the previous Thursday, Monica mentioned that her sister Deirdre, who had one 10 year-old daughter, wanted to see her nephews for a week or two and let Monica go on a short trip with a few of her friends down to the Jersey shore. In fact, Monica had watched her niece for two weeks while her sister and brother-in-law went to Florida last winter to visit friends in Tampa.

"Let's run it past her, but she's going to say no—she's proud and won't take any handouts. We both know that. Besides, we're probably going to be in her way. But, what the hell, give it a shot and see where it goes."

"You guys still here—can't get enough of me, right?" Monica laughed.

Pete blurted out, "Monie, you did a big favor for your sister by watching her daughter last winter, right?"

"Yeah, I did—my niece was fine and got along great with my boys. Like I said, what are you two plotting?"

"You told us you have a vacation coming, right?" asked Pete.

"Well, look, it's just that you never been on a cruise and your sister could probably take the boys up to Rhode Island if you come on a cruise with us. However, if you don't want the company of two distinguished gentlemen, why not consider a trip to the Caribbean—it's a place you said you'd like to go to, correct? We don't have to go all the way to England."

"You gotta be kidding," Monica said as she excused herself to take an order from two women at the adjoining booth. Coming back, quickly said: "Thanks loads, guys; you're real sweethearts, but I just couldn't. I don't have a passport; I'd worry about the boys and besides I'd need nice dresses with all that glitter and those rich broads on board."

Two gentlemen at the next table have been eavesdropping on some of the conversation and finally one of them came over to Pete and George in the presence of Monica and said, "Please excuse me, but my name is Lars Rasmussen of the Norwegian Lines. You may have seen our ship docked or on the TV commercials. I get the feeling that you're considering a cruise—well we have a great deal that I don't think you should pass up. Let me give you a few of the brochures on our Caribbean trips, which allow children under 12 to travel free. You can't miss. In fact, if you don't mind me saying, I think we can work out adjoining rooms for you and give you a good price. What do you say?"

"These two are just blowing steam. I would love to go, but I don't think I can." Monica again walked away to give a menu to a single patron sitting across from Pete and George.

Rasmussen talked to Pete and George and before returning to his table, gave George the brochures from his attache case.

"Sir, promise me you'll read the brochure and also don't forget to fill out the entry form—you can win a free cruise. Even if you don't win, the round trip with an inside cabin ranges from $499-599 for a six day cruise. You can see the islands they stop at—Puerto Rico, Jamaica, the Virgin Islands and Bahamas. I know you'd enjoy it—I've taken many groups there and never had bad reviews. There are a lot of activities for kids and the beaches are great at the ports of call. Tell your friend, the waitress, that the children's program we offer is considered the best in the Caribbean."

"You're quite a salesmen. I hope the casino is as good as Foxwoods," Pete said as Lars rejoined his friend at the booth. Lars laughed and gave him a thumbs-up.

Three weeks later, after filling out the entry form with Monica's name on it, Pete got a call from the Miami office of Norwegian Princess indicating that he was one of 10 prizewinners. His winnings included a trip on the Princess from New York on July 14 for a six day Caribbean cruise in an outside cabin. Visiting all the islands they had discussed at the table! He had never won anything! This was great news and it couldn't wait until morning. Pete left a message on George's answering machine and within 15 minutes, George told Pete that Monica was working at the Westway until 9 PM, as it was Saturday. They decided to see her right away.